GNOSIS!

SEAN BYRNE

GNOSIS!

AGE-OLD
BOOKS

Publisher:
Age-Old Books,
1 Martello Terrace, Holywood, Co. Down, N. Ireland. BT18 9BE

ISBN: 978-0-9540255-2-6

A catalogue record for this book is available from the British Library.

Cover picture: David Roberts (1796-1864), *The Departure of the Isralites*,
courtesy Birmingham City Art Gallery.

Printed in N. Ireland by Clandeboye Printing Services

Author's note

Fact is very often stranger than fiction! This may help the reader understand that while the following is a work of fiction, many of the strange and unusual incidents and situations depicted in it are based on recorded history and ancient, authentic, and, in some cases, recently re-discovered manuscripts. Most of the main characters and the various authors, philosophers, etc. referred to in the text, are historical personalities, and the contexts in which they appear, historically accurate. Also, while a keen student of the recorded biography of Origen may note some minor deviations from the known incidents and important events of his life and travels, these do not, in the author's view, alter the actual and historically-accepted biography in any substantial way.

*Truth stills lives in fiction, and from the copy
the original will be restored.*

- Schiller

PROLOGUE

In 336 BC a young man named Alexander became ruler of the Greek Macedonian Empire after his father Phillip was murdered. Alexander had been educated by Aristotle, one of the wisest and most intelligent men the world has ever known. Inspired to spread abroad the wisdom and ideas he had learned from his teacher, at 20 years of age Alexander set out on a great mission to unite the various peoples of the ancient world under the enlightened ideals of Hellenism, and by the time of his death – which occurred only a little over a decade later - he had created the largest and most diverse empire of the ancient world. Alexander the Great, as he is known, built various cities during his conquests, but the most famous and influential of these was Alexandria, named after him, a city which soon became the veritable Mecca of Hellenic culture and learning.

Alexandria was built from scratch on a strategic site jutting out from the north coast of Egypt which allowed for the construction of two large harbours, one giving access to the Mediterranean in the north, and the other to the Nile in the south. The new city was populated by immigrants from various parts of Alexander's Empire, as well as the indigenous Egyptians. Thus, it soon became the most cosmopolitan city of the ancient world where a great variety of religions, cultures and ideas freely and fruitfully interacted. From the south, along the Nile, blew the magic winds of Egypt; from the east the more mysterious ones of the vast Orient; from the north poured down the purest and most refined impulses and achievements of the Greeks themselves; and more indirectly and to a lesser extent perhaps, from the west, the robust, unlearned but later-conquering tribes of Europe had an input also.

For Alexandria was, quite simply, the great crossroads and cultural melting pot of the ancient world! And by the time the Romans annexed it in 30 BC, a unique, thriving and independent culture had fermented in Alexandria; one rich in diversity, straddling the whole gamut of human experience, and articulated in the doctrines and philosophies of hugely assorted cults and sects who practised everything from pure atheism to the most intricate kinds of spiritualism and mysticism; from popular, stout Stoicism and refined Epicureanism to the most indulgent and erotic kinds of pagan religions.

Thus Alexandria, at the beginning of the new era, marked by the birth of the Christ, was not only the crossroads of the ancient world - it was that very world in microcosm!

The great Event in Jewish Palestine, centred on the Christ, had, by the middle of the first century of the new era, set the entire Hellenic world alight with all kinds of mystical, philosophical and religious speculations, and out of this a whole new

1

socio-religious movement began gradually to take shape. Forming itself originally as an offshoot of the restrictive and tightly-knit Jewish community in Jerusalem, it steadily freed itself from them. First known as the Ebionites, or 'poor men', the followers of this new movement later became known simply as Christians, and in time they became as much a thorn in the side of the Romans as the Jews were before them, because they refused to recognise anyone or anything as God other than their own Christ.

From the beginning and by its very nature therefore, this new movement was very diversified. It sought to bring people together on a basis never before attempted in the history of the world; that is, it aspired to create a cohesive community of souls through an actual historical event rather than through tribal blood-bonds, book-based doctrines or written laws, a systematic teaching, some tradition or other, or just a mere story. Anyone at all could join it! Thus the movement could absorb into itself influences from very many directions, and the deepest of such influences came especially from the ancient Mystery Religions of the Hellenic world, many of which, however, by the 2nd century, had become thoroughly decadent and profaned, much to the dismay of religious men and women everywhere.

The new movement sought to incorporate into it the best of the old ways, while fostering also an attitude of total freedom and openness to the new mystery of the Christ. Nevertheless it soon saw that its adherents easily fell into two distinct types: those who could only, or needed only, to relate to the Christ Event on a simple level, and those who through their learning and culture, and previous spiritual training, could find in it unfathomable depths of wisdom, knowledge, and revelation - a division you could say into 'shepherds and kings'.

Thus, within this diversified spiritual/cultural milieu, with its inevitable and great tensions, with its struggles and aspirations, a new world body was actually being formed. At first they called it simply *Kyrios* – meaning Lord – or the Body of the Lord, (only much later did it become known as the Church). If one includes the hugely expectant period immediately leading up to the Crucifixion of the Christ, it was a time that is nowadays known to historians as The Gnosis - from the Greek word meaning 'knowledge'.

One of the early followers of the Christ, called Mark the Evangelist, came to Alexandria in the middle of the 1st century and brought with him two documents which recounted the life of Christ. Any such document in circulation then – and there were many - was known as a 'Gospel' (meaning 'good' or 'health-bringing news'). One of Mark's documents was for the 'shepherds', the other for the 'kings'; that is, a public one, and one aimed at those who were considered capable, for whatever reason, of assimilating the more mysterious or philosophical aspects of the

2

Christ Event. Soon after Mark's arrival the Christians became a strong group in the city. They taught the new Way enthusiastically, acquired meeting-places and built shrines, developed communal festivities and procured a steadily-growing following. In this way Alexandria became not only one of the strongest centres of the new movement, but also the very hub of The Gnosis itself.

The Gnosis was a spiritually potent *potpourri* of cults, creeds, teachings and teachers; mind-blowing in depth and variety, but often seriously lacking in logic and direction, and sometimes even spurious in intent, but all, nevertheless, inspired in one way or another by the mysterious Christ Event. It was a time when the leaders of the new *Kyrios* movement had to fight hard to establish and maintain a pure and clear identity for it. And into this milieu, in Alexandria in 185 AD, was born a man in whose destiny lay a most important mission: this was not only to battle against ignorance, error and deceit, but, amidst the acute spiritual fervour of the times, to root the new movement firmly upon the Earth while at the same time maintain in it as open an attitude as possible to the magic and mystery of the starry cosmos, from which realm he believed, most firmly, he and his Great Master had descended to take up their cross upon planet Earth.

This man set out to fulfil his mission through both his exemplary personality and his voluminous writings, the intentions of which were never to dictate new religious laws or to impose new dogmas, doctrines or articles of faith, that is, to produce a new kind of Torah; but rather to kindle in all human souls possessed of goodwill the joy of true spiritual friendship and to offer the peoples of the world a way of replacing their seemingly endless warring propensities with, at least the hope of, a true and lasting peace.

That man's name was Origen. And this is his story.

1.   THE MASTER AND THE NEOPHYTE

There was so much he could not say, so much he could not put into words, no matter how hard he tried. But the important thing was to know and to preserve the essential truth, the barest essentials. That was the challenge! Many had tried, but St. John had done it best. *In the beginning was the Word* he wrote, and then at the end of his short book he said that all the libraries in the world would not be able to hold the books that would have to be written if the real truth about Him were to be known.

He was sitting on a pebbled slope, looking out over the Great Port, with his back to the steps leading up to the magnificent, white marble edifice of the Serapeum, temple of the great god Serapis. He had been attending a lecture by an exciting new philosopher and had been so stimulated by him that he eventually found it hard to keep track. All those ideas, words, thoughts! Sometimes it was all just too much! He had left quickly after the lecture and now needed nothing but to rest his mind, his eyes upon some soothing image – and what was better than this shimmering, sapphire purity of the Mediterranean Sea. He bathed his eyes and his soul in it, and it helped a little, but still his mind raced.

Hippolytus did not know; Justin Martyr did not know; Irenaeus he simply could not stand; and as for Celsus - it was obvious *he* simply did not even want to know. It was just amazing! It was only old Tertullian who seemed to have *some* idea. They had any amount of words of so-called knowledge; on the one hand either refuting or on the other upholding the value of Greek philosophy, and yet they did not seem to know *Him*! If they did they simply would not talk or write the way they did. They would think differently, would know differently, nay, they would actually *see* differently. That was it! They would *see* differently. They were missing the central point! They didn't know the core truth; something stopped them from seeing that. It was so confusing.

He was distracted by a long, creeping shadow on the ground to his left.
'Origen,' he heard from behind.
Origen closed his eyes rather than turn, for the voice made him freeze – for a moment he thought it might be *him*. Jesus Christ! He was about to bless himself, but opening his eyes he was relieved to see that it was his earthly, not his heavenly Master, Clement.
'You cast the shadow of Rome,' Origen said nervously.
'Never!' Clement returned brightly, and gathering up his toga seated himself carefully beside Origen. 'Never!' he repeated. 'Rome is a beast, an empire built on cruelty and murder. It spreads vice and violence everywhere it goes and, ironies of all ironies, they actually call it law and order! Humph.'

Origen sighed deeply, picked up a pebble and threw it down the slope.

'I jest, Master Clement,' he said.

'I know my child.'

'Even your shadow it pleases me to see.'

Clement leaned towards him and said in a lighter tone, 'I'm not a Roman, I just dress like one, that's all. Demetrius, our pope, now there's a true Roman for you.'

In silence they both gazed out over the shimmering azure. The harbour was like a sheet of bright blue glass framed by two curved white fingers. Another white finger pointed heavenwards: the majestic, three-hundred-feet-high Pharos lighthouse, Alexander the Great's invaluable legacy to countless sailors and one of the Wonders of the World.

After a while Clement pointed to the ground in front of him. 'Your shadow is darker than mine,' he said. 'Do you know why?'

Origen studied their shadows intensely for a moment, then frowning he said, 'No.'

'Why, your light is stronger than mine.' Clement smiled cryptically and searched the fresh young face for a reaction. 'After all, you have the name of a god – Origen: son of Horus, the God of Light.'

'Master Clement, I know the meaning of my name – but I'm not sure that my shadow is darker because of this. In fact I'm not sure that it's darker at all.' Origen threw another stone down the slope.

Clement went very serious then and turning his face to the sea asked, 'What's the matter now, my child?'

Origen was Clement's star pupil in the catechetical school for Christians – the Didascaleon – located near the city centre, which had been founded many years ago by his own Master, Pantaneus, who had appointed Clement to succeed him after his death. Clement looked upon this young man sitting beside him with great love, affection, but especially hope, for in him he perceived a soul upon whose destiny the future not only of his Christian School, but of the entire *Kyrios* itself, depended.

Although Origen was of Egyptian parentage, like Clement himself he spoke excellent Greek, the language of wisdom, the language of the future. Clement had a great vision of the future. He was indeed an initiated seer into the new mystery of the Christ, and knew the Great Master intimately, stressing often that he could actually converse with Him. Clement was a free spirit, and he saw his School as a training-ground for similar free-soaring spirits, those kinds of people who could build upon the troubled Earth a true Christian community based on love. His School, he felt certain, could lay the foundation of such an ideal of the *Kyrios*. Moreover it was a hope and a vision that provided a very necessary antidote to the coarser, repressive kind of Christian entity that was, he noted with growing trepidation, being increasingly promulgated by the literalists and their militarist allies. Such people, he felt, were motivated far more by love of power than pure spiritual love of Christ, and all of them were scheming for the might of Rome to back up their suspect and often heresy-hunting theologies.

Origen was certainly not of that school! For, he had the mind of an angel. Anyone who was initiated like Clement himself into the mysteries of the Great Master, anyone who had even a modicum of that great, archetypal Seer's spiritual capacity would know that here was a God-sent child if ever there was one. Origen had the soul of a prophet and the potential to fully and properly establish the *Kyrios* in the world in the way the Great Master wanted: a movement based entirely on love, and one that would outlast all empires and their armies; an antidote to the divisiveness of all those cults and creeds too numerous to count; a human community that would unite all men and would last to the very end of time itself.

Yes, Origen had great potential all right. But he was still so young, so terribly young, and so tender.

Clement had known Origen's parents long before he was born to them sixteen long and eventful years ago. They had become converts from paganism and had been instructed in the new faith at Clement's school, mainly by Clement himself. Over the years Clement had joyfully watched them turn into the most devout followers of the Christ. They had had a Christian marriage and baptized Origen, the first of their seven sons, on the day he was born. Many signs had accompanied his birth and baptism which suggested that this was no ordinary soul placed into their care. And when they looked into his huge, flashing, violet eyes they knew for certain he was sent by God into the world to accomplish a great mission. Thus they had prayed fervently for him day and night ever since, that he might be a powerful servant of the Christ.

Origen turned to Clement with a tear in his eye and said, 'There is so much confusion, Master.'
'Where is the confusion, my child – inside your head or outside, down there?' Clement flicked a finely-boned finger in the direction of the gleaming white city spread out below them.

Origen cleared his throat noisily and ran his hand through his long black hair.
'I don't know' he said, trying to firm his voice. 'All I know is that the confusion is getting worse.'
After a short silence Clement said as if quoting: *In the beginning was the chaos –* when I was still a young pagan they taught me that.'
Origen slanted his eyes on his Master in anticipation of elaboration.

7

'Do you know who brought harmony into it all?' Clement asked.

Origen shook his head.

'Eros.' A faint smile appeared on Clement's thin, pink lips.

'Hesiod?' Origen earnestly suggested.

But Clement didn't answer. Instead he began to observe the contours of Origen's lean but athletic young body, outlined beneath his idiosyncratic, black tunic.

'Do you have a girl friend?' he asked.

Origen blushed deeply! For suddenly Sarah stood before him in all her freshness and intoxicating beauty. It was a most unexpected question from his Master! Origen couldn't answer and lowered his eyes shyly to the ground.

'Women are tricky,' Clement went on, carefully scratching his shiny white beard with his index finger, 'but wonderful. Among many other things they soften a man's zeal for God.'

'Master, how can they be wonderful if they soften a man's zeal for God? Surely you would put zeal for God above..........women?'

'I almost heard you say *mere* women, did I not?'

Origen smiled, and Clement returned it.

'Never underestimate them, my child. The Great Master himself loved them dearly. Remember that always.'

'My problem, Master Clement, the source of my confusion, has a more complex character than that of *mere* gender.'

Clement bowed his white head and pondered these words awhile.

'Mere gender,' he repeated at length. 'You are aware I'm sure, from your study of Genesis, that in the beginning there was *only* man.'

'Oh yes, of course, but provided man means human being.'

'Agreed. But *one* nevertheless.'

'So......?'

'And he divided the man, the human being, if you want, into two, did he not?'

'I think I can see the direction of your logic Master.......... a man must get married.'

'Yes. Your mind works like lightening! However, I would not use the word *must*, my child. But for most it's the healthier, happier option.' Clement pointed to Origen's feet. 'And they mend the straps of their spouses' sandals in their spare time.' With this Clement gave Origen a broad smile.

In silence they watched in the distance a tall ship with huge golden sails slip serenely past the majestic, white column of the Pharos lighthouse and into the deep, still waters of the Great Port.

As it drew up to the harbour's edge, Clement suddenly clasped Origen's shoulder and said, 'Come, let us go and meet with your father. We can further discuss your chronic confusion later. At the moment there are very pressing matters to be dealt with. I fear that the mob is about to be stirred up, yet again, against our fragile young movement. Your father should be aware of this.'

2   THE FATHER AND THE SON

Leonides, Origen's father, was a big man with a curly beard that seemed to be stuck to his face. His brown complexion betrayed the Egyptian blood in his veins, a thing of which he was secretly proud. Despite this, he wore the toga without any scruples.

He was sitting, reading quietly in his small but well stocked-library when Clement and Origen entered. It was late afternoon and cool in this back room of Leonides' modest *domus* which was in Rhakotis, the Egyptian quarter, tucked away on one of the side streets running parallel to Canopius Way, the great main street of Alexandria. Leonides spent many happy and quiet hours sequestered here, away from the busy life of the city as well as his large family, reading, studying, but mostly reflecting on the beauty, majesty and spiritual promises of his Great Master.

The older men embraced warmly, and after seating themselves on two old but elegant armchairs began chatting, while Origen drifted away into a corner where with his back to them he immediately started scanning the shelves.

'I found him sitting outside the Serapeum again,' Clement said quietly, nodding towards Origen.
'What is it that attracts him to that pagan place?' Leonides asked, shaking his head disapprovingly.
'Oh, many things I expect, Leonides. Probably some visiting famous lecturer I never even heard of. I didn't ask.'
'And what were *you* doing there, Clement, may *I* ask?'
'Aha, now that's an easier one to answer, Leonides. Nevertheless, I'm afraid I cannot tell you precisely.'
'School business?'
'Something like that.'
Leonides stirred restlessly in his armchair. His double chin quivered as he spoke. 'Personally I hate the place. Gives me the creeps.'
'Does something strange to him too,' Clement said nodding towards Origen who was by now deeply absorbed in a scroll. 'But it doesn't stop him from going there.'
Leonides ran his fat hand nervously around his curly chins. 'Serapis – the strangest god that ever was,' he muttered.
'Yes,' Clement agreed, 'a god created by a committee – a first in history I'd imagine.'
'I think that's why he gives me the creeps. At least Osiris is a *real* god.'
'Yes, you were a great believer in him once, Leonides, were you not?'
'I was.'
'You even went so far as to call Origen after him.'
'Yes. More or less. But Clement, my good friend, what are you suggesting?'

'I'm suggesting, I suppose, that it is very hard to leave the old gods behind, is it not?'
Clement nodded towards Origen. 'He's the same. He wants to know *everything*.'
'The old gods can teach us many things.'
'But hardly about love, Leonides, hardly about *Love*.'
'Yes. But Clement, I must remind you of my child's full name: Origen Adamantius. Does this not suggest to you something of God's creative love?'
'Indeed, Leonides. Forgive my probing. You chose the name well. It is symbolic of a link between the old and the new. Moreover, his name, like his soul, is deep, rich, and full not only of the ancient wisdom of God, but of his love-light too.'

After this, Clement became very serious. He looked deeply into Leonides' eyes and said with great emphasis, 'My friend, I'm afraid I carry some very bad news. There is trouble brewing again.'
Leonides wrenched his hands, 'My God!'
'Yes. I have heard it from the very best of my sources, some of those attached even to the Senate itself. Some so-called ambassador, inspired no doubt by Satan himself, has got the ear of our Emperor and is filling it with the wickedest, the filthiest kinds of rumours and mythologies about our movement. We are being made pawns in the great game of power, yet again.'
Clement got up, and paced. Leonides started sweating profusely.

'We live, Leonides, in very crucial times,' Clement went on. 'Crucial not only for ourselves, but for the Empire, nay, for the very world itself. The Emperor is nervous. He knows not where his true power lies. He listens to everyone and everything - astrologers, magicians, soothsayers, and even those who call themselves philosophers, but many of whom are little more than charlatans. And one of these, one whom the Emperor thinks no doubt very wise due to the effected learning and carefully-crafted phrases that are the hallmark of these so-called ambassadors – one of these self-seeking people has apparently told our Emperor that members of his Praetorian Guard stationed here in Alexandria are...... Christians!'
Leonides narrowed his worried eyes. 'And we are *religio illicita*.'
'Precisely! And not only that, Leonides, but Severus is an intelligent man. He knows that despite being illegal we have a kind of power over him. For he knows very well that he himself is no god, despite the fact that the people are supposed to worship him as one, but that our God is a real one, or at least that we truly believe in Him! Understandably he is worried.'

Clement sat down again. 'Now,' he continued, 'there may, of course, be some tiny truth in what our conspiring ambassador says about the Guard, for many good men in the army are deeply attracted to the Christ. However, they must practise their belief in total secrecy. But I have to say that personally I am not aware that any of the Guard here has been baptized. But all of this is not the main point. The worst part of it all is that this same advisor has also told the Emperor that these supposedly-Christian Guards are actually plotting to murder him, to form a phalanx to back yet another upstart soldier-politician that nobody, to my knowledge, has ever even heard of; the same person then to take over the entire army and rule the Empire from here in Alexandria!' Clement sat back in his chair. 'Do you see the situation?'

'This is truly evil, the voice of Satan,' Leonides gasped.

'A twisted rat-bag of lies and certainly the work of our enemies! Yes. What devilish ideas are really behind all this, only God himself knows. Politics always stinks to hell, doesn't it? I fear, Leonides, there may even be some kind of distorted reasoning at work here to actually get us, I mean the *Kyrios*, eventually declared *religio licita* by the Emperor. For this legitimization would no doubt be very profitable to many people. But at what cost, Leonides, at what cost?'

'Good God almighty!'

'Yes, surely. But the most pertinent and cogent point to be kept in mind at present is that Septimius Severus *believes* in this cocktail of pure lies. And because of it, I have been told, he is about to issue an Edict against us. And you know what *that* means.'

'Christ have mercy upon us all!' Leonides cried, and blessed himself.

Clement sighed. 'Yes, my friend. You know your history well. You have read about Nero, Domitian, all the rest of them. Anything is possible, Leonides, absolutely anything. We must prepare, be on our guard. You, as a presbyter, are particularly at risk. Our *Kyrios* is in the greatest of danger.'

Becoming slowly aware through the tone of the conversation of its very serious content, Origen by now had lowered his scroll, turned and faced the two older men. They stared back at him in silence. Standing in the shade, with his worn black tunic falling loosely to his knees and tied simply at the waist with a bright red cord, his shiny black hair just touching his shoulders and the yellow scroll in his hands held out like a silent offering of the Word, Origen suddenly reminded Leonides of John the Baptist, a lone, crying voice in the wilderness, but a most true, pure and promising one.

Suddenly, the chiming of a distant temple bell filtered through the open window and broke the sombre silence of the room.

'What are you reading, Origen?' Clement asked gently.

'Plato. The Symposium.'

'Socrates is a bad example for you,' Clement suggested good-humouredly and winked at Leonides.

'Why, Master Clement?' Origen asked.

'He had a very bad sense of time, my child.'

'Had he?'

'Well, he turned up late for the Symposium for one thing.'
Origen frowned at Clement who immediately stood up.
'Time is of the essence you see, the very essence.'
'Master Clement, what is the matter?'
Clement cast a patristic glance at father and son.
'I've already told you, Origen. Your father will fill you in on the details.'
'Oh, the mob..........'
'Precisely.'
'Now, it's five o'clock. I must get back to the School and prepare my evening lecture'.

Leonides pulled himself up heavily from his armchair and Clement put his hand on his shoulder. They exchanged a knowing glance. Leonides' eyes moistened.
'We must be prepared, my good friend,' Clement whispered, 'to suffer the greatest sacrifices for Him. He, and no one else, is the great, the ultimate Example in the perennial fight against evil.'

Clement and Leonides went out of the library and walked slowly through the dining-room where Leonides' petite wife, Miriam, was busy preparing supper, and the many boisterous children scattered about became suddenly very quiet as they watched their father pass with the elegant white man who visited their house regularly. They chuckled, as they always did when he lifted his hand to bless them, and their mother smiled at how sweetly they all received it this time.

Origen stayed behind in the library and flung himself into his father's still-warm chair. Immediately he began to think of how it was that the mob had killed his beloved Christ. He sank himself deeply into this thought; so much so that eventually he had to ask himself was that actually *anger* he felt in the pit of his stomach? And if so, against whom was he directing it? Deeper and deeper he went into this, searching for an answer, until his thoughts licked his anger like tongues of fire. And it was then that that Voice came through again, that familiar Voice, deep and velvety, the Voice that reverberated in his soul like the very lyre of Orpheus, so sweet it was. But never had he heard it so clearly before.
Did I not die willingly for them? Why then are you angry?
Paradoxically, it was then also that the anger seemed not only not to go away but to swell. Confused, Origen did not know what to think or do. He buried his face in his hands and soon he could hardly think at all. Then slowly he was able to let the anger slip away until eventually it turned into tears. Now it was these he let swell; big warm, wet and lovely tears; tears of pure love......oh yes, love..... but love for Him alone.

12

When Leonides returned, Origen stood up embarrassedly but Leonides laid his hand gently on his shoulder and pressed him back into the chair. Leonides then sat down beside him.

Leonides still adored this, the eldest of his seven boys, and one of his great regrets in life was that he could no longer kiss Origen's breast every night as he used to when Origen was younger. He was too old for that now. Yet he still cried; indeed Leonides could see he had been crying just now – no one ever knew why. And experience had shown there was little point in ever asking.

'Why were you up at the Serapeum, my son? Clement tells me he found you up there again.'

Recovering his accustomed serenity, Origen said, 'A very learned man was speaking, father.'

'What is his name, pray?'

'Ammonius Saccus.'

'I have never heard of him.'

'No, but you will, father, if you live long enough, that is. The whole world will know of him eventually.'

'Why, my son? How can you tell such things?'

'Oh, father, that is difficult to say. I just *know*. Everything he says........his words..........his words are like.............drops of fire. He is just....... amazing!'

'Is he a Christian, my child?'

'I am not sure......but it doesn't matter to me.'

'The fire in his words is not the fire of the Holy Spirit if he is not a Christian. Is it, my child?'

Origen smiled condescendingly. 'Father, you surprise me sometimes with the depths of your wisdom.'

'A lot of it I get from you, my son,' Leonides ventured.

'Father, I will not argue with you, about the Holy Spirit. We have had such arguments before. The matter is very complex. Let my Master speak to you about such fine points of Christianity, not me. All I will say is that Ammonius Saccus has a power in his words that strikes a note so deep in my soul I cannot but listen to him, whatever his deepest confession may be. He is the wisest man I have ever heard and I have heard many of them here in Alexandria, and read many more. As yet, only a few know of Ammonius Saccus. But because he has such profound, majestic and wise things to say, because he has such *gnosis*, he cannot but shed more light on our Great Master himself. And that, father, is why I listen to him.'

'What kind of things does he say then?'

'This is another point about him, father. Like the Christ, Socrates, and many of the very wisest of men, he commits nothing to writing. All is taught through the word, and the word alone – not a copied, printed or some second-hand version of it.'

13

'Well, then, you have listened to him. Tell me what he says.'

'Father, the point I am trying to make is that Ammonius Saccus requires secrecy of his students. We must, in order to be admitted into his lectures, give an oath of secrecy regarding his teachings.'

Leonides' expression had become steadily more disapproving.

'He cannot be a Christian!'

'What do you mean, father?'

'There is only *one* secret now, my son, and you, more than most, know what it is.'

'You mean the Christ?'

'Certainly. As Paul said, "Christ is the world's great open secret." And *I* say mankind needs no other. You must tell your Ammonius Saccus *that*, if ever you get the chance.'

With that Leonides got up and left the room.

3   THE MADMAN AND THE MOB

In the cool of the evening, after supper, Origen slipped away from his family, half intending to go to Clement's evening lecture in the Didascaleon, but really wanting to be on his own after the hectic business of supper was over and his filial tasks as eldest son were completed.

He took a shortcut to the canal and walked slowly along its salubrious banks watching the brightly-coloured ships laden with their rich cargoes returning from distant lands, some from as far away as mysterious India, and others setting off on equally long journeys. They went to all parts of the Empire, but chiefly to Rome with the corn of Egypt, that delicious golden grain which seemed to keep the Empire from total disintegration nowadays.

It was the time of the 'forty days' during which the etesian winds blew, keeping the city cool during the day despite the heat of the sun, so that now, in the calm of the evening, Origen could feel the air caress his face as softly as a woman's hand. But as he was passing under the great bridge which linked Canopius Way to the Gate of the Moon, he became aware of a noise above him which jarred with what, up to that, was the normal, rather somnolent mood of an Alexandrian evening.

Curious as to the cause of the commotion, Origen ascended the huge granite steps onto Canopius Way and saw a crowd gathered about a furlong down the wide, white street, halfway between himself and the Gate of the Moon, that great arched opening in the high wall marking the city's western boundary.

Drawing closer, Origen saw that the crowd was assembled outside the temple of Aesculapius. Casting his eye quickly among them he saw that it was quite a ragbag of people – Greek, Jewish, Egyptian and others, from many different levels of Alexandrian society. From their clothes he could clearly make out sailors as well as merchants, craftsmen as well as philosophers. But Origen's shrewd and educated glance was also quick to discern a preponderance of one overall type – for these undoubtedly were mainly Ebionites, the most disaffected, unruly, and unpredictable of all the various groups, religious sects and racial types that comprised the immensely varied and variegated texture of Alexandrian society.

Raised by the steps of the temple a few feet above the crowd and standing in the shade of its portico, Origen saw a man who was shouting and responding with great animation to both the provocation and encouragement of the crowd below him. Drawing closer still, Origen saw that the man was tall, bearded, with pointed ascetic features, and wearing a hairy, full-length, cowl. He looked as if he had just returned

15

from a long sojourn meditating in the desert, and Origen reckoned he had the eyes of a vulture.

'They are the scum of the Earth,' the man was screeching, 'blasphemers against the Law, consorting with devils, worse even than the blackest cannibals, claiming in a hideous distortion of sacred scripture to commune in their love-orgies with the great unknown God himself...... by..........by.........eating and drinking him!'

At this point a roar of 'Blasphemy! Shame!' and 'Kill! Kill! Kill!' went out enthusiastically from the crowd causing the man's pitch to shift into a new, higher gear whereby an even sharper, hate-filled invective flowed from his increasingly distorted mouth.

Away from the crowd but well within earshot of the speaker and leaning calmly against the column of a nearby civic building Origen spotted a lone but familiar figure. It was Lukas, a good if sycophantic friend and companion. Origen approached him, but as they embraced their words of greeting were totally drowned by another spontaneous cheer from the crowd.
'Who is he?' Origen asked, when the noise died down.
'No idea,' Lukas responded.
Lukas was a true seeker after *gnosis*, very impressionable, but utterly sincere. He was a little older than Origen but they both usually attended Clement's evening lectures together. Lukas worked during the day in his father's carpentry shop near the *agora*, and still had on the slightly soiled, blue tunic he wore there. He had been on his way home when he was stayed by the commotion.
'Have you been here long?' Origen asked.
'Half-hour. The crowd is getting bigger all the time.'
'He can really stir them up, can't he?'
'He's possessed, Origen. I've been watching him most carefully.'

But Origen was secretly admiring Lukas' golden curls. His face always reminded him of a lamb.
'What is possession, dear Lukas?' Origen asked nonchalantly.
'Bah, Origen! Why do *you* ask? *You* know what it is.'
'I'm not sure that I do. Anyway I would like to hear it from you.'
'It's.......it's......just look at him,' Lukas responded, pointing. 'That's possession.'
The man's entire face was now thoroughly distorted and his voice shriller than ever. He was continually jabbing his index finger across the street towards a modest building a few yards to his right. Origen suddenly realized to his horror that this was one of the main meeting-places of his *Kyrios* community, the house of Theonas.

'They're in there this very moment,' the man shouted,

16

'these…..these….Christians…..having one of their………their love orgies. They are trying to drag the whole of Alexandria down into the gutter with them. If they're not soon stopped, the Emperor himself will blame us all and punish each and every one of us severely. He will get……..'

'Are there really people inside?' Origen asked anxiously as the rising invective of the crowd focussed more and more on the house.

'Think so.'

'Don't you think then we should go and tell Clement?'

'Yes, Origen. You're absolutely right. Come. Let's hurry. This could turn ugly very quickly.'

In the short while Origen had been with Lukas the crowd had swelled further, and was becoming ever more restless. Origen and Lukas took off swiftly along Canopius Way, in the opposite direction of the crowd, towards the Gate of the Sun. They soon reached the huge central square of Alexandria formed by the intersection of Canopius Way and the other main street, the Street of Soma. This great square was dominated by one of the Empire's best-known architectural wonders, the Soma, a huge rectangular building of gleaming porphyry and marble with a multiplicity of arches, and a complex inner structure topped with a glistening, blue-slated dome, on the pinnacle of which stood a shining white statue of Alexander himself. This building was, in fact, the mausoleum of Alexander the Great, the man who founded the city over five hundred years before Origen's time and who had, by now, become a semi-divine hero. The building still contained Alexander's body, embalmed in a glass coffin for all to see, and drew pilgrims from all over the world.

Origen and Lukas turned eastward along the Street of Soma, away from the mausoleum, and in about ten minutes reached the Didascaleon.

The Didascaleon was a spacious, elegant building, set amidst pleasant gardens in the style of the ancient Greek academies. It had been founded by Pantaneus about forty years previously and funded by generous contributions from the many rich Christians of Egypt. Pantaneus himself was now dead but he had appointed the learned and wise initiate, Clement, who was also a very able administrator, as his successor. The School was situated quite near the community meeting-house of St. Mark.

Alexandria was famous the world over for many aspects of its life and culture, but especially for its Library and the scholars of its Museum. So also with the Didascaleon. For it too inherited the great philosophical and learned traditions of Hellenism, even taking the Museum itself as its blueprint, and thus taught a wide variety of subjects. Of course, as a Christian school, the Bible formed the bedrock of its studies. But alongside this its students were also exposed to an eclectic mix of

17

intellectual disciplines which included subjects such as philosophy, history, geography and mathematics, but more importantly they were also instructed in many aspects of the ancient spiritual path, and its accompanying emphasis on contemplation, prayer and especially meditation.

Thus, for many of the searching and idealistic youth of the city, who came from various backgrounds – pagan, Jewish, Stoic, Epicurean, and others - this School proved very attractive and its curriculum a potent mix, but one that also made the newly-emerging ecclesiastics of the *Kyrios* community, especially those living in Rome, nervous. Pope Demetrius, for instance, the patriarch of Alexandria, kept a very close eye indeed on it, for from its direction whiffs of Gnostic heresies were forever irritating his large, red nose.

Clement had already begun speaking by the time Origen and Lukas reached the Didascaleon. About thirty students, mostly boys, but including a generous sprinkling of girls, were assembled around Clement in the smallest, but nonetheless elegant and spacious of the three green-and-white, marble lecture halls of the School.

Clement was addressing them from a large raised area with his back to a beautifully coloured mosaic of the resurrected Christ which filled the entire length and breadth of the northern wall. Some of the students leant against the columns that lined the walls, others sat on the floor, and yet others loitered on the steps near to Clement.

'We dare not interrupt him, Origen,' Lukas whispered as they entered.

Clement, seeing them, stopped momentarily and deftly motioned them to take a place, which they immediately did.

'Now,' Clement continued, beginning carefully to pace again, 'to develop Plato's analogy: what we see, what we *know* through our physical senses *cannot*, repeat *cannot* be the truth, my friends, the ultimate reality. It simply cannot be! We have proven that. The truth is not to be rendered into either signs that I can make with my hands or feet, or whatever part of me, or sounds I emit with my mere tongue of flesh. Tongues of flesh are too fallible to convey the truth of the higher things, of the higher beings, of the things and beings that Plato knew........ and knew intimately. Pictures, *living* pictures, my young friends, can only do this. We, Plato said, are like men living in a cave, living, that is, with our backs permanently to the entrance, the very place where the light comes from, the place of the sun. We never know it, for we don't even know that we are turned the wrong way round! Worse, we don't even know *how* to turn! All we ever see, therefore, are mere shadows, shadows of our own selves projected onto the wall at the opposite end of the cave........ our very

18

own shadows! Do you see?'

Clement came down the steps and mingled among the students, directly addressing many of them. 'Why, what we take for reality is nothing but our own shadow! Do you see?'

The students looked at one another in perplexity. But Ambrosius, the precocious nineteen-year-old son of a wealthy merchant, and friend of Origen, nudged Origen from behind and said, 'Go on, Origen, ask him something.'

Origen smiled back shyly over his shoulder at Ambrosius, but remained silent.

Suddenly a girl's voice sounded clearly from behind the partial cover of a caryatid. She was perched neatly at its feet.

'Master, do we see the shadows, or the light that the shadows are made of?'

Clement threw up his hands in delight.

'Ah,' he said, 'what an excellent question! Do you see boys, do you see the lovely light of the female brain, rooting out the unexpected angle, coming as it were from nowhere, but sharp and sure as lightening. What Elizabeth means of course is can there be shadow without light? But an even better question would be, can there be light without light? Eh? For what is light? Now, my young friends, as you all know so well: *In the beginning was the Word*. But what does St. John go on to say that the Word actually is? It is, he says, the Logos, the very same fiery Logos of the most holy Mysteries of the ancients. This solar, this sun Logos is then, as John says, the Light of the World. And this Plato knew too. Not the mere ball of fire we can all see with our physical eyes. No! No! No! No more a mere ball of fire in the sky than you or I are a mere ball of flesh and blood. For we all have *souls*, my friends. The soul is the key to *all* truths. And the sun too has a soul. Everything has an inside. Behind, within the flame there is always a spirit working, *Agni* as they say over there in the mysterious Orient. They know lots of things in the Orient, of course, but listen to me very carefully now, my friends. The difference between us and the many other groups and sects clamouring for followers in our time - and I mean not only in this troubled city of ours but all over the Empire, and indeed the very world itself - is that we teach, we believe, *we know* that this very same Logos, this Sun-Word of God Most High, this Light of the World is no dream, no mere shadow, ghost or phantom. No! For we know that the *Word has become flesh. That* is the point.'

Clement then stood to one side, and gestured towards the majestic mosaic behind him, suddenly shining now like a sun due to the brilliancy of its flaming colours. He pointed and said, 'And there it is.'

All eyes now rested on the beautiful work of art. The central motif of the mosaic was in the form of a spiral, the lower part of which was a brightly-coloured serpent's tail which sank deeply into a raging, scarlet fire that was teeming with hellish demons, but the upper part of which expanded majestically into the body of the Risen One, his pierced hands outstretched triumphantly, his face shining like a thousand suns, his long, thick, golden hair flowing like wings in the air of heaven, and his huge round eyes drawing the onlooker inexorably into his realm.

Origen, as always, when he gazed at it, was more deeply absorbed than most. But as usual also, his own searching eyes soon wandered from those huge ones of his Saviour down into the flaming depths He had risen from. For there was an equal or even greater attraction here for Origen, stimulated as he was by the artist's intense feelings and thoughts regarding the various demons and their fascinating, if fearful habitats.

'Origen!'
It was Clement! Having spotted Origen's mind drifting, he spoke decisively, intending to pull it back immediately, 'What do you think? Eh?'
'Think about what, Master?'
'About the Light of the World. What else? Is it pure light, or is it merely something that smokes and burns like wood, papyrus or charcoal?'
'You mean, does it possess the darkness of matter?'
'Precisely.'
'Can I conceive of light without a source?'
'I didn't say that; I did not ask that.'
'Then where *is* the source, Master?'
'The source of what?'
'Why, we speak of the light surely.'
'Yes. But what light?'
'The light of the Logos.'
'From the Father.'
'Oh yes, of course. I forgot.'
'You shouldn't forget, Origen,' Clement said. 'You should remember. *Re-member.* Everything. Especially yourself. Keep it together, all in one piece. Don't be drifting away.'

Ambrosius suddenly shouted, 'Master, is the Father all-good?'
'Of course.'
'Marcion says he is not.'
'Marcion!?'
'Yes.'
'My, my, Ambrosius, I can see that you have been spending a lot of time, perhaps more than is good for you, in your father's well-stocked library. Anyway, Marcion didn't say that.'
'Forgive me, Master, but he did. I have read it on this very day.'
'Pray, my friend, what *exactly* did you read?'

'He said………..well……..that Jehovah could be, was often so……….cruel.'
'Yes. But is Jehovah God the Father?'
Ambrosius remained silent as Clement continued, 'No, he is not. Abba is the Father, or as some say, Sabai, and *He* is the all-good, only He'.
'Who is Jehovah then?' Ambrosius asked, sunk now in deepest perplexity.
'That is for another time.'

A young man suddenly burst in through the door at the back of the hall, and all heads turned. The young man remained in the doorway, beckoning and panting heavily.
'Master Clement,' he blurted. 'Come. Come quickly. A mob has attacked the house of Theonas.'
The students stirred uneasily and some of those seated stood up.
Clement's face darkened.
'Come in, Rufinus,' he said to the young man, 'and close the door.'
The young man closed the door and drew near.
'Now. Tell me again…..slowly…….. what you have seen?'
The young man took a deep breath. 'Master, I was on my way home, walking along Canopius Way and I came upon a big crowd. They were very noisy and shouting all the time. I drew nearer, but as I did so I saw them suddenly charge the meeting-house of Theonas to which I and my parents go regularly for the *Agape*. I saw them break down its wooden doors. Many of the crowd then rushed inside and I heard screaming and fighting. I could not look any more. I turned and ran straight to you, Master Clement, for I was so afraid, and anyway I knew that you would want to know, and that you would know what to do.'
'Thank you, Rufinus. Sit down.'
Rufinus sat down reluctantly while Clement paced for a few moments with his head bowed, and everyone watched him in suspense. Clement then lifted his hand in a calming gesture and said, 'There is little we can do now. I advise all of you to get to your homes as quickly as possible. Do not *dare* to get involved in any aspect of this disturbance. Do you hear me? Do not *dare*. In the times ahead there will be great difficulty, as so often in the past, for those of us who wish to pursue knowledge, true knowledge of the Lord. We have enemies *everywhere*. But, my friends, remember, the greatest enemy is always within. We must overcome ourselves, our desires, our fighting, our warring, bloodthirsty nature. Be not aroused, my children. Be true pacifists as we are called on to be, as we are all taught to be by Him.' Clement pointed to the mosaic again. Then turning once more to the students he lifted his hand in a priestly blessing and said, 'Go in peace.'

Outside the Didascaleon, on the steps leading down towards the Street of Soma, some of the students loitered and talked animatedly. Lukas stayed very close to Origen. Ambrosius came up to Origen and clapped him on the back.
'Hey! You come with me,' he said loudly.

'The Master advised us all to go home, Ambrosius. Remember?' Origen replied nonchalantly.

'I know. I know. But he also said not to get involved, didn't he?'

'Yes.'

'Well, if you go *that* way,' – Ambrosius pointed southwards along the Street of Soma - 'which is towards your home, you'll surely meet the mob, my friend, and how can you not get involved then? Now I live *that* way,' – he pointed then in the opposite direction towards the Great Port.

Origen looked into Ambrosius' pleading eyes and nodded approval. 'All right.'

'May I come too?' Lukas asked. Ambrosius was standing between Origen and Lukas and placing his hands on both their shoulders he boisterously drew them down the steps saying, 'Yes, of course. Come friends, let us get as far away from the mob as possible, and talk some more philosophy.'

4   THE LOVER AND HIS LOVE

Ambrosius lived with his family in a beautiful *domus* set on a hill in sumptuous gardens with panoramic views over the busy Great Port, towering above which permanently soared the majestic and ever-shining Pharos lighthouse.

Ambrosius' father, who was a lukewarm Stoic with strong pagan leanings, had, in middle-age, become very wealthy importing for the general populace of Alexandria, silk, ginger, spices and scents from far-away and luxuriant India, as well as precious gems and stones from more accessible Persia for Alexandria's aristocrats.

The flaming, majestic ball of the Egyptian sun had sunk into the deep-blue Mediterranean, gilding the clear sky with an angelic afterglow as the three young friends passed under the palm trees and through the full-scented front garden of Ambrosius' elegant home. As they went through the open entrance of the *atrium* they saw that some guests were already there. Ambrosius then stepped forward enthusiastically and greeted in turn Philemon and Joshua who were stretched out lazily on couches near one another, eating and drinking, and talking animatedly. Origen's attention, however, was arrested by Sarah, Ambrosius' sister who was standing with another girl in a corner of the room.

As Origen's and Sarah's eyes met they exchanged quick, warm smiles, but did not speak. Sarah was a tall eighteen-year-old, almost a year older than Origen. She had tan Ethiopian features and these, together with her flashing white teeth, caused Origen to think her the most beautiful girl in the entire city. He had known her through his friendship with Ambrosius almost since the time of his sexual awakening and had observed her own development with growing interest and attraction ever since then.
'Friends,' Ambrosius announced, 'Lukas and Origen have come to stay with us this night,' and added facetiously, 'for fear of getting...... stabbed!'
'Stabbed!' Philemon exploded. 'Who would want to stab such a wise man as our good friend Origen? It's preposterous.' Philemon laughed loudly as he popped a grape into his mouth.
'And of course he is wise,' Joshua added good-humouredly. 'For, a man with broken sandal tongs is *always* wise.'
All eyes then fell upon Origen's poorly clad, plebeian feet. His worn, black tunic soon too began to stand out in contrast to his finely-clad, toga-wrapped, rich friends.
'Pay no heed to these jesters, Origen,' Ambrosius said, handing both him and Lukas a glass of sweet, red wine. 'Here. Drink. Be seated.'

Sarah and her friend soon came forward and joined the circle of young men.

'Have you met Herias?' Sarah said to Origen.

'I think I may have seen you occasionally at Clement's lectures,' Origen said surveying Herias, who blushed deeply. 'Is that so?'

Herias nodded shyly.

'Yes. She is a Christian,' Sarah said. 'Aren't you, sweet Herias?'

Herias blushed and nodded again.

'There you are now, Origen. One of your very own,' Sarah continued in a slightly mocking tone.

How bold and confident she is becoming, Origen thought. But how intoxicating!

'But I thought you, Sarah, were a Christian too,' Philemon interjected. 'Don't you attend the Didascaleon?'

'Oh, yes, I do occasionally. But that, dear Philemon, doesn't mean I'm a Christian.' She turned brightly to Origen. 'Does it Origen?'

'No. Sarah is right, Philemon,' he said. 'You don't have to *be* a Christian in order to attend. But I think it's only fair to say, Clement expects you to at least think about *becoming* one. It's the first step on the Way.'

'The way?' Joshua challenged. 'The way to what, to where?'

'To Christ. Christ said, "I am the Way",' Origen replied.

'How do *you* know?' Joshua asked.

'It is written in St. John's Gospel – John the Evangelist. He knew the Great Master intimately, personally.'

'Mmm. Your Gospel. I've heard of that all right.'

After a pause Philemon said, 'But, Origen, you haven't answered Joshua's question. The way - it implies *going* somewhere – *I am the way* – that's far too vague for me.'

Origen sipped his wine, preparing an answer, but Philemon continued, 'What I would like to know, Origen, is, would your Christ take *me* to the Elysian Fields? For if that is the way he is talking about, I, too, shall start going to the Didascaleon tomorrow.'

Sarah forced a laugh. 'I think you have your eyes more on the Senate than the Elysian Fields, dear Philemon,' she said.

Slightly ruffled by Sarah's remark, Philemon asked, 'What makes you say that?'

'Why, I believe you have been selected as a candidate for initiation in the Temple of Eleusis.'

Philemon looked astonished, but Sarah went on, 'And everyone knows that that is the first step on the road to the Senate these days. You haven't a hope otherwise.'

Swallowing nervously Philemon asked, 'Who told you that I was a candidate for the Eleusinian Mysteries?'

'Oh, you know…..I have friends in…..well…….. in all kinds of places.'

After a few moments Philemon relaxed. 'Actually,' he now suddenly confided, 'I am more than a mere candidate for selection - I have already passed through the Lesser

24

Mysteries.' He grinned proudly.

Sarah laughed loudly. 'Why, this is excellent, dear Philemon! For one who not only doesn't believe in the gods, but not even in God the singular, how in the name of Serapis did you manage it, eh?'

'It is not true that I do not believe in the gods,' Philemon asserted, nervously fiddling now with a bunch of purple grapes, one of which he popped into his mouth. He chewed rapidly as Sarah, with eyebrows raised, encouraged a response from Origen. Origen, however, remained silent, for he wanted to hear more from Philemon first.

'I have been converted,' Philemon announced stubbornly.

'Well, that's a sea-change from the last time we had a conversation like this,' Sarah said. 'Of course, that was before you became a candidate.'

'Come on, Sarah,' Joshua interrupted, 'give the man a chance.'

'Oh, Joshua, you know our good friend Philemon here better than most of us. He knows perfectly well that these days you haven't a hope in Hades of getting elected to the Senate, the softest job in town, unless you have first been initiated into the Mysteries of Eleusis.' Sarah turned to Philemon again. 'Come on now, Philemon, be an honest neophyte. Tell us how much you paid, or rather how much your father paid the Hierophant, to get you in, eh?'

'Sarah,' Philemon said, becoming quite exasperated, 'it is not good to ridicule the sacred Mysteries like this.' He turned for support to Origen. 'Is it Origen? Tell her, pray.'

Origen was about to say something, but Sarah went on, 'Seriously, Philemon, I am not ridiculing the sacred Mysteries. Such a thought would never enter my head. I am merely setting out the facts, the plain truth, as I know it. I follow these things with a keen interest. And I know that our poor, deceived, innocent little Persephone becomes ever more scantily clad with each passing, yearly ceremony up there in the Temple. So much so that in no time at all I fear the ancient and elaborate ritual of her raping will become so easy that they will even allow the butchers of the *agora* into their so-called sacred rites, if, that is, the same butchers can save up enough money from their slaughtering to buy their way in!'

Philemon by now had become quite as purple as the grapes in his hand! He stood up angrily and looked as if he was about to leave when Ambrosius rushed towards him and put his arm around his shoulder.

'Sister Sarah is a bit too bright for her age, I'm afraid, good Philemon,' he said. 'And what is more, she's at her very best after the sun goes down. But don't let her get into your hair. Believe it or not, she actually means well. She seeks the truth. She has the great Mother Demeter's interests at heart, always.'

Philemon reluctantly allowed Ambrosius to press him back onto his couch.

Lukas, who was mesmerized by all these exchanges, looked worriedly to Origen who continually trawled his brain for something suitable to take the sting out of choleric Sarah's provocative rhetoric.

25

'Philemon,' he said eventually, 'you don't have to admit to us the sin of simony. Anyway, the concept of sin hardly exists in your pagan cult, does it?'

Philemon frowned at first, and then shook his head.

'Have they actually revealed Demeter to you yet?' Origen asked.

'No. They have spoken of her only.'

'Then I do hope you will believe in *her* when they reveal her to you, dear Philemon,' Origen went on, looking now at beautiful Sarah. 'She is intimately related to the one whom we – I mean us Christians – call Sophia.'

'And I hope they have her properly clad,' Sarah cut in, 'for if they strip *her* down too, that would truly make me angry.'

'Oh, I love it when you get angry', Ambrosius said, forcing a laugh. Turning to Origen he said, 'Origen, why don't you take this simmering beauty out for a walk in the cool of the garden before she gets too hot. I want to have a few private words with Philemon.' He immediately drew Philemon to one side, and Sarah and Origen stood up.

Sarah, who was slightly taller than Origen, surprised him by gently but firmly taking his hand. She led him into the garden, while Lukas sidled closer to Herias.

Outside, the cool evening air was heavy with the scent of sage, hyacinth and honeysuckle but spiked by delicate, stray whiffs from the numerous, lemon-scented roses. Origen breathed in deeply as he strolled with Sarah, but it was the softness of her hand that he was most conscious of.

Sarah had on a full-length turquoise *stola* made of the finest Indian silk, and her jet-black hair was plaited in an intricate, artistic loop which touched the nape of her long, smooth, coffee-coloured neck at which Origen was longingly gazing.

After a while Sarah let go of his hand to pick a yellow narcissus which she held to her nose.

When their eyes met again Origen saw how playful they were, how inviting, and so full of warmth. Sarah was suddenly no longer the girl he used to know, but a woman now. And, he realized, he was in love with her all the more, because of it.

And was this, what he had just witnessed, an example of the woman taking over from the girl? He had never known her to be so consciously provocative towards anyone before – the way she had spoken to poor old Philemon, and so cleverly ruffled his fine, self-satisfied feathers.

Origen decided to be bold himself. 'I've just had a wonderful idea,' he said.

26

'Oh, Origen, you are so rich in ideas! Come, let me *have* it,' she said exaggeratedly widening her huge blue eyes. 'I am so greedy for wisdom.'

'Yes, I know. And, dear Sarah, you will get as much of it as you earn. But if you are really so interested in the Mysteries of Eleusis, and if it is so very easy to get admitted – and I think on balance you are probably right in what you say in this regard – then why don't you ask the Hierophant yourself to be initiated? That way you would find out *everything*.'

Pondering, Sarah put the flower down from her nose. 'Origen, you astonish me! How can you say such a thing? Women are not allowed into the Mysteries!'

'But Demeter is a woman, is she not?'

'Yes, of course.'

'And is she not the key figure in the sacred rites?'

'Yes, you know she is.'

'Well...........?'

Sarah turned from him and pensively looked out across the harbour. 'You mean, *I* could play.....be..... Demeter?'

'Who better?'

Astonished, she turned back to him. 'But.....but Demeter is a Goddess?'

'She is surely.'

'And I am just a ....a *mere* woman.'

'Are you, sweet, sweet Sarah, just a *mere* woman? Truly I sense something more than a *mere* woman in you........ this.....this special evening.'

Origen was slightly unnerved at the trend of his thoughts, the brevity of his ideas, the suggestiveness of his words. But it was her, in her intoxicating beauty, who was sucking them out of him now.

For a long while they looked deeply and longingly into one another's eyes and absorbed themselves in a mysterious, musical silence, their hearts wonderfully vibrating in tune like the strings of an Orphic lyre. They drew their faces closer, but as they did so the magical silence was suddenly broken by the harsh sound of shouting in the distance. The two friends then reluctantly turned their faces once more towards the city below them. The shouting was intermittent, but got steadily louder.

'It's the mob most likely,' Origen said at length. 'They are looking for blood again.'

'Blood?' Sarah asked, her face now suddenly full of anxiety.

'Of Christians. I witnessed the beginning of it earlier. They're being stirred up, yet again, by some madman who blew in from the desert. However, I fear that this time it is going to be much worse for us than ever before. For now the Emperor himself is actually encouraging them.'

'Oh, no! Dear Origen.' Sarah took his hand and squeezed it tightly. 'No'.

'Yes. So, will you come to the Didascaleon tomorrow, Sarah?' Origen asked after another loud burst of shouting had died down.

The question unsettled Sarah. She released his hand. 'Origen. You know I am trying. I want to believe. Really I do. But I am not yet prepared to commit myself to the Christ as fully as you. I can't be false to myself, false with myself. I must know the *truth*.'

'You sound like a Gnostic now, Sarah.'

'Perhaps. In any event, I admire *you* deeply, Origen. Personally, I mean. You must know that. I love what you and your colleagues are doing there in the Didascaleon. And whether I attend it or not, that will always remain the case. Everywhere we look nowadays we see naught but decadence, decay, betrayal, corruption and utter confusion. Even Ambrosius, I fear, will fall into it. But Clement - no one can fault him. He is totally pure, the most virtuous man in Alexandria, nay in the whole of the Empire, I would guess.'

'Then let us support him, dear Sarah, with all our heart and all our power.'

Origen sighed deeply as the words fell from his lips, and he thirsted fervently to seal them upon hers with a pure, sweet kiss. But just as his face moved inexorably towards hers once more, he heard the loud voice of Ambrosius call from the entrance to the *atrium*: 'Friends, it's time to eat.'

5   THE GREAT MASTER

A light meal had been prepared by the servants upon Ambrosius' instructions and was served by them to the gathered friends in the dining-room. They ate it, stretched out Roman-style on soft couches, along with cups of light, red wine. Origen, however, preferred to sit on a wooden folding stool.

During the meal the atmosphere and conversation was entirely dictated by Ambrosius who, determined not to let his choleric sister provoke his friends further, spoke almost continually about his extensive and growing knowledge of the great Gnostic, Marcion. Origen gladly let him carry on, although he could easily and successfully have challenged him on several points. But Origen's thoughts were being pulled in too many directions at once. He could get neither Sarah out of his mind nor the thought of the madman preaching hatred and venom against his community.

And all this, augmented by the strange noises that still occasionally filtered up from the city below, echoed in his ears when later he was shown to the guest-room on the upper floor, which he was to share with Lukas for the night.

The room was small, clean and freshly decorated but it had only one bed. However, a black servant soon arrived with a brightly-coloured mattress and placed it carefully on the floor. Origen insisted on having this despite Lukas' many efforts to get him to take the bed.

Origen slept uneasily and had strange dreams. Many times he woke up sweating, sometimes struggling desperately to cry or shout aloud. As he lay awake between each fitful dream he could make no sense of them, nor could he barely remember them, all except one, that is, the very last one. This was as clear as crystal and he would remember it always, for in it the Great Master came to him.

It was not the first time the Great Master had appeared to Origen, for he had a deep, personal relationship with Him, and He came to him not only in dreams but in many other ways as well.   Such things, however, Origen kept entirely to himself – especially about his dreams and visions he spoke to no one, apart from Clement, that is.   But even to Clement he merely dropped hints occasionally rather than speak freely and openly.   For it was a most difficult subject to put into words, so open to misinterpretation.   The world, and especially here in Alexandria, was awash with magicians, both amateurs and accomplished; seasoned and unseasoned soothsayers; naïve and acclaimed philosophers; as well as pure tricksters of every conceivable sort. On any street corner you could meet someone willing to sell you the perfect philosophical system, a neatly packaged religious doctrine, a magical method, a safe swift passage to the spiritual world, to the stars, to heaven, to God himself, if only you believed the purveyor, believed in his visions, in his miracles or his philosophy, believed, that is, in his own personal and guaranteed way to the master. Origen at all costs did not wish to be bagged with such people. He did not claim to know everything, and often suffered great anxiety regarding the deepest and truest nature of his Great Master's being. But he also knew for certain that his awareness, his growing knowledge and informed understanding, and especially his way of seeing the Great Master was not based on any false, naïve, or questionable systems, on mystical visions, on half-baked doctrines and the like, but on the truth; and this truth, to Origen, was the truth of the Gospel.

Origen's relationship with the Great Master was based primary on a deep and growing *love*, as shown in the Gospel. It was taught to him by both of his parents, but especially his father. This love was deepened in Origen's youth through a growing faith, so that in his teenage years and especially as he began to take in what Clement had to say, he saw the Great Master in a light so clearly and lovingly that he was afraid almost to speak of Him at all; afraid he'd say the wrong thing, lead people away from Him rather than to Him. And *that* surely would be sacrilegious. On the other hand, Origen fully realized that eventually he would simply *have* to speak openly. He could not keep locked up in his breast forever what he knew to be so true. That much was certain.

This time the Great Master came more like an angel than ever before. He was standing outdoors on a small hill. It was dawn, and the huge, golden sun was rising behind the hill. The Great Master was most beautiful, tall and majestic and dressed in a long, shining robe which was tenderly woven from the first golden rays of the morning sun. He smiled, ever so benignly, at Origen who felt himself almost melting away out of pure love for Him. Origen concentrated then on the Great Master's eyes which flashed in many colours. Slowly the Great Master lifted His hand and pointed to one side. Origen looked and saw a drawn, saffron-coloured curtain which was billowing in a gentle breeze.
'Is this a dream?' he heard himself asking.
'The answer lies in the fact that you can actually ask me such a question at all,' the Great Master responded in His familiar, velvety tones.

After a pause the Great Master continued 'I want to show you something,' and He raised His hand again, this time to draw back the curtain slightly. Immediately, however, the shouts, shrieks and cries of the mob returned to Origen's troubled ears.

The Great Master then stepped aside completely and the curtain opened fully, and although Origen could no longer see Him, His presence remained overwhelming throughout the entire dream.

A great drama then began to unfold before Origen's night-time eyes, a drama in which he wanted desperately to be fully involved but realized, with growing frustration, that he could not move at all, being fixed like a plant into the ethereal ground of his strange, waking-dream, so that all he could do was helplessly observe.

First he was looking down like a bird on white Alexandria from high above, and saw that its streets were clogged with people who clamoured about in great confusion but who nevertheless seemed to move in undulating waves in one definite direction. And gradually, as Origen's vision focussed, he also came to realize that that direction was none other than his own home!

The scene changed rapidly and he then found himself amidst the mob; still stuck, however, to his spot but now fighting off attackers on all sides. Suddenly he became horribly and fully aware of what was happening; he had to get to his house before them, for he knew for certain now that the mob was intent on destroying his family!

Origen then looked up, and above him he saw the mad preacher who had earlier been stirring up the mob outside the temple. Now, however, he was not preaching but hovering weirdly in the air, totally naked, with his arms outstretched like huge bats' wings, and his body encased in angry, spurting flames. His eyes were wide open but blank as a statue, and around his feet were iron chains. He had no words, but he did not need them, for fiery smoke fumed from his mouth with a much greater power. And, silently, Origen watched as with his sulphuric venom, this demon fanned the entire mob onwards like a single, huge, angry beast.

'O Great Master, help me!' Origen cried in desperation.
'I am here,' the Great Master responded invisibly.
'Help me, Master!'
'Deliver my people, my child. And keep awake always. Watch and pray.'

The next thing Origen saw was his father being dragged by his head by the mob out of his home while his mother looked on in horror and utter helplessness, his many little brothers clutching to her and howling with fear.

Origen's vision then started to sway and swell as if he was looking down from a tall ship's deck into a great dark sea, lashed and whipped by a mighty hurricane. He felt as if his head was being pulled right off him.
'Master! Master!' he cried again. 'Help me!'
'Feed my sheep.'
'Yes, Master, yes. But help *me*..........help......please.'

31

'Origen! Origen!'

To Origen's great relief the Great Master then stepped back fully into his vision, momentarily cancelling out his horror, fear and frustration. Origen immediately flew towards him like a bee to a flower. The Great Master's face then spread out in a fan of softest, brightly-coloured flower-petals before Origen's dreamy eyes. These petals, however, soon began to dissolve and the contours of a different, more ordinary, human face began to emerge.

'Origen! Origen!'

Origen awoke to see the familiar face of Lukas hovering anxiously over him.

'Origen! Origen! Wake up!'

Origen sat up and looked about him panting. Outside, the first steaks of dawn were colouring the eastern sky but the room was still grey.

Lukas sat down beside Origen and put his arm around him. 'You have been dreaming?' he asked, tenderly now.

'Oh, yes, Lukas, I have.'

'I have heard much disturbance throughout the night, Origen, but *I* was not dreaming.'

Origen, who had slept in his tunic, got up from the mattress and went over to the single, small window of the room. He could not see much but what he did see was ominous – wisps of smoke coiling like black snakes above the white, flat rooftops of the city. Origen reckoned it was still far too early for this to be the smoke of breakfast fires and turned to Lukas anxiously.

'I must get home at once,' he said. 'I fear something terrible has happened.'

'What do you fear, Origen?' Lukas pleaded.

But Origen did not answer. Instead he seized Lukas' hand and said, 'Come,' and he drew him swiftly down the stairs of the *domus* and out into the fresh morning garden.

'What do you fear?' Lukas asked again, hurrying after him.

'Let us not speak further,' Origen advised and they set off down the hill on which the beautiful *domus* of Ambrosius was set. At a turning where Lukas had to go in a different direction Origen said, 'You, Lukas, must get to your own home too, at once. I pray that your family is safe. Go.'

Origen gave him the Kiss of Peace and set off alone.

At that moment Origen saw the golden orb of the sun, known, to the nomads of the vast desert beyond the city and even to some of the sophisticated city dwellers of Alexandria itself, as the Eye of the great God Ra, lifting himself from his nightly sojourn in the underworld and setting out on his daily journey across the blue face of heaven.

Origen was not one of those who paid homage to Ammon Ra but this never prevented him from acknowledging and respecting Ra's great power, majesty and beauty. This morning, however, Origen could see little majesty or beauty in him and felt no warmth either, for the closer he got to the city-centre the colder he felt and the more the smell of death began to fill his nostrils. Then turning onto Canopius Way, where about halfway along he saw a great pyre burning, he knew for certain that whatever name and power one may ascribe to that great orb up there in the sky, a different one was now being unleashed upon his city. A dark angel from hell had descended upon it and was in fierce and gluttonous pursuit of its most peaceable and innocent community, that of the Christians.

At that moment also, Origen knew for certain that his life had been changed; changed utterly, and forever.

6   A WEALTHY MATRON

When in 30 BC Caesar Augustus marched with his army into Alexandria and ended, once and for all, the power-mad, love-drunk, and opium-fuelled dreams of Anthony and Cleopatra, he finally realized, through this decisive action, one of the most deeply-held ambitions of Rome: that of absorbing this great and independent city of Alexandria into its growing Empire.

One of the first Edicts of Augustus, regarding the consolidation of Alexandria, was to dissolve the city's most important civic institution, the Senate. Over 200 years later, when Origen was still a young boy, another Emperor came to the city, albeit in less bellicose circumstances. This was the soldier who had recently manoeuvred himself, with great skill and cunning, onto the throne of the Emperor after the reigning one, Didius Julianus, was murdered, like the one before him, after only a few months rule. This new, relatively strong Emperor was called Septimius Severus and he visited Alexandria three years after his installation, in the year 196AD when Origen was eleven years old.

Given the shortness of the rule of his predecessors and the constant threat of assassination, Septimius Severus was, of course, anxious to consolidate his newly-won power and position and he shrewdly realized and correctly valued the growing importance of Alexandria in this regard. Thus, in his various strategies concerning the great but increasingly difficult business of maintaining order in his Empire, he gave centre-stage to Alexandria. So that on his state visit there he announced, to the great enthusiasm of the crowds, that he was restoring to them the privilege of their long-abolished but highly-valued Senate.

After another few years however, rumours began to reach the hypersensitive ears of Severus about a strange new sect called the Christians whom, he was told, were secretly infiltrating every department of his Empire's administration. This, understandably, alarmed Severus who, nevertheless, instantly recognized that in such rumours he had hit upon a perfect scapegoat. For, clever politician that he was, he was instinctively aware that if he was to continue to cunningly manipulate and exploit, for his own aggrandisement, the Demos of the Empire, to control its restive and ever-warring factions and keep the balance of power to his advantage, a scapegoat, an enemy within, was the ideal tool he needed.

Apart from its run-of-the-mill work, the new Senate of Alexandria had, of course, the task of acknowledging the Emperor's wishes but even more importantly of enforcing his various Edicts. And in one of these, Severus duly denounced the Christians as conspirators, idolaters, and blasphemers against the traditional gods of Rome, trouble-makers whose sole purpose was to subvert the established laws and order of the Empire. The Christians, in this manner, were offered to the mobs - not only the most degenerate ones of Rome itself but to the mobs of all the cities of the Empire - as prize meat for their most blood-thirsty and devilish appetites, appetites which decadent Rome itself was expert at both fuelling and satisfying. The Emperor knew, of course, how to rule because he knew how to please the citizens! These are always the basis of political power and in the enforcement of his Edict against the Christians some of the most enthusiastic of these so-called 'citizens' lived in Alexandria.

In the very first wave of attacks, which lasted for a few months, Origen's nightmare actually came true! Leonides, his beloved father, was preaching one evening at the *agora* when suddenly and very unexpectedly someone in the small group of his listeners threw a stone at him. It struck Leonides on the forehead and this was the sign for a disparate but obviously conspiring group of anti-Christian fanatics, who, up till then, had been loitering in various parts of the *agora*, to congeal quickly into a mass. They grabbed Leonides and dragged him viciously onto the nearby street where, in a diabolical frenzy, they hacked off his head with sharp hatchets and machetes, while a growing crowd of onlookers cheered them on enthusiastically.

During the following weeks and months, about a hundred other Christians were dragged from their homes, workshops, and meeting-places, and either beheaded in a similar way, or else burned on great pyres outside the Soma in the central square of Alexandria amidst great celebrations which often went on for days after each atrocity. Because they were acting on strict orders from their centurions, the many soldiers, who were carefully watching these spectacles from a distance, only interfered if they thought the mob threatened to damage the property of the citizens.

Months later, when his own and the deepest grief of his mother began to lift (most of Origen's brothers were too young to fully appreciate the horror of the tragedy that had befallen them) the fact that Origen had become the head of his large family began to sink in. He shuddered at first but then prayed most earnestly. He asked God, day and night, for strength, understanding, and especially for forgiveness for those misguided souls who were carrying out such awful deeds. Often, then, he took to his father's old chair in his library (his mother had little interest in the books) and sat there quietly in the evening like his father used to do, pondering deeply his own future, the future of his family, the School, but most of all the *Kyrios* of Alexandria and its important place in the growing new World Body. This latter was the broadest of all his concerns and often occupied his troubled mind even more deeply than many of his more immediate ones.

During this time he was also chronically missing the soul and spiritual sustenance he always received from attending the celebration of the *Agape*, or love-feast, which was the central act of worship and celebration of the Christian *Kyrios* community. Because of the pogroms, it was difficult to celebrate it. However, this loss meant that he applied himself all the more diligently to prayer, meditation, and study.

The *Agape* was a community commemoration/celebration of the very last supper which the Lord had had with his intimate disciples. This had taken place during the time of Passover in Jerusalem just before the Lord was crucified, and was a meal at which He had miraculously poured out His body, soul and spirit into ordinary bread and wine and offered Himself, in these purely vegetarian substances, as a replacement sacrifice for the animal one of the lamb and its blood, with which the Jews had always celebrated God's covenantal relationship with man, up to this point. By this miraculous and revolutionary act of the Lord, however, He was able to establish a totally new kind of relationship between God and man, and one binding, not only on the Jews, but, He said, on all men and for all time to come.

Many of the presbyters who usually celebrated this meal had either been murdered during the pogroms or else had their lives threatened and had, therefore, stopped holding it, temporarily at least. Clement was also a presbyter. But, due to the good offices of a wealthy Roman matron who was very interested in the Christ and to whom Clement always took a particular delight in talking, he was able to continue to hold *Agape* occasionally. For this matron, Paula by name, was of the Patrician class and owned a spacious villa situated outside the city walls in the suburb of Eleusis. Clement, who normally lived in an *insulae*, a large building comprising numerous individual apartments, situated near the Didascaleon, had had to flee the city at the height of the pogroms during which the Didascaleon itself had been attacked and plundered. Clement had found safe, secure, and very hospitable hiding in Paula's. And in a clandestine manner, he occasionally sent out word from there about the next *Agape* and surprisingly large numbers of people usually turned up.

The *Agape* feast was always broken into two parts: one open to everyone but especially the catechumens under direct Christian instruction, and one for the baptized only. It was during the latter part of the event that the initiates or enlightened ones gathered around the sacred Cup and consecrated bread and wine, and at which the Lord himself often appeared, especially in the first seventy years after Pentecost. It was this, also, that gave the Christians the reputation of being a secret society.

Origen, however, although far more advanced than an ordinary catechumen and a long-time baptized member of the community, he had not yet been admitted to the most sacred part of the *Agape*. One could attend this inner part of the celebration by invitation only.

He felt certain that this invitation would at some stage be extended to him and he looked forward to it with great hope and joy but he was continually reminded and instructed by Clement that the key ingredient, the key virtue that all the initiates must, above all other virtues, have, is *patience*.

During the pogroms Origen took to visiting Clement occasionally in Paula's villa and one evening he was sitting with him in her delightful garden. They had been talking quietly of different things for a long time and during their many and long pauses they deeply absorbed the rich sounds and scents surrounding them – the humming of insects, the sweet perfume of abundant roses, the haunting hush of the breeze among the trees. Occasionally they were jolted by the startling squawks of large but unseen birds, which caused Clement to keep his eyes firmly slanted on a brightly-coloured parrot that was perched on a branch of one of the trees in the small wood directly facing them.

'They may burn our bodies, Origen,' he said, 'but they can't touch our spirit. Never! In fact, for every one of us they burn, a thousand new souls line up immediately to follow Him.'

'How can you be so sure of such things, Master Clement?'

Clement turned slowly towards Origen. 'There are many ways, my child. But one of the very best is simply to look into *your* eyes. For there I see a myriad of souls, all pleading to be baptized and waiting to be breathed upon by the Spirit-Word so that they may enter into the new life.'

'You see so much, Master. I wish I could see like you!'

'Yes, I can see, Origen. And in ways most men only dream of! And yet remember this: I am merely a shadow, albeit a conscious one.'

'Can you explain that to me, Master? I know you are not a shadow or a mere ghost. I touch you; we regularly exchange the Kiss of Peace. I do not understand.'

Clement stood up, gathered his toga about him and took a few careful steps onto the grass. Turning back towards Origen he said, 'The world is not as it first seems to us, to our untrained, physical senses. We have, as it were, to take them in hand, discipline them, purify them. For, in our uneducated, which is, by and large, our so-called normal state, we truly see only shadows.' Clement pointed. 'Plato has made all this as clear to us as that parrot sitting over there on the tree.'

They gazed on the colourful, silent bird for a few moments.

Clement then suddenly pointed to the ground and said, 'See that?'

Origen looked at Clement's long, lean shadow.

'It is nothing without me.' Clement went on, 'That shadow is as much a part of me as my hands. And I am conscious, am I not?'

Origen smiled. 'Certainly, you are, Master'

'Well then, so is that shadow.'

With raised eyebrows Clement watched Origen's suddenly perplexed face. After a few moments he continued. 'Now, my young friend, hear this. Something has happened recently in Palestine and you know what it is – it is all there in the Gospel. A Being has come down from Heaven, as Plato knew perfectly well he would, eventually. And this great Sun or Logos Being has infused this Earth and everything in it, including me, with a new, incorruptible light. This is the light that Plato was talking about in his cave story. We call this great Being, the Christ. And it is *His* light that now lights up everything, so that, whereas, what you may see with your ordinary senses is still a shadow, now, my friend, it is a shadow of Him. The whole world has become a shadow through Him but we, by following the Way, must break through this, pierce it, through to His Being which lives behind this shadow. We live in the very valley of death. Nothing less! But He, as I told you before, is the Light of the World, and this,' – Clement pointed to himself – 'as with all other things, is but a transient image, a thrown, dark reflection, a shadow of Him. See? He has become, through His Great Sacrifice, the triumphant archetype of all, the source, the Light that renews all things, and makes them visible in a new way, and I mean the material things as well as the spiritual.' Clement waved his hands about him. 'I have learned to *see through* all this, to *see through Him*. I have learned to walk with Him, literally. He is as real to me as you are, my precious young friend. Believe me. Now *you* have to learn to see through me.'

'I do, Master,' Origen said feebly. 'I see, through you.'

'Yes,' Clement agreed, 'I know. But in time you will see more and more. In time no more will you see only this' – Clement pulled his cheeks – 'this decaying dying flesh, but Him in His Risen flesh. Of this I have no doubt whatsoever.'

Origen let his Master's wise words continue uninterrupted, let them sink down deeply, as deeply as he possibly could, and, as so often before, felt them play like warm and gentle fingers of flame upon the strings of his searching soul. He listened quietly to this celestial music and gave himself up to it in utter ecstasy and remained thus, silently, for a long time. Eventually, however, he heard a single discordant note, whether inside or outside him he did not know, but with it he did know that the music also ceased abruptly!

Origen looked up worriedly. 'Master,' he asked, 'who am I?'

Clement looked deeper than ever into his shining violet eyes. Then, lifting his hand and tenderly stroking Origen's cheek with the back of his delicate fingers, he declared, 'A beautiful boy. Truly the very spirit of youth.'

Origen was shivering now. He had heard his Master speak wonderfully clearly many times before, about the Christ, but seldom had his words been so penetrating. Origen's esteem and love for Clement grew more and more.

Clement then embraced him and gave him the Kiss of Peace. The Kiss of Peace was a holy sign given by the Risen One to the Apostle Paul who had given it to the *Kyrios*. In the gesture the lips were tenderly placed upon the brow of the recipient, the seat of the soul.

After this, Origen began weeping and Clement considered it best to let him be. He got up and for a while walked in large circles on the grass, deep in thought. When he saw that Origen had stopped weeping he sat down beside him again.

'Soon, you too will be initiated into the Great Mysteries, my child,' he said gently, 'and then you will know fully what I mean. Not only will you learn how to serve Him but also to see Him, truly, not in dreams and visions, not as a mere angel, phantom or some such being, not like so many of our so-called knowledgeable Gnostics see Him, but *truly*, as He is in His crucified, but Risen and fully redeemed *flesh*.'

'Clement! Clement!' A deep, female voice boomed across the garden in which Origen and Clement were sitting. It was Paula, the matron-owner of the villa.

Clement turned and saw Paula's imposing form sweeping swiftly towards him on the rose-bordered path which led directly to the broad portico and courtyard of her villa. Her bright-orange *palla*, which was draped loosely but elegantly about her shoulders, billowed fulsomely in the cool, evening breeze.

If Ambrosius' *domus* was beautiful, Paula's villa was positively palatial. Paula had been widowed during the reign of Marcus Aurelius, in whose army her husband had been a long-serving *legatus*, or legion commander. He died, during the great plague which devastated parts of the Empire during Marcus' time, while on duty defending the borders of Pannonia and Dacia against the increasingly restless Germanic tribes there.

Paula, who had lived in Rome before she settled in Alexandria, had bought her villa here with the generous grant given her by Marcus upon her husband's death. She had chosen it with great care. The setting was quite pastoral for Alexandria which, because of its sea and desert surroundings, had very little variety in landscape. But whatever woods there were, were in the region close to Paula's villa, the grounds of which comprised at least five acres of exquisitely-kept gardens as well as fruit orchards. And it was not by accident either that, although it could not be seen from her gardens, the Temple of Eleusis lurked mysteriously within these woods, and its varied and seasonal activities intrigued her greatly. Indeed the activities surrounding the Temple gave Paula's active and searching mind endless food for speculation.

For Paula was fiercely interested in all things religious, and in the Christ in particular, and she loved dearly to hear Clement speak about Him. But she had never taken any steps towards actually becoming a Christian herself, and had never, Clement carefully noted, even *hinted* that she wished to become a catechumen which was merely the very first step on a path which led eventually to many souls becoming fully initiated into the Great Mystery.

Clement stood up and greeted Paula with a slight curtsy.
'Come, Clement,' she said. 'You two have been speaking long enough.' She threw a maternal glance at Origen. 'And I can tell by your young friend's eyes that his soul has been fed quite enough spiritual meat for days to come – and we must not over-feed the young, must we. Their digestive system is still only forming after all.' She laughed at her own wit and beamed a broad smile at Origen who, however, remained silent, serious and seated.
'Origen,' she prompted, 'you could do with some freshly-roasted pheasant in orange sauce, couldn't you?'

Origen, who had actually made his very first acquaintance with Paula earlier in the day when he arrived to speak with Clement, pulled himself up awkwardly from his seat and tried to act politely.
'Er...I do not eat animal flesh, Madame,' he said with some embarrassment.
'Aha......like the great Pythagoras. Makes you think better, does it, eh?'
'Animal food does not engage our digestive organs in a healthy way,' Origen said, trying to defeat his embarrassment with wisdom, 'whether we are young or old – it is, in a certain sense, already pre-cooked or at least pre-digested food, that is, in terms of the natural food chain which we, as human animals, cap. As such, animal flesh actually causes our digestive organs to become lazy, atrophied, heavy. And thus yes, you are right, not eating the stuff helps me think better.'
'Ouch! Clement, help me. Was I being *that* serious? Are these words of revelation, wisdom, or merely juvenile idealism? *You* didn't tell him not to eat meat, did you?'
'No, Paula, I did not. This young man arrives at many conclusions which, I have to admit, often makes *me* think hard, sometimes, too. And I have not heard this one before.'
Clement smiled proudly at Origen, 'But he will, I'm sure, eat some vegetables.'
'Yes, come, my dear friends. Let us all eat *something*.'

They walked off slowly then, along the beautiful path leading to the wide, white colonnade of the portico.
'Clement, I have someone very special for you to meet at dinner,' Paula said.
'Paula, you know so many special people. Pray, is this one *extra* special or just plain common-or-garden special?'

40

Laughing heartily at Clement's jibe, Paula said, 'Clement, my dear, I will let *you* decide on that philosophical nuance! My guest is a namesake, of sorts. He is called Paul and is from Antioch. I met him there last year while visiting some friends and I invited him to Alexandria for a spell. He has finally arrived. He can lecture...........oh, just wonderfully. He will give lectures here in my villa,' and she added in a whisper, 'I hope.'

'On what, pray, Paula, will he, does he, lecture?'

'Oh, you know............he has *immense* knowledge.'

'Immense knowledge of what?'

'Everything.'

'Does he believe in the Christ?'

'Ah.........Clement. That, I have not asked him ......yet. Anyway, belief! - pray, what is it? It's such a tricky one, isn't it? He certainly speaks about the Christ sometimes.' Paula closed one eye, turned towards Clement and lowered her voice conspiratorially. 'You, Clement, at the right moment during the meal, ask him *that*. I will be most anxious to hear his reply.'

'I will find out quickly enough if he is a Christian or not, Paula.'

As they passed under the red-roofed portico they immediately saw a tall, imposing figure with a long, bushy grey beard. He was standing perfectly still in the middle of the courtyard, and looked to Clement very much like a Roman senator except, he noted, he did not have the telltale purple on his toga which actually was shining white all over. He seemed to be carefully studying a large, stationary insect on the ground in front of him.

'That is Paul of Antioch,' Paula whispered excitedly to Clement.

Apologising for disturbing his contemplations, Paula proceeded to introduce her two new guests to Paul and after they had exchanged greetings she duly announced that they were already running far too late for dinner and straightaway led all three of them into the dining-room.

Paula's dining-room was spacious, predominantly orange in colour (her favourite), with shining white marble busts of Homer and Plato at the entrance, and other, more obscure but equally shiny statuary of Greek, Roman and Egyptian divinities doted about in various niches.

During the first course of the meal, in which Origen was forced, to his chagrin, to recline like the rest of them on a separate couch (for he was far too shy to ask for a stool!) there was little talk, excepting the usual pleasantries that invariably accompany such new encounters. For a while as they ate, Paula's lean old poet recited some of her favourite verses from Callimacus, Ovid and other poets, but when, during the intervals between these verses she noted, with a well-disguised despondence, that they did not produce the desired philosophic effect on her guests, she suddenly clapped her hands and the poet disappeared like magic!

'Paul, tell us what your journey from Antioch was like,' she asked. 'Was it pleasant?'
'Awful!' Paul replied abruptly in a deep, resonant voice but went on picking with his big white teeth at the wing of a roast pheasant.
'Oh, dear! Was the sea rough or something?'
After putting down the bone and carefully wiping his mouth with his hand, Paul leaned back on his couch and said, 'No. No, Paula, the sea was fine. Calm mostly, for the whole week, actually. No. You see, the only passage I could procure, in order to fulfil my long-term promise to you, was on a ship with a cargo of.....slaves of all things!'
'Slaves! Good heavens, Paul. What a bore! But tell me........ I am so surprised. Do they really export such things from the heavenly city of *Antioch*?'
'Well, trade is something I have little interest in, Paula. But let me see..... do they export slaves from Antioch? Oh, I suppose not. The creatures, I would guess, were gathered up from all over the place. You know how these businessmen operate. They have their middlemen who engage well-armed, mercenary raiding parties that go deep into the Barbarian lands and collect up these savages. Oh Paula! I was looking at chained gangs of them for a whole damn week! There was little else to look at. But sometimes, when I had the stomach for it, I could actually pass my time tolerably well by *studying* them. I think most of them were either Armenian or Caucasian. I could tell by their features.'

Clement, who was watching Paul and listening carefully to him, while picking at a little bowl of juicy black olives near his main plate, said, 'Poor souls. What a life! What a destiny!'
'I was glad to get off,' Paul said.
'I hear it's not such a lucrative trade anymore, at least not here in Alexandria. It's falling off,' Clement suggested.
'Why?' Paul asked, licking his fingers. 'Have you enough of them here or something? My personal experience nowadays is that it's very hard to get a really good one.'
'Oh, no. It's not that. Some of us here in the city have been.........well, shall we say, encouraging the senators to *think* about this so-called trade.'
'Some of us?..........think?........this so-called trade?'
'Oh, yes, pardon me. I mean us Christians.'
'Christians!' Paul looked shocked.
'Er, yes,' Paula interjected embarrassedly. 'I should perhaps have told you, Paul. Clement is one of our.........ahem.....foremost Christians, here in Alexandria. He is actually the head of the Christian School.'
Paul raised his eyebrows, looked a little less shocked, and picked up another

pheasant's wing from his plate. 'Christians,' he repeated, and started biting again.

On tenterhooks, Paula watched him in silence, but when it was obvious that he was not going to say anything else she turned to Clement and said enthusiastically, 'Clement, I must tell you that I attended every lecture I possibly could by Paul during my stay in Antioch last year. And I can honestly say I learned more in that one month than I did in my entire life up to then. He knows *so* much about.........about, well especially....er... Aristotle.' She fluttered her eyes at Clement and then beamed a big, motherly smile at Paul who, however, remained quite serious.
'What is your special subject, Paul, may I ask?' Clement ventured.
'The Categories,' Paul responded between bites.
'Aha! Very interesting. Very important. And the Temperaments?'
'That too.'
'Lovely. What about the Organum?'

Paul slowly began to eye Clement more directly now and Paula, finally scenting the arrival of her dearly wished-for philosophical encounter, clapped her hands enthusiastically for more wine.

Origen, who had been watching with a measured detachment all of the proceedings around him, tried hard to keep up an interest in what they were actually saying but he found that even the small amount of wine he had been sipping was already making him sleepy. He wished more and more for a stool. Clement, however, educated through his profession to be attentive to the mood-swings of youth and always, through his empathetic nature, anxious to include them in his conversations, spotted Origen's difficulty and threw a sudden question in his direction.
'Origen here has read Aristotle, haven't you, my boy?'
Origen became suddenly awake. 'Yes. I have.'
'He spends half his time in the library, up in the Serapeum, you know,' Clement said to Paul.
'Mmmm. It's one of the places I shall visit during my stay.'
'It is famous the wide world over, our library,' Paula said proudly.
'But Origen has his own library too,' Clement went on boldly. 'He is a most enthusiastic student of philosophy. Origen, ask this learned gentleman a good question, will you?'
'About Aristotle?'
'About anything under our wonderful, god-given, Egyptian sun.'

Origen looked sideways at Paul who had by now firmly put down his pheasant wing, wiped his hands on his toga and was determinedly if reluctantly readying himself for some kind of contest.

43

Origen said carefully, 'Paul of Antioch - is this golden, Egyptian sun of ours god-given?'

Paul scratched his beard and looked up in a slightly bored manner. After a few moments he said very slowly, 'Is a projected visual effect, produced in my brain's atoms when I open my eyes outside on a sunny day, something which I can, most aptly, define as the trajectory of a great ball of fire across a thing we call the sky, god-given?'

Paula was delighted with the answer and enthusiastically searched both Origen's and Clement's face for suitable responses. Origen's expression was blank.

'Everything is god-given,' Clement affirmed.

'Only if you include *nothing*,' Paul said humourlessly.

'I don't. Nothing is nothing.'

'Except a word.'

'Precisely. The Word is everything.'

'Oh......I did not mean......well then......do you mean............'

'Yes. I mean the very word, the idea itself, creates; *eidos* – it means 'to form'. See? The Word is magical. You just have to use it in the *right* way, that's all. We know for instance...........'

'Wind!' Paul interrupted irritably. 'This is but wind.'

'Pardon?'

Paula, spotting possible unwelcome difficulties, decided to change the conversation's direction.

'It's that they have such a love of their John, these Christians, Paul,' she said with uncharacteristic coyness. 'John, you know, said that Christ is the very Word made flesh – a human being he means, I think.'

'My dear Paula,' Paul replied emphatically, 'I am well aware of the Christian's philosophy of the Logos.'

Origen, sitting up suddenly on the edge of his couch, said, 'Christianity is not a philosophy, Paul of Antioch.'

'It's nothing if it is not a philosophy..........ah.......what's your name again?'

'Origen.'

'Origen. Yes. Look. Greek philosophy is the cream, the very finest fruit of mankind's entire civilizations – note the plural. Through it, and nothing else, we can come to a true knowledge not only of the ancient Gods and their various meanings, but also we learn of the relative, yet true, places in the world of the leaders and the led; that is, of the kings and the shepherds, the princes and their slaves, the heroes and the villains. We learn of everyone and everything: of the composition of the rocks, the dynamics of the rivers.........the.....'

'Christ can explain all these things too,' Origen interjected bravely.

'Then *he* must be a philosophy,' Paul said with a rare, forced smile.

Clement was smiling too, but joyfully, and at Paula. Then he turned to Paul and said,

'Pray, Paul, give me an ear. Christianity, as our good young friend here has said, is not a philosophy. But it will in time absorb *all* philosophy into it, Greek or otherwise. Of that I, for one, am certain. Christianity is best described as a *Way*, something which Christ actually describes himself as, in St. John's Gospel, *I am the Way*. He means it in the old, oriental sense that everything you are, and do, can become part of a work that leads to a certain peaceful place, a certain goal, a still point, a sphere, a utopia, a perfect ending, you know, and a perfect, new beginning.'
'What can be better than philosophy? Philosophy *is* the way,' Paul said irritably.

Paula decided to change the direction yet again. 'It is terrible,' she said, 'the way the Christians are being tortured and burnt at the moment. What is it like in Antioch, Paul?'
'Regarding these.........Christians?'
'Yes, of course. We talk of them.'
'Well, they are, you know, Paula, more prominent there than in any other city in the Empire.'
'Even more so than here in Alexandria, or Rome herself?'
'Yes. In fact I can tell you they are becoming quite a.........a...........'
'Problem?' Paula reluctantly suggested.
Paul made no response except to pout his lips and look forlornly into his wine cup. Paula clapped her hands again and directed a young slave, standing nearby, to fill Paul's cup. Then she went on, 'Problem or no problem, Paul, the Christians are the most sensible and peaceable group of people I know. I abhor what this Severus is trying to do. Marcus Aurelius must be turning in his grave. *There* was a principled man for you! Do you think such acts as Severus is committing would have even entered his head? Our current Emperor is, I fear, profoundly *evil*.'
'Evil!' Paul gasped.
'Yes!'
'Come, Paula, what is evil?'
'Oh, Paul. We have discussed such questions before *ad nauseam*. Let us not go into details. You know *exactly* what I mean. You can't just go chopping people's heads off, or throwing them to the lions for the enjoyment of the degenerate, city rabble just because you are Emperor and you disagree with what these good people believe.'
'Oh, I don't know about that, Paula.'
'Paul, tell me, what is the situation of the Christians in Antioch?'
'We hear so many things about them, Paula. The Emperor *hates* secret societies.'
'So I take it they are being burnt and butchered there too?'

But Paul did not answer.

'We are not a secret society Paul,' Clement said emphatically, breaking the strained

45

silence. 'No more secret, that is, than any one of numerous other Gnostic and mystery groupings or schools here in Alexandria, and all over the eastern Empire. So why are *we* being singled out? I'll tell you. The Emperor senses that we, more than all the others, possess something he needs but can't get his grubby, greedy little hands on, and that is the *spirit* of knowledge and Truth. For this cannot be bought with gold, cannot be seen with physical eyes nor coerced by physical force. But we have it as our primary power in the world! *That*, Paul, is why we are being persecuted! And as far as secrecy is concerned, it has been known from time immemorial that once an individual reaches a certain level of philosophical and spiritual development, he or she also comes to a kind of threshold, and experience from that point onwards takes on a character and a quality that simply *cannot* be conveyed in words. Human language is simply inadequate when it comes to spiritual experience of this kind. It can, at best, only be conveyed by occult signs and symbols. For, Gnosis is a mysterious, magical process *by its very nature.* Surely you, Paul, as a learned man versed in modern philosophy, as well as in the wise ways of the ancients, must know what I am talking about.'

Paul remained silent for a while, giving the impression of seriously contemplating Clement's words. But eventually he said with stubborn emphasis, 'I do *not* condone secrecy among groups, any groups, in our Empire.'
'We are *not* secret! Quite the reverse! *Anyone* can join us,' Clement retorted in an uncharacteristically impatient tone.

Paula, somewhat unnerved now by the excitement she had stirred up, decided to try to ease the tension a little with a plea for compassion.
'They beheaded this poor boy's father, you know Paul,' she said, looking with great sympathy upon Origen. Paul's eyes, however, remained sullenly fixed upon his wine.
'Pray, tell us, Origen, how is you family now?' Paula went on.

Origen, who had been slanting his eyes more and more carefully upon Paul who himself rarely looked at anyone when he spoke, turned to Paula and replied, 'My mother is a good Christian, Paula, but she also possesses fine stoic qualities. So she is coping quite well, thank you.'
'But surely the family income..........where does it come from now?'
'We Christians share, Paula,' Clement interjected. 'That is another thing the Emperor hates about us. He wants to be the father of *all* the handouts. That way he wins the approval of the idle, city mobs.'

'The Emperor is a strong ruler and has brought peace to the Empire,' Paul said dryly.
'Peace! Some peace!' Clement countered.
Paula turned to Origen again and said, 'Origen, I am certain you could do with some

money. How many are in your family?'

'Seven boys, all younger than me.'

'Oh dear. Look, Clement, why doesn't Origen set up a little tuition group here in my villa? He is *so* learned for such a young man. Why, he could teach grammar, geography, history........I'm sure he could easily find some pupils. And Paul could.........'

'Yes, Paula?' Paul asked coldly.

'Well, the students could come to your lectures in the evening too.....'

But Paul merely looked into his wine cup again.

'Paula, what an excellent idea,' Clement said slapping his thigh enthusiastically. 'Origen what do you think?'

'I will think about it, Master. I will. I think, actually, I would like to teach grammar perhaps.'

'Good. And this learned gentleman has given me, Paula, a whopping good idea just now. I suddenly feel I would like to........ to write a book!'

Paula clapped her hands in utter joy. 'Goodness gracious, Clement! How terribly, terribly exciting! What will you call it, pray?'

Clement looked across at Paul who despite his patron's growing enthusiastic response to Clement's proposal, remained quite aloof.

'Let's see,' Clement pondered aloud. 'How about *The Exhortation to the Greeks?*'

7   CONVERSATION BENEATH THE SPHINX

After a few months, the attacks against the Christians in Alexandria abated and Pope Demetrius, who, like Clement, had to flee the city, was able to return to his residence. Soon after this, Clement too was given the all-clear and after organising a clean-up of the Didascaleon, to which happily no major damage was done during the pogroms, he went back to his beloved teaching there. While continuing to attend as many of Clement's lectures as possible, Origen also took up Paula's offer and began, in the garden of her villa, to teach pupils himself, most of whom were directed to him by Clement.

Origen enjoyed his new task, for he found it helped him to focus his mind and prevented him from brooding on matters way beyond his control. He prayed most earnestly for the strength to forgive those who had not only so brutally murdered his father but were causing so much suffering to the followers of the true Way, not only in Alexandria but by all accounts, almost everywhere in the Empire now.

To Paula's delight, Paul of Antioch decided on an extended stay in Alexandria! For his lectures were unusually successful, and invariably well attended. Paul was, in fact, a minor master of oratory and rarely failed to give weight and power to whatever subject he chose, even those which held little personal interest for him and upon which he spoke merely to please a particular audience. He held his lectures every evening in the spacious *atrium* of Paula's villa. But after the first few, he imposed a strict condition that she must keep her beloved peacocks well away from the always-open entrance of the *atrium* through which the curious birds were want to wander during a lecture and upset everyone present, but especially Paul, with their noisy and far-too-awakening shrieks.

While Origen enjoyed his new teaching task, he was also uneasy about it, for Paul's proximity disturbed him. Despite Paul's experience, confidence and knowledge, Origen had a growing dislike for everything he said, either publicly or privately, for he always seemed to challenge Origen's own ideas, his teaching, even his very way of thinking. In his antipathy, Origen even went so far as to actively deter his students from either meeting Paul or attending his lectures; all of which was difficult, given the closeness of the illustrious and popular visitor, and his patron's wish that there be as many as possible at Paul's lectures.

Although Origen was ever anxious to deepen his love for and understanding of the Christ through hearing learned people of every possible persuasion speak of Him in the context of religion and philosophy, in Paul he found or saw nothing but a painful, professional pedant, albeit sometimes quite an erudite one, but by dint of that, one all too capable of luring souls most subtly away from Origen's beloved Christ.

But if Paul of Antioch repelled Origen, another recent arrival in the city made up for him. This was the exciting new philosopher, Ammonius Saccus. Thus, in these months also, Origen found himself attending more and more lectures by this teacher whom he considered one of most unusual and wisest men he had ever met. Origen was most curious of all as to how this man would regard the Christ – for, so far, he had not, to Origen's mind, said much of substance about Him.

Ammonius Saccus' lectures were given in the prestigious Serapeum and Origen was so fascinated with him that he sometimes felt a clash of loyalties when both Ammonius and Clement were giving lectures at the same time!

One bright evening Origen was sitting in the grounds of the Serapeum after attending a lecture by Ammonius Saccus. The subject of the lecture had been the significance and meaning of the Temptation of Eve. In the lecture Ammonius had displayed an incredibly knowledgeable command of the various world gods and mythologies, but especially those appertaining to the ancient Greek civilization, the one most familiar to Origen himself. Ammonius had expounded with uncanny and fascinating dexterity on the various relationships between these gods and their mythologies, and then went on to compare these *en masse* with the Creation story written by Moses in the Bible book of Genesis which the Hebrews took as historical fact.

Origen was sitting facing the great yellow Sphinx which had been there in front of the Serapeum from time immemorial, long before even the Serapeum itself was built. While musing on the lecture with one half of his ever-active mind, Origen was with the other half contemplating the heavenly serenity of the human face of the Sphinx which seemed so firmly fastened to its huge, crouching, bull-and-lion torso. Origen soon found himself secretly envying the command that these ancients had over their various and obviously huge animal passions, a command which he felt the Sphinx itself was meant to portray and emphasise, a power which, the more Origen looked, seemed consummate, if this heavenly face, mounted on such magnificent animal limbs, was anything to judge by. But, he wondered, could such unearthly mastery have been a *reality*? Or did the monument merely articulate a dream of it; the dream say of the master artist who actually sculpted the Sphinx, or, if not, the dream perhaps of the Pharaoh who instructed him to make it?

Origen was suddenly roused from these deep musings by the crunch of approaching, heavy footsteps on the gravel. It was Ambrosius who had also been at the lecture. He sat down and clapped Origen jovially on the back.
'Pray, tell me, wise man,' he said, 'are we allowed to speak of this extraordinary enlightenment we have just received, or must we twist our tonsils into a Gordian knot and hermetically seal our lips forever regarding it. Eh?'

'I believe we are allowed to speak with one another,' Origen said nonchalantly.

'Good. Except, I don't know what to say!' Ambrosius retorted and laughed. After a while he went on, 'He has an inner circle, too, you know. That's where you get the really secret stuff, I'd say. Will you join?'

'He must ask first, I think.'

'Well then. If he is as wise as he sounds he will ask *you* at least,' Ambrosius said. He buried his hand deep inside his light-green toga and scratched his fulsome belly. 'Ammonius Saccus. Saccus – the sack-carrier. Is it because he carries that little bag around his waist all the time, I wonder?'

'Yes. I suppose so. I've noticed too. Mercury, you know, always carries a little purse.'

'What! Mercury! You don't mean to tell me you think the man is a flipping god, do you?'

'Come, Ambrosius. I did not say that. I said *like* Mercury.'

'Mercury – that's a Roman derivation, isn't it? Let me see......so his real name is Hermes, right?'

'Very good Ambrosius, yes, the Greeks use that name. But they speak of roughly the same divinity, the one who teaches the magic arts. The Egyptians here call him Thoth. But the Greeks, I think, know him, knew him, best of all.'

'And you think our Ammonius Saccus has a kind of special, say spiritual connection with this divinity then, is that it?'

'Well, yes. It explains many puzzling things about the man to me.'

'So what's *in* the little sack, or bag, then, eh?'

Origen smiled. 'Do you mean in the bag of Hermes or Ammonius Saccus?' Ambrosius' blank face was a cue to continue. 'I don't know. But I reckon whatever is in there is talismanic. Can you not see the power in the man's very eyes? Indeed, can you not *feel* it? I reckon he uses whatever is in the bag in the same way as the Hebrew High Priests would have used their Urim and Thummim - in the old days I mean; that is when these things really had magical power, not like nowadays when they have, for the Jews, become sort of cold, dead leftovers, things once charged with real life, but now quite devoid of soul and used more or less just for show because those who possess them have no knowledge of whence they came and why they were even given in the first place.'

After a short silence Ambrosius said, 'They say his parents were Christian, you know.' Ambrosius turned with a puzzled look to Origen, 'But *he* is not.........is he?'

'Christian? No, I do not think so.'

'Are you sure?'.

'He seems to me to disavow the historical nature of the Christ drama, but most especially the Resurrection.'

Ambrosius exaggeratedly scratched his head. 'Wow! So that's the definition of a non-Christian, eh?'

'It's the *main* reason, Ambrosius. Paul, I mean the Apostle of course, made that perfectly clear.'

'I have not heard Ammonius Saccus say such things.'

'Well, I am reading between his lines; I can hear behind his speech. He may be fascinating and have tremendous wisdom but I believe he lacks faith in, or has any real knowledge of, the Christ.'

'Ah, Origen. Now *you* speak! Of faith! Yes. That's a thing and a half all right.' Ambrosius sighed. 'Where, pray the gods, does it come from, eh?'

'Nowadays from the spirit of Grace and Truth, spoken of so eloquently by St. John.'

In silence they both mused on the giant Sphinx in front of them for a while. Eventually Ambrosius said, 'Do I have some of that faith stuff in me, Origen, do you think?'

'I think you have, Ambrosius. Some. But you need more. And you can increase it – easily.'

'Easily! How?'

'Pray!'

'Pray! Oh, my God, Origen, my good, my precious friend, I can do many things - I can ride, study, sing, write, sail, make love, make money for my father, and tables and chairs for my mother - but one thing I simply cannot do is *pray*. I know. I've tried many times.'

'Well then, you shall have to learn, Ambrosius.'

'How? How?'

'Like making chairs, money, or……. love – you must *practise!*'

Ambrosius gripped Origen by his shoulder. 'Hey, listen, you are *good* today. Jokes like that could make a pot of money for you if you put them into books, or better still, plays. Become a latter-day Aristophanes.' He laughed heartily and touched Origen's old black tunic with his sandals, adding, 'In no time at all you could buy yourself a brand new tunic.'

Origen blushed.

After a few moments Ambrosius continued in a quieter tone. 'You know, my most beautiful sister, Sarah, is talking a lot about you these days. She complains that you do not visit us anymore.'

'Well,' Origen said, 'I have had to be most careful of my movements over these recent months. You must know the reason for that. And, surely, Sarah knows it too.'

'Oh, I suppose she does. But you know women. It probably wouldn't enter her beautiful head why a whole bunch of you people getting burnt or beheaded or whatever would keep you from seeing *her*. She is very aware, you know, that you love her.'

Origen stiffened a little at the unexpected directness of Ambrosius' statement. He swallowed nervously but did not speak. After a while Ambrosius went on dreamily. 'You know what, Origen, I'll tell you something that maybe even Ammonius Saccus wouldn't tell his own inner circle if he was in a similar position to me. It is this: I actually envy those old Ptolemies who used to rule this great city of ours in days gone by.'

'Whatever do you mean, Ambrosius?'

Ambrosius looked directly at Origen and said with uncharacteristic seriousness, 'I mean the way they could marry their sisters.'

Origen stared back at him with astonishment. 'You mean...?'

'I mean she is a most remarkable and attractive creature, my friend, and I have my difficulties with her precisely because of that. And if *you* have any equivalent sense in those parts of your body which are not under the direct control of your obviously very well-controlled and wise brain, you should act on their sound promptings before she, my sister I mean, gets distracted from you.'

Ambrosius got up and walked slowly over to the Sphinx. Origen's eyes followed him, pensively at first, then becoming more alert and amused as he noted, comically, how even he, Ambrosius, an unusually large man, was so totally dwarfed by this magnificent Sphinx. Ambrosius ran his hands slowly along the yellow sandstone of its monstrous limbs, as if caressing them. Then he stopped suddenly, looked up at the serene face, way above him, turned back to Origen and shouted, 'What is it that first goes on four, then on two, and finally on three?'

Origen smiled. 'Excellent, Ambrosius. You know the Riddle all right. But do you know the answer?'

'I do,' Ambrosius returned confidently.

'What?'

'You. You are the answer. Origen of Alexandria, the wisest man in the Empire. First he crawled on all fours, then he walked on his two legs, and finally he will have to carry a stick. Man himself is the answer.'

Ambrosius then brushed back his toga, bared up his arms in a proud display of his masculinity and shouted, 'Animal power. Man. Man.'

'Woman,' Origen retorted weakly.

'Balls!' Ambrosius shouted. He laughed heartily but Origen felt unable to respond further, for he was trying desperately to hold back a strong, almost uncontrollable desire to laugh also.

After a while Ambrosius came back and sat down again. Origen was sitting with his knees crossed and his tunic was arranged in such a way that one of his white knees showed. Ambrosius slapped it gently and Origen pulled down his tunic modestly, blushing again at Ambrosius' behaviour.

'Listen,' Ambrosius said, 'have you heard of the Ophites?'

'Oh, yes. Who hasn't?'

'Have you been to any of their.........ahem......rituals?'
'No. But I have a good idea of what they do. They worship the Serpent.'
'Yes. But not Mercury's, I can tell you, at least not to my mind. I've been to them. You wouldn't believe what goes on there, my friend. You should come and see for yourself. It'll toughen you up, do you a power of animal, manly good. With respect, it's better by a mile than your................. I mean your Christian..... *Agape*.'
'Nothing is better than our *Agape* love-feast, Ambrosius.'
'You want to bet? Why don't you come with me next Sunday?'

Origen felt a frisson going through his entire body. He instinctively recognised that Ambrosius was offering him an important opportunity to learn more about the Gnostics. Of the Gnostics generally the Ophites had the most widespread reputation and following in Alexandria, many of them claiming to be Christians, a thing Origen wondered about most deeply, and one which often troubled him also.
Hesitantly, he asked, 'Are these Ophites of yours........Christian?'
'Yes. They are. That's the laugh of it, my friend. Knowing you personally, and then seeing these people I could hardly believe my pretty little eyeballs............and....er............as you know,' he added as an aside, 'I myself attend for legitimate reasons, of course; the study of the various parts of the body, and how these can lead to enlightenment and so on........but I could hardly believe I was dealing with the same thing as you people ......I mean Clement, Demetrius, the Didascaleon, etc. That's why I feel you should come - for your own education and information, apart from anything else.'
Origen considered his words in silence for a while then Ambrosius went on, 'You know, too much book stuff can be bad for you if you do not augment it now and then with a juicy little bit of worldly wisdom. Know what I mean?' Ambrosius winked but Origen merely frowned.
'Yes, yes, do come, Origen. And afterwards if *you* call these people Christian, then I promise you I'll call my beautiful, blue, Persian cat an initiate of the Eleusinian Mysteries!'

But Origen still said nothing. Suddenly Ambrosius jumped up. 'Look. don't answer me now. I've got to go. Business calls! I'll come and visit you in Paula's garden tomorrow evening after your class. Tell me then if you want to come. The place where these Ophites have their most........well, shall we say, *exciting*.........ritual, is actually hidden in the woods not far from Paula's villa.'

With that Ambrosius bent and embraced the still-seated and deeply-frowning Origen. Then he took off rapidly down the hill towards the sprawling, gleaming white city below and Origen's eyes did not leave him until he became no bigger than a bird in the distance.

8 MASTER, WHAT IS THE VOICE OF CONSCIENCE?

Origen was delighted beyond belief to see that not only had the pogroms not affected adversely the attendance at Clement's lectures but that the numbers there were actually increasing all the time. This, despite the fact that sporadic sectarian attacks continued against the Christians.

As he moved discreetly about the city on his business, Origen continued to see the madman from the desert trying to stir up the people. But his novelty, and thus his power, had by now fallen off somewhat. Origen made careful enquiries about the fellow and found that he had been a stylite somewhere in the Arabian desert-fringes of Syria and had come down off his twenty-foot pole after seven solid years of meditation! He had done this apparently upon instructions of none other than the Archangel Gabriel himself who also, it was widely reported, told him to come to Alexandria on a special mission, the generalities, if not the details of which were most obvious to Origen at least: kill the Christians! Thus he was known in Alexandria as Simon the Stylite.

Simon's activities went totally unchecked, albeit carefully monitored, by the obedient, ubiquitous soldiers who always watched with cold detachment the movements of the masses. And, whether directly the result of Simon's ranting or of one of his growing number of 'inspired' imitators, they also watched coldly as every so often some poor man or woman, who was widely known to be a follower of the Way, would be dragged from their home and either brutally beheaded or burnt amidst great cheering in the central square. If the demand on the particular evening was for an entertaining burning, very often the pyre would be built up with cartloads of wood willingly supplied by one of the many local fuel merchants, upon public affirmation by an on-the-make senator who happened by the scene, that the Senate itself would foot the bill! More cheers all round!

Afterwards, when the excitement of the killing had died down, but still amidst fierce taunts from straggling onlookers intoxicated by the lingering smell of blood or burning flesh, it was often Clement himself who led a group of dedicated, brave followers of the Way in giving the latest martyr a Christian burial. If it was a beheading they were allowed by the soldiers to remove, without interference, the decapitated bodies and take them in carts to their meeting-house of St. Peter which was situated outside the city walls in the western necropolis. There they held the funeral rite for the soul of the martyr amidst both tears of grief at the loss of yet another beloved follower of the Way, and tears of hope that the departed soul would strengthen them in their resolve to defeat the evil beast in their midst. Later they would inter the body in the nearby catacombs with a growing, communal feeling that each martyr's death was ultimately no death at all, but yet another candle lit in the darkness of the world proclaiming, with an ever-expanding radiance, the light and power in it of their beloved, Resurrected One. And if the martyr had been burnt, they would ritually take some ash from the pyre in a pottery vessel and scatter it with a similar ceremony upon the deep, blue Mediterranean, north of the necropolis, or else upon the placid waters of Lake Mareotis, just below the gate in the great southern wall of the city.

Origen missed not a single one of these ceremonies but noted with increasing unease the conspicuous absence always of Pope Demetrius. However, at these times, Origen was moved not into any kind of remorse or hatred for the enemies of the *Kyrios* but actually into an ever-deepening love of his Great Master, for invariably during these rituals of the dead martyrs he felt an exquisite power of devotional love welling up in him and saturating his body and soul. He strove hard to keep this supremely devotional mood alive throughout the days following each martyrdom. However, despite his greatest efforts in this regard, he always had to experience the sadness of it slipping away again. It was then also that he became increasingly aware of a singular difficulty with regard to his inner life generally. And with increasing desperation he wanted to bring this into a conceptual clarity but could not.

For he felt something blinding and terrible stirring deep down in him, in his guts, as if he was bound up with the birth of some monstrous, dark, and unspeakable deformity. He increasingly felt that his own soul was becoming a battlefield upon which a monumental struggle was taking place, a struggle against the lower, animal lusts and passions which were everywhere and always so ready to rise up and destroy that purity and intensity of devotion which he knew to be the key to the Door of Initiation into the great mystery of his Master; and it was on this alone that he wished to focus and base the entire direction of his life.

Yet now, as he moved about the city, he felt prey at every turn to all those temptations which the bright light of the Alexandrian day so easily brought to a man. Ever and ever again, even if his eyes did not wish to, he found himself looking upon the enticing, dazzling contours of flesh, the displays of fine foods and assorted wines from every part of the world, the ubiquitous allure of oriental luxury and opulence, and the huge variety of the pleasures of the senses that were cultivated more, perhaps, here in Alexandria than in any other city in the Empire.

Through this ever mounting inner tension, Origen, in his natural and in-bred capacity for spiritual and devotional love, longed more and more for the night and its cool security - the serenity of prayer, the strength of meditation and the clarity of thought that it brought. For, most especially, it was in the night that those sweet, temperate breezes blew and those impossible-to-describe feelings came, fleeting but so welcome; more like visitations, bordering often on visions, but always harbouring pure and lasting spiritual insights and offering precise and ever-clearer directions for his life's destiny - the whisperings of the mystic, inner voice.

One late autumnal evening after the burial ceremony of yet another martyr, Origen was walking with Clement along the wide, deserted Canopius Way. The air was cold, the sky dark and the stars in the east exceptionally bright. Farther along the horizon the white moon hung huge and low over the city, casting a silvery glow upon the white, flat roofs of the dwelling-houses, and causing the marble and porphyry facades of the many and magnificent civic buildings and temples to shimmer and glisten eerily as they walked passed.

The occasion had been a particularly sad one for Origen, for they had just scattered upon the moonlit, indigo waters of Lake Mareotis ash from the pyre of Plutarch who, although he was somewhat older than Origen, had, nevertheless, been an ardent student of his in Paula's garden. He was one whom Origen loved, both for his enthusiastic reception of the Gospel as well as his eagerness to deepen his knowledge of it. Origen's lessons were mainly secular in content – grammar, history, geography – but he always coloured them with relevant references to both the Hebrew Bible and the new Gospel of Love, for he simply could not tea h in any other way. But his method also allowed him to discern which of his students might be potential catechumens. And Plutarch had shown great possibilities in this regard. But it was this very enthusiasm for the Gospel which had gained him the attention of his pagan and other colleagues at the *agora* where he worked as a potter and had, in the end, caused him to be singled out by one of the bloodthirsty mob there who had overheard his excited talk.

As Origen and Clement were passing the Temple of Isis, the ornate capitals of its numerous Corinthian columns caught Clement's eye. He stopped. After a few moments he raised his hand rather tiredly and pointed to a very bright star in the sky directly above the Temple.
'You know that one, I hope,' he said. (The persecutions had taken their toll on Clement: his movements were slow and his voice hoarse.)
'Yes. It is Sirius.'
'That's the *real* sun, you know.'
'What do you mean?'
'I mean that it's the centre of the *universe* as opposed to our *planetary system*. As a budding astronomer you surely must see the difference. That's the reason also why they made it the basis for their calendar here in Egypt. The ancient ones here knew far more than most of our modern Gnostic intellectuals give them credit for nowadays, you know.

They actually gave this star, the Dog, the Guide of the Dead, to Osiris, their most beloved god. They even called it after him: Osiris – Sirius – same name.'
'Osiris - god of the dead,' Origen said melancholically. He was thinking of Plutarch again.
'Yes, or turn god around if you like and say: dog of the dead,' Clement said with a cryptic smile. 'Still is god, for lots of them, of course. Just look at the beauty of this architecture here,' Clement went on, pointing now to the sculpted ornamentation of the Temple's columns which stood out clearly in the angled light of the moon.
'It will take a long time for the old dogs, er…gods to die,' Origen offered facetiously.
'Yes, centuries. No! Millennia. But they *will* die eventually. The will have to - no choice, quite simply. Of course, gods are good fighters……… and their dogs even better.'

They moved off slowly again in the direction of the Soma. After the burial ceremony Clement had asked Origen to stay with him for the night, saying he wished to talk to him about important matters next morning. Origen was delighted to accept the offer of such intimate company of his Master.

And now, as they walked slowly along the enchanted street, Origen felt a great desire to say those kinds of things to his Master that he had never touched upon before; things to do with his volatile inner life; his often tortured spiritual striving; his great concerns for the *Kyrios*; his love of his Great Master; his love of Sarah even. And yet it was so hard to pull all these thoughts and feelings together and put them into the precise kind of questions that would draw a crisp and clear answer from Clement. For Clement always demanded that questions be good, correctly thought out, and most importantly, properly phrased. If the question is asked properly, Clement had said on numerous occasions, then the answer is often contained within it.

Tonight Origen felt not only brave but strangely compulsive.
'Master Clement,' he said in an uncharacteristic firm tone, 'what precisely is conscience?'
Clement looked at him directly. 'Conscience?' he repeated.
'Yes. What is it?'
Clement surveyed Origen for a few moments in silence and walked for another twenty yards or more before responding. Then he merely repeated the question yet again. 'So, what is conscience?' but his tone this time impelled Origen to answer, 'A voice, Master.'
'Good. But come…. more….'
'An *inner* voice.'
'Yes, and…….?'
When Origen failed to respond Clement continued, 'It's surely not *simply* an inner voice, is it? The whole concept of conscience signifies something more.'

'Oh, yes, of course. It prompts one towards the good.'

'Yes. That will do.'

'But where does it *come from*, Master?'

'Why, from one of the angels, of course, but one of the good ones, as you have just inferred. Why do you ask? Are you hearing voices or something?'

Origen was slightly taken aback at the directness, the intuitive ability of Clement to know what he was getting at. But he was used to this, so that he recovered quickly and said, 'Yes and no.'

Clement said, 'It's nothing to worry about so long as it doesn't become pathological; meaning if your mental balance is disturbed by it, or your ability to act in the world, in a relatively normal way, is impaired. It is a most complex, yet common phenomenon, for it is intimately connected with the power of the word and the very way we think. But to discern the voice of conscience, that is, the spirit-word - to hear the one true voice of your good, your angelic self within the, shall we say, constant internal chatter – this is an *art*, my young friend. Nay, it is more. It is a spiritual *science*. And, as in all other things spiritual, here too we receive our most palpable and profitable help from the spirit of Christ. For some people this help comes relatively easily, for others it is difficult. But it is available to all. And, furthermore, it is good to know that even the Christ Himself, before He was baptized by John, had to struggle intensely hard to find His own true inner voice.'

'How do you know this, Master?'

'When I was young I travelled extensively around Palestine, and much farther eastwards also. I spoke with many people: remarkably old men and women, hermits, ascetics and saints, some of whom actually knew the Lord, believe it or not, who spoke with Him. These people told me many and very remarkable things, things which will never be put into books, I can tell you.'

'Things to do with conscience?'

'Yes. But the conscience of the Hebrew people - that most mysterious voice which empowered the prophets, and who, through their constant calling to account the sins of the people, kept the old covenant alive, through thick and thin. After Malachi, however, this inner, angelic voice went more or less silent. But it came back again with a greater and purer power and clarity than ever before through the soul of the Christ.'

Clement stopped, and turned directly to Origen. 'He, you should know, had direct access to the Bath-kol.'

Origen frowned deeply. 'The Bath-kol, Master?'

After a long and ponderous silence Clement said, 'Yes. You should hear this right now. This is the name given by the ancient Jewish scribes to the last whisperings in the human soul of that wonderful, ancient Hebrew voice, the inner spirit-voice that, as I have just said, inspired all pious people, but especially the greatest of the prophets. The doctors and the scribes actually thought by Christ's time that this was dead. But the Great Master could hear it clearly! He did not say so directly to the doctors and scribes of course – then they would've killed Him sooner than they did – but many of them were so astounded with His answers to the almost impossibly complex questions that they loved, perversely perhaps, to heap upon Him, that they were quite ready in the end to believe it! He was only fourteen or fifteen at the time, you know. In later life He told all of this to some of the people that I actually met, and He said quite categorically to them that He could hear the Bath-kol.'

After a long silence Origen asked, 'And can one hear the Bath-kol now?'

'Yes, through the Risen One. The Word has been made flesh and lives within us. He has renewed it.........renewed it for *everyone*, believe it or not. We can all become priests and prophets, after a fashion, from now on. We just have to listen exceedingly carefully, that's all. Listen, Origen, my young friend. Listen, and believe me, you will hear it, Him. But you must listen very carefully'.

'*Be still and know that I am*.........'

'......God. Yes. I Am. Very good. Psalm 46. I AM is indeed His name, the Tetragrammaton, as indicated very clearly in Exodus, chapter 3. You are right. Listen. Make yourself still enough to listen, through prayer, meditation, fasting. Don't, as the great St. Paul commands, get caught up in this,' - Clement swung his arms about him indicating the entire city. 'It is full of utter distraction, little else. They have so little love or knowledge of the one true God! It's so strange! Even many of the so-called Gnostics are more licentious than ordinary folk, you know. But *you* have the golden key, my friend. And that is self-discipline. Discipline – disciple. Same word virtually. You are a true disciple, and self-discipline is the greatest of all the many gifts God has given to you. For you cannot know him without it. You may know *of* him, but that is something quite different from what we call *gnosis*, real knowledge, real and personal experience of God. God is not just an idea. He is a reality and we must learn to *experience* him. To achieve this you must curb the lower passions, the lusts. There is no other way. Remember what Socrates said: *The greatest wealth lies in poverty of desires.* Practise this always, and the magic of His voice, His Word, His spirit will fill you up – you will feed on Him, literally. You will lust, forgive me, after *Him* then - you will need no one, nothing more, ever, for ever...you will be free!'

A secret smile of ecstasy was fixed firmly on Origen's fresh young face now and he walked for many paces alongside Clement with his eyes closed, carried along and directed by the sheer power and beauty of his Master's voice. Yes, he must pray more. He must listen more and ever more carefully. He must put down *all* temptations. He must become like a sphinx; get totally on top of his animal and draw whatever beasts were lurking down there in his bowels up into the full light of the day; tame them, and then either drive them out or drive them before him like a team of horses, all galloping wildly heavenward, with no one ever telling him or them where to turn, or what to do, no one, that is, except the sweet whispering voice of the Lord Himself.

9   MASTER CLEMENT'S STORY

Next morning over breakfast in the dining-room of his small but spotless and neatly furnished apartment near the Didascaleon, Clement spoke to Origen in a manner he had never done before.

He began by telling him of his widespread travels in his youth and how in India, in his twenties, he had been happily married to a most beautiful daughter of a powerful Raja, who owned vast estates near Bangalore. He had always, he said, since childhood, been deeply interested in religion and later on in philosophy also, and had, even before he went to India, practised various pagan religions and had even been initiated into some of their mysteries. But none of them every fully satisfied him, and so too with the various Hindu deities he became familiar with through his marriage to Devaki, for that was his wife's name.

Then one day by chance he met a very old man sitting alone by the seashore near a small village north of Bangalore. This old man told him the most amazing story he had ever heard! He spoke of a great being, a god, who had actually walked among men on Earth, exactly like a man. It happened in Palestine about a hundred years ago, the old man said, and it spelled the end of all of the ancient ways. The old man seemed to speak out of an unfathomable depth of faith, wisdom, serenity and knowledge. Clement immediately made further inquiries and very soon afterward he was fully converted to Christianity.

Clement then gave details of his increasing absorption into the truth, beauty, majesty and mystery of the Great Master Jesus. After this, he said, he began to feel so different to Devaki, it was as if he had been virtually transformed into a new person. Increasingly then her family and tribal connections and traditions became alien to him. And in the end he simply had to divorce her. It was sad, he said, but he got over it. Luckily there had not yet been any children. But he was more than compensated for her loss by the ever deepening insights and inspirations he acquired both into himself and the world through his new life in Christ.

Eventually after many more years of study and meditation he had come to Alexandria - he believed under divine guidance - for he felt certain there was someone there he had to meet. This turned out to be his great friend, teacher and master, Pantaneus. It was through Pantaneus that he had become fully initiated into the Great Mysteries. And soon after this, Pantaneus made him co-responsible for everything connected with the School he himself had founded many years before, the Didascaleon. And it was especially since this time that the Didascaleon became one of the most important organs of the *Kyrios* devoted as it was to the task of making the Gospel take root and become ever more alive both in the city of

Alexandria and in the world at large. By now, Clement said, the School was known and highly regarded virtually everywhere in the Empire, to Christians and pagans alike, as the most important spiritual and cultural institution in the world, and students came from all over to hear him lecture, and study under his guidance. Many of these went on to become instructed in the ways of the Lord, became good Christians, and a lesser number to be fully initiated into the Great Mysteries.

Since the establishment of the School, Clement said, he had given all his time and energy to spreading the 'good news' of the Gospel, and he had not regretted one single moment of it. Now, however, he was deeply worried, not only about his own future, but especially the future of the School. He had spoken, he said, to Pope Demetrius only a few days ago and informed him that because of the jeopardy his person was in, due to the current wave of persecutions against the Christians in the city, he was recommending Origen himself as his successor should anything happen to him. Demetrius, however, Clement went on to say, did not fully disclose his feelings on the matter and had, in fact, said very little throughout the meeting. When leaving he had merely informed him that he would summon him again in due course. Demetrius, Clement confided, was difficult.

Origen listened to all this silently but with a growing sense of unease. He did not believe he had the power, knowledge, or experience to take on such a momentous position of responsibility, despite Clement's faith in him. And he did not know what to say when Clement eventually stopped talking.

'It is not really a question of experience, power or even knowledge, Origen,' Clement said after the long silence, guessing Origen's unease. 'It is a question of destiny, a question of a calling, of divine grace and guidance.'
'Are you divinely guided to appoint me as your successor?' Origen asked with a brevity that surprised him.
'Yes,' Clement responded with an uncanny air of certainty.
After a pause Origen said, 'I feel so unworthy, Master.'
Clement eyed him seriously. 'Perhaps the virtue of humility has got the better of you, my child?'
'It's not that. It's that.........I.......just feel.......... *so* many conflicts.'
'Well then, perhaps you are being chastened.'
'Or chased!'
'Chased! By what, whom....... the Emperor?'
'How about the Devil?'
Clement smiled. 'Ah! Yes. Perhaps. It's hard to get away from *him* all right. He has so many faces. But remember this, my young friend: *you* I can see better than you can see yourself. Not only I, but many can see that, young as you are, you have

61

the aura of a true initiate, even though you have much work to do yet before you receive initiation itself. But this will come. I put my trust in that and because of it I put my trust and faith in you too. Or perhaps I should put it the other way round. I put my trust in you that you will work hard and cut heroically through your conflicts, your uncertainties, triumph over all those things which, you should also remember, accompany *every* striving, whether one is young or old, towards the good. Yes, the beast of evil is hard to overcome. But you will rise up over it to the heights......I can see it, believe me, my friend, I can *see* it. Have more courage and faith, therefore. I will pray for you. And do not say more to me now. We can talk again in a few days' time.'

The following Sunday morning Origen visited his family in Rhakotis. He did not live with them much now for Lady Paula had generously offered him a small room for his exclusive use in her villa, and this allowed him, as often as he wished, to escape the topsy-turvy life of his family home. Therefore he slept there only occasionally but visited often and gave virtually all the money he received from his tuition classes to his mother, and assisted her in every other way he could But apart from being exceptionally pious, his mother was also competent and undemanding and tried hard not to interfere with his work or studies, or deflect him in any way from what she intuitively knew, even from the time he was a tiny child, was his primary mission in life: to serve the holy Christ, and Him alone.

After saying goodbye to his mother and many brothers, especially the youngest, John, aged two, whom he adored, Origen made his way quickly through the crisp, cold air of the Alexandrian morning to the beautiful *domus* of Ambrosius on the hill overlooking the busy Eastern Harbour. He found Ambrosius and Sarah sitting in their dining-room, talking and drinking wine. It was the first time he had seen Sarah in almost two months.

Ambrosius greeted Origen as usual with a warm embrace. Origen's eyes then fell upon Sarah. She was stretched out on a couch leaning on one elbow, and had on a full-length, white *stola* and a bright-blue *palla* draped elegantly across her shoulders. Her black hair was combed out and hung down low each side of her beautiful face. Origen had never seen her like that before. She inclined her cheek towards him and he kissed it delicately.
'Where have you been?' she asked. 'You are almost a complete stranger.'
'Dodging the mob,' Origen said nonchalantly. 'Saving my skin.'
Sarah demurred. She pointed to an empty couch beside her, upon the edge of which Origen awkwardly sat down.
'Do not be shocked, Origen,' she said 'that we are drinking wine so early in the morning. It is because the servants failed to light the grates of our heating system in

time. We are still trying to warm ourselves up. Poor Ambrosius had to help the servants, *himself*. Look, he got his hands all black!'

Ambrosius looked in embarrassment at his hands, picked up a napkin and wiped them.

Origen said, 'I am all right. I have warmed myself by walking quickly up here.'

Sarah turned and leant with both of her elbows in order to watch him more closely.

'You don't come to the Didasacleon any more,' he said to her.

'I've been busy exploring the Mysteries of Eleusis,' she replied, eyeing him over the lip of her wine cup.

Ambrosius laid his napkin down and began studying his sister's gestures most carefully as she continued to engage Origen. She went on, 'Origen, I know things are getting very rough for you and your friends. I even have to restrain myself most severely at times in order not to go down to witness one of these......these awful events. I can hear the whole commotion usually from my bedroom window, you know.'

'Well, then, why don't you go and look. You are a seeker, Sarah, and seekers should be brave,' Origen suggested.

'Yes,' Amrbosius said, 'we are all seekers, and listen to this, sweet sister, Sarah – we two, myself and my good friend Origen here, are going to learn something very special this morning.'

Not moving her eyes from Origen Sarah said, 'Pray, what?'

'The Ophites. We are going to attend their *Agape*, their love-feast!'

Astounded, Sarah turned to Ambrosius. 'The Ophites!'

'Yes.'

'Dear God, Ambrosius, what next!'

Ambrosius was grinning widely. Then forcing a serious face he cleared his throat and went on, 'Look, I go to the Ophites with good, not bad intentions. I have an eclectic mind. Believe me, sister, my main purpose is one of edification, enlightenment, illumination, *gnosis*.'

'Believe you! Are you sure now, Ambrosius dear, that your primary objective is not just yet another cheap, exotic thrill? The Ophites of all people! And their *Agape*! How on earth did you manage that one?'

'Oh, I have lots of connections through the business. It wasn't that difficult, you know, once I set my mind upon it.'

'Origen,' Sarah said, 'are you really going with him to this wicked little orgy?'

'Orgy?' Origen retorted. 'Who told you that?'

'But isn't that what everyone says about them? Orgies with snakes! My God, it sounds disgusting beyond belief. I'm surprised at *you*, Origen, for letting my...my...Gnostic brother drag you into such practices. I would've thought that your mind, your soul, was a purer kind of vessel altogether.'

'My soul, Sarah, believe it or not, is, at bottom, like every other man's.'

63

'My dear Sarah, you can come too, if you want,' Ambrosius suggested.
'I wouldn't dream of it!' Sarah snapped but after sipping a little more wine she went on dreamily, 'However, I will be most interested to hear the report.' She turned to Origen and fluttered her eyes, 'From Origen especially.'

Origen felt her every gesture drawing him now. Every inflexion of her voice, every movement of her eyes, every ripple of her body whose soft contours he could clearly see outlined beneath her fine silk *stola*, was arousing him. Trembling almost, he fought the effects of her intoxicating, sensual beauty but his eyes, his hands, his whole body was hungry for her and with growing pain he felt his sweet love turning into a burning, ravaging lust.

Almost angrily he said, 'I will tell you every detail of my experience with the Ophites, Sarah. Where and when shall we meet?'

Sarah laughed out loud at his uncharacteristic brevity. Teasingly she said, 'Come to my bedroom tomorrow evening after supper,' and flashed her huge eyes playfully at him.
'I will,' Origen said. 'I will.'

10 THE SNAKE WORSHIPPERS!

About an hour later Ambrosius and Origen passed through the Gate of the Sun in the eastern wall of the city. At first they walked along on an open common but soon they joined a narrow, tree-lined, rutted track that, Origen knew, led eventually to the Hippodrome, a couple of miles away. A little farther on Ambrosius pulled a small piece of papyrus from his satchel upon which he had scribbled the directions to the Ophites' ceremony. At a certain point, along the track, indicated obviously on the map but unobserved by Origen whose discretion did not allow him to enquire where or what it actually was, they turned off the track and headed directly into the dense woodland.

Once in the forest Ambrosius began looking in all directions and eventually spotted what appeared to be traces of an animal track on the soft, moist forest floor. They followed this for a while and though the forest became darker, the track itself became clearer. After about fifteen minutes walking in the gloom, turning here and there according to Ambrosius' obscure directions, they eventually began to hear distinct sounds emanating from a distance in front of them. Soon a brightening ahead indicated that they were approaching a clearing in the wood. Suddenly, a thin, bearded man, dressed in old animal skins, dropped out of nowhere onto the path directly in front of them and seemed to block it purposely. He carried a tattered scroll in one hand and with the other he made a pointed gesture which demanded a response. Ambrosius looked at the piece of papyrus, cleared his throat and said firmly, 'Saraph'. The man nodded, turned, and silently beckoned them to follow. Ambrosius looked at Origen and smiled conspiratorially. 'That's the priest,' he whispered and winked. But Origen winced, for even from a distance he could smell the man distinctly.

In a short while they entered an expansive, pleasant glade unexpectedly filled with a large, mostly silent crowd. The bright morning sun poured generously down into the glade and upon the people, men and women of various ages who were sitting in a rough semicircle around a white cloth spread out on the grass. In the centre of the cloth there was a large, ornamented, gilded cist. At the opening of the circle stood a table covered in bright red cloth – obviously the altar. To the left of this a small fire was crackling noisily and filling the glade with the incense of sandalwood.

To Origen these were as mixed a bunch as he ever saw but he immediately noted from their facial expressions and bodily gestures that most of them, either through intoxication or shared expectation, had already sacrificed their individualities and were in the grip of some common spirit, eager for sensual experience. For, many of them, even of the same sex, were already arousing one another by uninhibited caressing.

Origen sat down beside Ambrosius after they were directed by the priest to the only free spot still left in the circle. They had obviously arrived just in time, for no sooner had they settled themselves than the priest approached the altar and began to mumble prayers. On the altar were a number of loaves of white bread, a large silver chalice and an unlit torch upon a tall stand.

After finishing mumbling, the priest unrolled, in a somewhat weary fashion, Origen thought, the tatty roll he carried. He began by saying, 'A reading from the Holy Gospel.' Origen did not hear a name but the priest had not gone very far with his reading before Origen realized this was not the Gospel he knew, but obviously one of the numerous spurious ones in circulation. Many of these Origen had read. Most of them claimed to be written under divine inspiration but it was plain to anyone with even a modicum of learning that few of them were little more than juvenile fantasising about the Christ, often in an openly pornographic way.

When the man had finished reading he made the sign of the Cross over the loaves of bread then broke them and sprinkled the broken pieces all over the white cloth on the grass. Still mumbling prayers, he lit the altar torch from the nearby fire and replaced it on its stand. Then he turned, lifted his hand as a signal, and from behind him, out of the darkness of the trees a masked figure appeared wearing a full-length, hooded, bright blue cloak.

The priest followed this unshod figure who walked carefully onto the white cloth among the scattered pieces of bread and then stopped by the cist in the centre. The priest then took away from the figure the mask and cloak to reveal a totally naked, well-proportioned woman with long black hair. The priest went back to the altar, laid the mask and cloak carefully upon it, and immediately began chanting in a high, piercing tone while the woman slowly removed the lid of the cist. Then Origen caught his breath as a huge, multicoloured cobra rose up like a flaming phantom from the cist. It responded sensuously to every nuance of the rhythmic cadence in the priest's strange, hypnotic chanting and began to coil itself tightly around the woman who held her arms worshipfully aloft as it did so.

With his mouth wide open Origen turned to Ambrosius. But Ambrosius didn't see him. In fact he saw nothing except what was now directly before his eyes and would see little else for a long time to come.

When the serpent had slid its pulsating body up the woman sufficiently to bring its huge, bulging head before her face, its forked tongue flicking all the while, she drew down her hands and caressed its head and kissed it passionately several times. Falling ecstatically to the ground with it she then allowed the snake to roll her all over the bread. Soon after this the snake began to free itself from her and slid freely over the broken pieces of bread. Often it came very close to the people, even wielding among them. Most of them by now were rolling their heads, murmuring or chanting along with the priest; many of them reaching out and touching the snake or even kissing its head as it passed, while all the time the woman rolled herself over the bread in the centre.

'Hail!' the priest was chanting, in what looked like a state of drugged ecstasy. 'Hail Jaldabaoth! Hail to the Mighty One! Hail to thee, oh Son of the most High God, the Word made flesh. Hail! our God incarnate.'

Origen's eyes moved quickly from the priest, to the woman, to the snake. He was deeply shocked, aroused, confused, and strangely angry, totally uncertain of what to do, yet not wanting to miss anything. He watched the woman closely and caught a glimpse of her face as she rolled passed him, and was horrified to see no eyes at all, only two holes as black as soot! But, as if to compensate, when the snake came close he felt the light of *its* eyes piercing him like a lance, so powerful, hypnotic and colourful were they.

Origen shuddered and then began to shake all over.

Still chanting wildly the priest came forward and began to distribute the bread to the people. 'The body of Christ,' he spoke to each one between his chanting. And no sooner had they put the bread in their mouth than they jumped up and started dancing wildly. One of them soon produced a loud, deep-sounding drum and started rhythmically drumming. Amidst the creeping snake and the rolling woman the people now gorged themselves on the bread and with the hypnotising rhythm of the drumbeat began dancing ever more wildly, many discarding their clothes, some shrieking, hissing and shouting in strange voices, and tongues.

Origen felt nauseous. He had remained seated even when Ambrosius, who was one of the last to do so, rose up from his seat and joined the ecstatic crowd on the cloth. With each new glance at the passing woman and snake Origen became ever more dizzy. He wanted to run but felt literally glued to his spot as if some invisible, sweaty hand was pressing him firmly down. Soon the whole scene began to sway violently, as if he was on a small boat among huge waves on a turbulent sea. He closed his eyes but the serpent's eyes he saw all the brighter; huge eyes like vortexes of light and colour, sucking him in, body, soul and spirit.

Origen rocked his head to and fro and felt torn between screaming and a fierce desire to join the orgiastic dancers. But still he could not move. Instead he gave himself up to a strange, deep rumbling; an energy stirring in the very depths of his bowels, an energy that slowly began to rise up in great, undulating waves through his whole body until, reaching his throat, he felt it actually forming itself into words. But there he, and they got stuck. He could not bring to birth the words of release, for the serpent's eyes still swirled before him, threatening to suck every ounce of him away into utter oblivion. He took one last, long, deep breath then suddenly, like letting go of an exquisitely aimed arrow from his unbelievably tense bow, he heard himself scream at the top of his voice, 'YOU ARE NOT CHRIST. YOU ARE LUCIFER.'

Then he passed out.

When Origen woke up again he found himself on his hard, narrow bed in his little room in Paula's villa. Ambrosius was sitting beside him, watching him and calmly smiling.
'I did not think anybody could sleep as heavily as that,' Ambrosius said when he saw that Origen was fully awake at last.
'How did I get here .... how long have I been here?' Origen asked.
'Five hours. I carried you on my back the whole way, believe it or not. But I had so much energy to get rid of, it wasn't actually *that* difficult. Anyway, the villa here is not very far from where we were.'
'Thanks,' Origen said with a sigh. 'You are a true friend.'
'Any time,' Ambrosius said. After a pause he continued, 'Well, that was something, eh?'
'Yes,' Origen said dreamily, 'something.'
'Hey, what happened to you? You missed the best bits.'
'Was I.......shouting........or something?'
'Oh..........I think I heard you say something all right, Origen. But I, and most of the others also, well......we took no notice of you. How could we, pray? It was so intense...........I felt........so.......well.........'
'Possessed?'
'Ah, Origen, come on. I didn't say that. Don't be so dramatic!'
After a pause Ambrosius continued, 'But phew, what an *Agape*!'
'It wasn't *Agape*, Ambrosius. Anything but.'
'What was it then?'
'It was...........' But Origen could not bring himself to finish.
'All right then. Look, was it even Christian?'
'No!'
'You sound so certain.'
'Yes, I am.'
'Why?'
Origen rubbed his face deeply in his hands then sat up and looked directly into Ambrosius' eyes. 'They are dangerous, Ambrosius. I warn you. You must be very careful. Truly, you risk losing your soul if you follow them.'

68

Ambrosius looked for a moment as if he was seriously considering these remarks but then suddenly brightening again he said, 'Hey, I enjoyed it, you know. It was interesting. Now don't tell me, Origen, it wasn't very *interesting*. All that bum! Eh? And you know, some of them afterwards ....' He broke off.

'What?' Origen insisted.

'Well, some of them...............they actually..........'

'Actually what?'

'.......... had the woman, in full view of all, and.... and the snake......and...'

Origen scoffed. He did not want to hear any more. He felt like spitting. He jumped up and started pulling on his sandals. 'Ambrosius, look,' he said, 'there are a thousand women you could have here in Alexandria. Two thousand! You are a man who has connections with all the very best classes here. And there are so many *good* women you can choose from.'

A faintly contemptuous smile now played about Ambrosius' lips.

'I've had a thousand,' he said wearily and looked away. But Origen laid his hand delicately on his shoulder and turned him back.

'Ambrosius,' he said, searching his eyes, 'all right, but listen. You don't need a holy whore as well. You, I know you ...... you are truly looking for the Christ, albeit in your own way. But, please believe me........ holy whores won't lead you to Him, never. They will lead you down..........up........'

'Pray, where, Origen?' Ambrosius prompted cynically. 'Do tell me *exactly* where they would lead me? I long to hear it clearly from your pure, white mouth!'

'Hell!' Origen snapped.

'Ha, ha' Ambrosius jeered. 'Hades! Is *that* the best you can do?'

But Origen did not answer. 'And anyway, listen,' Ambrosius said, 'I've never seen you so all fired up before. Maybe it's done you some good after all!'

Ambrosius then forced a loud laugh but as he did so Origen started nodding his head sarcastically.

'Yes, I have definitely learned something all right, Ambrosius. Definitely.'

'What?'

'I don't want to go into it now. I need to think more.'

'Oh, all right then. We can talk again later. But you must tell me your thoughts, remember, and tell me very clearly. I want to know *precisely* what you think. That's the main reason I wanted *you* to be there after all.'

'Yes, of course. But on one condition.'

'That I don't go back again, right?'

'Right.'

Origen started to tighten the red cord he always wore around his black tunic and brushed some lingering grass from it. As he was doing so, Ambrosius put his arm around him.

'My friend, listen. I know you have gone through something..........well.... let's say difficult. But if it hurts too much, then please, blame me.'

Origen smiled shyly and Ambrosius went on, 'Knowledge, *gnosis* is painful. That much is as plain as the noses on our faces. Nevertheless, I'm certain that it does us good. Seekers, after all, must also be experimenters. Right? And look, do not worry about having to tell my beautiful sister about all this stuff. She'll be demanding to know all the fine details, of course. But I'll tell her myself.' He winked at Origen who, however, could only manage to acknowledge his offer by knitting his brow deeply.

11   THE DEVIL'S ADVOCATE

In the weeks that followed, Origen became increasingly preoccupied with the problem of how to preserve the truth of the Gospel. Ambrosius was right! The Ophites had certainly stirred him up. They had catapulted him into a mood more intense than he had ever experienced before, a mood of deepest-possible questing and longing for Truth. Apart from practising with renewed intensity the many spiritual exercises taught to him by Clement, day in and day out he unceasingly taxed himself with deep philosophical questions regarding the Gospel and the problem of belief in God generally.

He went so far as to consciously evoke a devil's advocate in his imagination, carefully building up this psychic being during long hours of meditation until he could see it almost as clearly as Clement himself, and then he allowed it to hurl at him every possible objection to Christianity under the sun. Sometimes this advocate became so real that Origen felt he was going mad. But he didn't! Instead, with each new objection, once he had met it courageously and honestly, he felt his faith, like yeast in fresh dough, expanding rather than diminishing. More and more convinced he became that the Gospel, upon which he was reared and nourished, bequeathed a truth to mankind that no other book, no other system, teaching or teacher, no other Being in the entire world, could. So that eventually he felt confident enough to be happily able to dispense with his devil's advocate altogether.

However, once thus fully renewed in his personal faith and belief, another equally troubling but less personal problem - for it was one to do with the broader Christian community of which he was a part - began to shape itself in his consciousness. It was this: how was it going to be possible - given that the kind of practices he had just witnessed with the Ophites were widespread - to preserve the grace, beauty, wisdom and especially the truth of the Gospel, not only for his own generation, but for all the generations to come?   For the truth of the Gospel surely demanded such an impersonal, worldly work.   But the mere thought of such a task was momentous, and at times it made Origen tremble and feel faint, for it was a task that sometimes seemed to be almost unfathomable in its complexity. But something terribly deep in him told him that he must, that it was in his very destiny, not only to address it, but to solve it.

True, this particular band of Ophites he had been party to may have been an extreme example but similar types of groups were proliferating all over the Empire.   How was it going to be possible to ensure a unified, uniform, and healthy growth of the *Kyrios* community in the world in the face of such........such downright diabolical masquerades?   These groups, their leaders and so-called priests were, in Origen's eyes, doing little more than jumping on a profitable, spiritually titillating, bandwagon. They offered, at most, only half-truths regarding the Gospel, and half-truths, he fully realized, were always more insidious than pure lies!

Everywhere in the Empire the old ways, the old gods, their meaning and truth, their customary laws and common forms of justice, were being questioned or ignored. This state of affairs had its origin in Rome. For the simple fact was that the very centre of the Roman Empire, the city of Rome itself, was nothing more nowadays than a seething mass of debauchery and corruption and was in fact falling apart at its seams. Thus, no Emperor felt safe anymore. Every day in that city there were rumours and counter-rumours of conspiracies to topple the Emperor and replace him with some ambitious, strong soldier who, somehow, somewhere in the outlying districts of the Empire, had managed to make a name for himself. In such a milieu the ordinary people were increasingly exploited, felt more and more exposed, alienated and unprotected, and were becoming desperate for something real and stable to hold on to. And it was into this stew that the sublime and precious Gospel was being poured. But for many people, precisely because of the disintegration, the figure of the Christ was often little more than just another straw god to be clutched at, amidst the prevailing anarchic winds. But Origen knew that his Christ represented for mankind something much more enduring than any of the gods of old. He must be considered an entirely new kind of god or not at all. To Origen, Christ was the absolute King, a brand new and a fully divine one, a Godman to be contemplated, and the more he did, the more convinced Origen became, He was destined eventually to rule the entire world.

During this time Origen took to re-reading as many of the Gnostic texts as he could lay his hands on but especially he studied the great Alexandrian teachers Valentinus and Basilides. He paid particular attention to Valentinus' *Gospel of Truth.* He taxed both Clement and Ammonius Saccus at every possible opportunity with piercing questions regarding the teachings of these famous Alexandrians and became ever and ever more convinced through the answers he received that direct access to the knowledge of God, that is, the unmediated contemplation of and absorption in the Divine Light, a state that was often and graciously visited upon himself in his night hours of meditation, should not be lost to the general *Kyrios* community in its efforts to maintain uniformity of purpose and teaching. This teaching of the direct, personal relationship with the Great mediating Master and the methods and disciplines by which it was to be achieved, should *at all costs* remain part of the ethos and general teaching of the *Kyrios.*

In this regard Origen, ever more clearly, began to see that the very influential old literalist writer and bishop, Irenaeus, who was still alive and working in Lyon in Gaul, was dangerous. For in his intense hatred of the Gnostics, Irenaeus had gone to the extreme of including among them the great Christian teachers, Valentinus and Basilides. He did this simply because they had taught the *inner* way, the individual path which some called secret but this was simply because it was not possible to put such forms of knowledge into words with a general meaning. Individual guidance was all important. Irenaeus' zeal for orthodoxy had led him now to fiercely oppose such a way of knowing the Christ at all, arguing, often, to Origen's mind, with a woeful logic, that such a teaching did nothing more than perpetuate various forms of magic and superstition.

This, to Origen's way of thinking, was a great error, a total misconception. Moreover, Irenaeus was becoming increasingly popular among those so-called Christians, in the seething city of Rome, who wished to use the growing power of the *Kyrios* community to benefit from, at a merely worldly, political and opportunistic level, the fall-out from the tottering Empire. Thus they were busily promoting the books and teaching of this narrow-minded, hard-headed zealot, a trend which Origen regarded as harbouring the greatest of dangers for the future of the entire community. He worried deeply as to what to do about all of this, a mood that lasted many months.

One evening, when the intensity of this searching mood and the euphoric effect of his renewed evaluation of and enthusiasm for the truth of the Gospel of Christ, was wearing off, Origen felt relaxed enough to visit Ambrosius, who, since the episode with the Ophites, he had seen only once, and then quite accidentally on Canopius Way. For, during this intense period, Origen kept to himself as much as possible, not wanting his meditations to be unduly disturbed. Unusually, also, Ambrosius rarely turned up at Clement's lectures during this time.

The accidental meeting with Ambrosius occurred on one of those days soon after a huge cargo ship had arrived in the main port. The street, therefore, as always on such days, was buzzing with the liveliest kind of commercial activity as camels, asses, elephants and even giraffes, all moved about in various directions, jostling one another and laden with goods of every conceivable kind. The merchant-owners of these animals and goods were often far too fat to walk and were thus usually carried about in the midst of this activity on shaded, sumptuously decorated palanquins, from where they continually shouted in a variety of languages to their slaves and others, as they made bargain offers to all and sundry.

The intense activity on the street had squeezed Origen and Ambrosius into a doorway and in the short while they had been together there, they spoke quickly and excitedly of many and different things. Ambrosius had said, on that occasion, that he had seldom been so preoccupied with his father's business as lately, and seemed to Origen to be sincerely, if uncharacteristically, apologetic that he could not even afford to attend any lectures for the foreseeable future. Sensing some anxiety, which discretion and modesty prevented him from enquiring into, Origen sympathised with him saying, in a somewhat trivial aside that work was good for him. In this conversation Ambrosius confessed, to Origen's delight, that he had not gone back to the Ophites, and Origen then, as promised, delivered some of his considered opinions and conclusions regarding them. Ambrosius listened carefully to him with bright, open and enthusiastic eyes, saying that he had waited patiently for this moment. And when Origen mentioned Valentinus whom he had been studying in order to form his opinions regarding the Ophites, Ambrosius immediately snatched out of his satchel a piece of papyrus and jotted down the name.

'I shall get Valentinus' *Gospel of Truth*, Origen,' he said, 'as soon as possible. He sounds like a fellow on my particular wavelength. Thanks.'

'He is an excellent teacher, even though since his death he is fast acquiring the reputation of a Gnostic,' Origen replied.

'And you disagree?'

'I am undecided about that, as yet. There is much good in the Gnosis. It is not *all* about snake-worshipping, you know. But you don't need me to tell you that. You will profit by reading Valentinus, I feel certain.'

'You are a genius, Origen. I have always said it, and I will continue to. Listen, you simply *have* to come and visit me and my big, beautiful sister again soon.'

Quickly pulling another piece of papyrus from his satchel as he spoke - his itinerary – Ambrosius gave Origen some appropriate dates and times for such a visit. And, partly out of respect for and loyalty to his rich friend but also because he wanted so much to look again upon the face and lovely lips of Sarah, Origen went to them on one of the first dates that Ambrosius had given.

On that evening, as Origen walked from his little cell in Paula's through the cool winter air, rarely had he seen the stars shine so beautifully. After all the recent turmoil in his soul, his heart was light and happy again, and as he approached Ambrosius' *domus* and could see clearly the Pharos lighthouse shining in the dark, he thought it a mighty symbol for something he had to do, some great and wonderful mission he had to fulfil, something that he was, by destiny, intrinsically part of and that was to come out of his own soul and that of Alexandria's, and would bring to the dark, disintegrating world beyond the city's walls and embracing harbour a ray of hope and the promise of eventual peace for the ever-warring tribes of human kind.

He found his friends in their dining-room, stretched out on rugs and cushions on the floor which was amply warmed by the hypocaust heating system of the *domus*. After greeting them, Origen sat down and there, freed of the servants, with the room lit by two gold and glass lanterns that hung on long brass chains from the high, brightly coloured ceiling, the friends talked way into the night as they slowly sipped sweet Antyllan wine. Surprisingly, the conversation rarely touched upon the Ophites but remained throughout mellow, searching, and free of troubled or complex emotion. It was a mood that suited Origen deeply. He was relieved and warmed by the company of his friends as they talked with increasing openness and frankness about their individual hopes, dreams, and fears. Origen had, in fact, never seen or heard Sarah in such a light before and his love for her was kindled anew. But as the darkness of the night slowly dissolved into the grey of yet another dawn and the time for parting once more drew near, Origen's attention began to linger ever more fixedly upon Sarah's sensuous lips, and with an ever increasing frustration he longed to give them not a kiss of peace, but a kiss of deepest and purest possible fleshly desire.

12 ANGELS, DEVILS, GODS AND MEN

The matron Paula decided to give a very special dinner party!

It so happened that Paul of Antioch's sixtieth birthday fell during Ludi Megalenses in April, the festival of the Great Mother Cybele, whom Lady Paula never failed to honour. Paula felt that this coincidence was auspicious and because of it decided to mark the festival in an extra special way – a surprise dinner party for Paul of Antioch with roast veal in peach sauce as the main dish!

Origen received an invitation, and although he disliked such events he nevertheless could not refuse his patron who promised him faithfully some extra-special vegetables, cooked in some even more special sauce, she said. Origen thanked her and accepted the invitation. However, sensitive to his unease, Paula allowed him the liberty of bringing along a friend of his choosing, if he so wished. She also said that he may be very surprised at the identity of some of the other guests; one in particular, whose name however, she would not reveal under any circumstances. However, she reassured him that among those present would be his beloved Master, Clement.

Origen was at first tempted to ask Sarah, for there were few opportunities in his life whereby he could be with her on her own; that is, apart from her home, where Ambrosius, his parents or their several servants were usually present. But in the end, and for reasons he could not rationally figure out, though he tried hard to do so, he did not ask her. Instead he asked Ambrosius, who was glad of the opportunity to rub shoulders with the cream of Alexandria's intelligentsia.

Paula, in issuing her invitation to Clement, had asked him specially to bring along, as she put it, one of his virgins, for she feared, she said, that she might not be able to manage if she was the only female present at such a large table!

Ambrosius and Origen, on the way to the dinner, lost track of time, for they were still trying to make up for their restricted meetings due to Ambrosius being so intimately and intricately involved with matters appertaining to the importing and distribution of large quantities of silks, perfumes, precious stones and other goods for his father who, he now divulged, had taken to drinking too much wine and as a result was neglecting important taxation and accounting procedures, much to the chagrin of his mother.

But this protracted conversation meant they arrived late for the meal! Paula graciously managed to conceal her annoyance and showed them to their respective places on an arrangement of large couches placed strategically around the low, already laden dining table.

Origen was flabbergasted when he saw Ammonius Saccus! This, he immediately concluded, must the surprise guest Paula was talking about!

Clement, who as always, looked perfectly at ease, had brought along Herias of all people, who was reclining beside him and who looked decidedly awkward on the crimson couch. Paul of Antioch, as usual, looked totally self-absorbed. Paula introduced everyone again and only one of those present Origen did not recognize, a man named Alexandros who was, Paula proudly announced, a senior senator of the Alexandrian senate.

The customary poetic recitation, which always occurred during the first course of Paula's dinners, had obviously concluded, for her lean and loyal poet was now nowhere to be seen. The conversation had in fact been in full flow before Origen and Ambrosius arrived, and no sooner had they sat down than Clement picked up where he had obviously been interrupted in mid-stream, 'I repeat. Give the Emperor what is the Emperor's. It is written very clearly in Mark's Gospel. The Emperor has little interest in anything other than money, which he calls tax. So just give it to him, I say. It is his, anyway. His head is on *all* of the coins! So it *must* be his. When I said we Christians want to abolish taxes I meant it in a spiritual as well as a material sense. If you follow the Way, I tell you most sincerely and out of the depths of my experience of the truth of it, that whatever taxes have to be paid to *anybody*, whether Emperor or devil, they will be paid by *Him*! Full Stop!'

The senator, a thin, lively-looking, middle-aged man, was chewing rapidly but listening intensely. 'The Great Master, you mean?' he queried.
'Yes,' Clement said.
'He will pay your taxes!?'
'Yes.'
'But he is dead!'
'If you have the eyes and the heart you can see Him, senator,' Clement said cryptically. 'He is more present than you think.'

Paul cleared his throat noisily. 'Does he pay your taxes weekly, monthly or yearly?'
'He pays, Paul. He pays, believe me,' Clement stressed.

Origen's eyes moved slowly and watchfully among the guests but inevitably came to rest on Ammonius Saccus. Ammonius Saccus was a small, bird-like man of late middle-age with a pointed jet-black beard. Origen had not seen him bare-headed before, for a little red skullcap always covered his close-cropped, shiny black hair when lecturing. He sat now almost motionless on the couch with his legs coiled up beneath his long, cream-coloured tunic, the full weight of his body resting, seemingly effortlessly, on one of his thin arms. His mysterious and famous little dark-blue bag which was tied to a silver cord around his waist, rested, even glinted conspicuously, on his hip. He held his eyes cast downwards, to one side, and said very little, but his overall posture and expression betrayed him to be listening most carefully to every syllable spoken.

Paula however, who was gradually becoming impatient with his long silences by the time Origen and Ambrosius arrived, now wanted him desperately to speak. She was most eager to hear, in her own select little salon, some of the wit and wisdom she had heard on many occasions flow from his mouth amidst the grandeur of the main lecture hall of the Serapeum where she, like Origen, was a regular attendee at his lectures.

'Ammonius, pray, what do you think?' she asked, missing Clement's earlier point. 'Why shouldn't the Christians pay taxes like all the other subjects of our Emperor? What makes *them* so special?'

After a few moment's silence Ammonius lifted his head and calmly, if somewhat obscurely said, 'I believe the Emperor *still* thinks they are Jews.' His voice was small but firm, and clear as a little silver bell.

'But we are not Jews!' Clement protested.

'What are you, then?' Paul interjected. 'A religion?'

'We simply call ourselves *Kyrios*, that is, the Body of the Lord' Clement said. 'Look, we consider ourselves to be living in a new time, a new spiritual, *Time-Body.* Believe me, a mighty, the mightiest of archetypes has descended upon us. Soon they will even have to change the normal calendar because of this spiritual fact. In fact we, in the *Kyrios*, are already doing this. We have begun to number the years, beginning with His birth. And soon the whole world will have to follow suit. I know it. But the Body is still young. So, please, don't label us yet. Anyway, we are not a commodity, putting ourselves up for sale or anything like that. Give us time and space and we shall become what we shall become.'

'Come. A religion or a state?' the senator demanded. 'One or the other.'

'A flower!' Clement retorted.

'Ha,' Paul said, 'with bishops and popes as petals. What a flower! It *must* be a religion.'

'Look,' Clement returned, sitting up on the edge of his couch and animatedly addressing all, 'we need to have some form, some way of regulating ourselves, and our authority, as in all proper families, comes from the *elders*. These names – bishops, popes, presbyters, whatever, they are unimportant – it is the spirit that we wield that makes us what we are and *nothing* else. We are a spiritual phenomenon, we are a spiritual flower.'

Paula was beaming. 'Oh, how lovely,' she cried, her moist eyes resting now on Herias who was restive and still trying to find a comfortable posture in which to absorb the wit and wisdom of the learned company Clement had so unexpectedly brought her into. She could hardly follow the conversation, but every so often Clement looked down upon her and smiled, and on these occasions she felt as if the sun was darting out from behind a dark bank of clouds.

'Did your Jesus ever get married?' the senator asked suddenly, as he bit enthusiastically into a juicy lump of veal that hung loosely and temptingly from a large bone in his hand. 'I mean before he was crucified.'
'Did he get married *after* he was crucified – that's what I'd like to know?' Paul added in a deep sarcastic tone to which the munching senator responded with a quick but uncertain smile.
In the pause that followed Clement slanted his eyes on Origen and smiled. Origen, however, merely blushed.
'No,' Clement said firmly.
'So! He died a virgin,' Paula said, looking at Herias. Then turning her meditative gaze to Origen she continued, 'Pray, Origen, why did your Great Master not get married?'

All eyes now, including Ammonius Saccus' turned directly upon Origen. He had never experienced such an embarrassing situation before, and was terrified. It was as if he was being strangled by a forest of invisible, hairy, spidery fingers! Words were waxing and waning in his throat, but they refused to be born into his mouth which to his acute frustration went suddenly as dry as the desert. Nevertheless he was surprised to hear himself get out in an unfamiliar tone, 'Perhaps Ammonius Saccus could answer that.'

Ammonius remained quite unperturbed by Origen's unexpected request, and as they exchanged a long, silent glance a quiet smile played about Ammonius' delicate lips. 'Angels can live without sex,' he said cryptically, his eyes remaining firmly fixed upon Origen.

A beautiful young servant slave-girl suddenly appeared with a large *amphora* of bright red wine and all watched and waited in silence as she poured it quietly into the now almost empty one already at the table.

Alexandros, the senator, said, 'So, Christ was an angel then, eh? Yes, now that makes some sense to *me* all right. You know my parents were Jews and.........I..........I myself am actually a Stoic.........but my.....my....'
'He is *not* an angel,' Clement interrupted.
'He is God,' Origen added bravely.
'But are not angels and gods the same sort of thing?' Paula asked frowning deeply.
'I must say all this angelology stuff does rather confuse me at times.'
'As it surely should,' Paul added. 'It's all a muddy hotchpotch of mad magicians'

fantasies, if you ask me. Celsus was right. He said it all as far as I'm concerned. Bagfuls of mumbo-jumbo based on misguided, totally unscientific speculation, or downright hallucinations, or a mixture of both.'

'Celsus was an arrogant poser with a little learning that went to his head,' Origen said, almost angrily. 'I have studied his so-called *True Doctrine* carefully. It should be called *The Untrue Doctrine*.'

There was a strange silence then in which all eyes remained on Origen, expecting him to continue, but he did not. He was too surprised with himself for having said so much already.

Clement sniffed. 'It's not all mumbo-jumbo if you know where, or better still *how* to look, Paul,' he said calmly.

'Where, how.... pray, tell me? I *have* looked.'

'Have you read Dionysius?'

'Dionysius?'

'Yes, the Aereopagite, Paul's disciple in Athens. He started a Gnostic School there after he was initiated into the Great Mysteries by St. Paul himself, and the School still thrives. I'm surprised you haven't come across it. But, needless to say, they do not proselytise. Anyway, there the teaching about the Nine-Fold Hierarchical Orders of the Angels is very clearly taught, and I am fully conversant with it.'

'Bah,' Paul scoffed.

Paula suddenly clapped her hands very loudly which was a signal for the man-servants to remove the table and bring on the next course.

Origen kept his plate of vegetables beside him on the couch, for they were still only half-eaten and he wished to continue to pick at them. Ambrosius, who had devoured his plate of veal with zest, belched loudly, and wiping his hands on a napkin leant towards Origen and whispered, 'Ask a question about Valentinus.' Origen grinned boldly in reply.

A new, low table laden with nuts, fruit, honey, and a huge assortment of colourful, iced cakes, was soon set down by two able-bodied men-slaves and each guest began to help himself accordingly. Origen continued to observe Ammonius Saccus as discreetly as possible. He noted how Ammonius had but rarely altered his almost meditative posture throughout the entire conversation and then usually only to place an occasional morsel in his mouth. Origen also noted with not a little pride that Ammonius was a vegetarian. Origen was intrigued with the way in which every time Ammonius spoke, which was rarely, he drew his free hand up from his side and placed it gently upon his little blue bag. Once or twice Origen actually thought that Ammonius had disappeared, just briefly, and this made him all the more eager to observe. But he was soon overcome by a strange feeling that the more he observed Ammonius, the less he was actually seeing the man!

'Words are what matters. The dialogue! Plato was fully aware of the value of it,' Clement offered in a quick response to Paula fluttering her huge, green eyes at him after a long silence, during the dessert, began to perturb her.

'With words we can make new worlds,' Origen said, feeling relaxed at last.

'Excellent,' Clement said. 'Who said that?'

'Origen!' Ambrosius said unexpectedly. (It was in fact the only word he spoke during the entire conversation!)

'Valentinus,' Origen corrected, smiling at Ambrosius cryptically. 'Valentinus said it.'

'Oh, yes!' said the senator enthusiastically. 'Now, I've heard of him all right. Wasn't he....?'

'Wasn't he,' Paul rudely interrupted, addressing Clement directly with a sharp glance, 'one of your popes or something, here in Alexandria, before he was sent off to Rome with his tail between his legs?'

'Yes, Paul. You are partly correct. But he was actually a presbyter. Valentinus is, was, one of the most learned of those initiated into the Great Mysteries.'

'Hmmm. But was he a Christian?' Paul asked sceptically.

'Of course! And a great one. He knew the Great Master *intimately*. How do you think he became a presbyter if he wasn't a Christian?'

'Like Paula, I get confused sometimes,' Paul said, throwing back half a cupful of wine and flashing Paula one of his rare, sardonic smiles. 'Why *precisely* did he go to Rome?' he went on, addressing Clement as he peered into his empty cup. 'I've heard various stories. What's your one?'

'In a nutshell?'

'In half a nutshell.'

'Our current pope, Demetrius, didn't like him.'

'That simple?'

'That complicated!'

'Why? What was the matter with him, Valentinus, I mean?'

'It's far too involved a story to retell here, Paul. I can tell you afterwards if you wish,' Clement said with an air of finality.

In the silence that followed, Ambrosius nudged Origen gleefully. Origen was eating rapidly now.

'What did Valentinus say about the Christ?' the senator put in. 'Did he say angel, or god, or prophet or...... or what?'

At this Clement remained conspicuously silent. But he raised his eyebrows to Origen, inviting him to respond.

Origen swallowed a mouthful of vegetables with difficulty and cleared his throat.

'Oh, Valentinus believed in the *one* nature of the Christ. There is no doubt at all about that.'

'The one nature?' the senator queried.

'Yes. He believed Christ was a singular and divine being.'

'That's not an angel then, right?'

'No,' Origen said confidently, 'definitely not. An angel is a lesser kind of being than a divine one, more akin to a man than a god.'

'So your Christ was *a* god then?'

'*Is* a God; *the* God – he is the new God of man, revealed fully only to man, or the Godman if you so wish. That makes him unique among gods, men *and* angels. He lived like a man and died like a god – the first god to die a fully human death. Nevertheless he remained at all times totally united with the highest, the Father Being, the Creator. He was a singular, uncreated and divine being.'

There was a long pause.

'Oh pray, *do* go on,' Paula pleaded, and then, instead, went on herself dreamily. 'In the beginning was the word, and the word was a god...........and....'

'Almost correct, Paula,' Origen said. 'Yes, He was the Logos. It's simple really. Angels are created, like men. Divine beings on the other hand *create*.'

'But there is more than one of them?' the senator queried.

'With an ancient confidence,' Origen replied, 'we can conceptualize them as being Three, a Trinity. That covers all possible mathematical permutations, philosophical speculations and astrological calculations!'

'And so Christ is one of these Three?'

'Yes. He is the divine Son.'

'Aha!' The senator closed his eyes and thought deeply about this. 'Yes, the Son.' Origen was smiling brightly.

'Well done,' Clement said. 'You see, Paul? I told you, before he arrived, that if this young man eats enough vegetables you will hear wisdom flow from his lips, pure wisdom. You've just got it.'

As everyone chewed and contemplated Origen's remarks, slowly, one by one, their faces began to turn in the same direction. For sounds of a sudden commotion, erupting elsewhere in the house began filtering in through the open, dining-room door. A few moments later a tall Ethiopian slave, who acted as Paula's porter, entered the dining-room and with a forced dignity nervously handed Paula a little note.

As Paula read this her expression changed gradually from beaming happiness to utter horror.

'Whatever is the matter, Paula?' Clement begged.

Paula put her hand to her mouth. 'Oh dear, Clement. Oh dear,' she blurted.

'Pray, Paula, come, do, please, tell us,' Clement pleaded.

'Clement, my dear. This is a message from Demetrius.'

'From Demetrius!'

'Yes. The Didascaleon. They've set it on fire!'

13   A SCHOOL FOR MAGICIANS?

There was a sudden, renewed and most vicious upswing in the pogroms! And in this latest phase Clement himself, who was after all one of the best known Christians in Alexandria, became a prime target. It turned out that a large part of the interior of the Didascaleon was damaged by the fire on the first night of the renewed attacks, during Paula's dinner. According to reliable accounts gathered afterwards by Origen and Clement, the fire was actually started by Simon the Stylite himself, albeit operating at the head of a supporting mob. The soldiers, as usual, looked on and did nothing. Civic efforts to quench the fire only began when it threatened to spread to nearby buildings. The smallest lecture hall of the Didascaleon, however, Clement's favourite, was least damaged, but even here the walls were daubed all over with death threats, written in the most obscene language, against all who attended it, and in which Clement himself was clearly named.

A few days after the fire, Origen was sitting in his father's library, his mind racing faster than ever before. It raced so fast he thought he was losing control and actually feared going mad. The only relief he could get was to close his eyes and roll his head in circles. He was experiencing utter anguish. On the desk before him lay five silver coins which he had collected from his students earlier in the day in payment for tuition, but each time he opened his eyes and gazed upon the five beastly heads of Septimius Severus he felt his anguish increase.

There was some relief in anger. How foul a fable it was, he thought, that this monster should be called a god – a god, of all things! - this apotheosis of blasphemers, this hater of truth, this despoiler of justice and peace, this absolute denier of the one true God, the Christ.

But as such thoughts multiplied in his head Origen soon became aware that if he was to speak them aloud, how easily he would sound like Simon the Stylite. How hypocritical of him! Was it not the Christ himself who counselled most strongly against the error of meeting evil with evil? Again and again Origen had to check and admonish himself. But each time he looked at the coins the urge to spit on them only increased. Where is your capacity for forgiveness now, he charged himself, where? Bah! Spit on the damned monster, spit!

As his inner turmoil mounted, his rolling eyes travelled from the coins up to the laden shelves of the little library. They were crammed with every conceivable author of note, ancient and modern, from before and after Plato; philosophers, historians, poets of every description, the very cream of Greek and Roman culture and learning, all there piled up in these rolls. And now in this most anguished of moods Origen found himself beginning to despise all this. For, what was it all when placed alongside the inestimable majesty of his Christ? Was it not all simply intellectual stuffing for a gluttonous, decadent Empire that thoroughly despised his God? Was not all this so-called learning and philosophy just a jumble of meaningless squiggles on reams of useless papyrus? For had not *He*, through His great, the greatest sacrifice ever, set all this worldly learning at naught? And what, pray, did a monster like Severus know of such a pure sacrifice? 'Absolutely nothing,' Origen said out loud, and banging his fist on the desk jumped from his chair. 'Nothing,' he repeated, and sweeping the coins violently from the desk scattered them in all directions. 'Keep your dirty filthy tax,' he scoffed, and in the same temper was about to start sweeping the rolls from the shelves when suddenly his mother entered the room. 'Mother!' he gasped, feeling utterly ashamed. Characteristically she did not comment, despite his obvious anguish, but rather her honey-soft eyes radiated complete empathy with his inner struggles. Her presence soon returned to Origen a modicum of his customary calmness.

'Son,' she said quietly, 'Clement is here to see you.'

'Thank you, mother,' Origen sighed, and she left quickly as Clement entered.

Clement came across the room to Origen and, spotting his anguished state, embraced him warmly. He looked deeply and empathically into Origen's eyes then gave him the Kiss of Peace. A little later he confided quietly, 'Demetrius wants to see both of us, together.'

'When?' Origen asked, holding back his tears.

'Right now.'

'Why?'

'He did not say precisely. He was, as usual, hurtfully curt. But so much is happening. Perhaps he has received some important information that we need to know.'

'But, Master, what does he want *me* for?'

'Come, Origen. Let us not speculate further. Let us simply go and find out.'

Origen gathered up the scattered coins and dejectedly replaced them on the desk. 'Rome calls,' Clement said with a glint in his eye as they went out of the house and set off up the narrow street towards Pope Demetrius' residence.

Demetrius lived in a shabby but spacious apartment on the ground floor of a crumbling old *insulae* in the Brochium quarter of the city where most of the civic buildings were located. Demetrius was indeed a very civic-minded man, despite his spiritual status as head of the *Kyrios* in Alexandria.

Before becoming a Christian, Demetrius had been a successful merchant (some rumours even suggested a slave-merchant, but Clement could never corroborate this) and Clement often wondered how much this had to do with Demetrius' sudden and strange rise to the position of spiritual authority he now held. For, notwithstanding the fact that Clement had tried, he could never come to terms with the incongruity, the ambiguity of Demetrius' position. As far as he could see there were, as yet, no clearly-established procedures in the Congregation for electing someone with the kind of supreme authority that Demetrius had somehow been able to arrogate to himself in Alexandria.

But then that perhaps was the real, albeit negative, explanation of it all! For Demetrius, Clement knew for certain, was not a member of any of the inner circles of the house-communities. And *there* lay the greatest incongruity, for it was only in the inner, initiated circles that one was certain of finding those who knew the Christ intimately, like Clement did himself. And these surely could only be the ones considered as candidates for carrying the kind of spiritual power and authority in the *Kyrios* that Demetrius supposedly possessed. But the truth was that Demetrius was one of the old, conservative types who still clung to Ebionite traditions, and had little idea of the incredible difference in the spiritual life of mankind that the Christ had wrought. But whereas he had somehow managed to get himself baptized into the *Kyrios*, it was as plain to Clement as the huge nose on Demetrius' face that he knew little or nothing of the pure fire-baptism of the Christ-spirit.

But, however it happened, Demetrius, the arch-philistine, was not only a lukewarm Christian, but also the *de facto* father of the community in Alexandria, and Clement, a true pacifist by nature and a pragmatist by design, tacitly accepted him. For Clement fully realized that to challenge Demetrius now would create more trouble than it would solve. It was also a fact that Clement, more than any other member of the *Kyrios* in Alexandria, realized the need for *some* kind of overseeing authority in the city, something which was indeed becoming more and more acute as the pogroms and general persecutions of Christians in the Empire increased.

When Clement and Origen reached Demetrius' *insulae* they were shown, by an untidily-dressed negro slave, into the study. This room was small, dark, and, as Origen immediately noticed, virtually bookless. In it Demetrius, an oldish, fattish man, was sitting on a worn but large, soft armchair. He was wearing a loose, light-grey toga and from his neck swung a huge silver medallion attached to a bright, bronze chain. This medallion depicted the sign of the Fish, a symbol of the Christ as Fisher of the souls of men.

Demetrius dismissed the slave and silently motioned Clement and Origen to sit down on two wooden stools in front of him.
'The Didascaleon is attracting far too much attention,' Demetrius mumbled, fiddling nervously with his medallion.
'Too much attention!?' Clement questioned. 'But it is world famous, more famous

now, I reckon, than the Museum itself.'

'Yes, but the Museum and Library are very widely *respected*.'

'The Didascaleon is widely respected also.'

'I mean where it matters, in Rome.'

'Rome! Bah!'

'Look, Clement,' Demetrius said, leaning forward with some difficulty and wagging his index finger, 'Rome is what matters.'

'Christ is what matters!' Clement retorted.

Demetrius sat back again. 'They are greatly suspicious about the School,' he revealed in a slightly menacing tone.

'And who, pray, are *they*?'

'There is a great need to bring order into the movement. You know that. They know how to do such things in Rome. And, I repeat, they are very suspicious of the School. I don't like it!'

'Why, Demetrius? Tell me. Why do *you* think that *they* are suspicious?'

Demetrius fiddled with his medallion again.

'They say it teaches.......secret......secret practices......magic........'

'But, surely, you know that that is the very height of nonsense, Demetrius?'

'What I know is that I have to keep the interests of the *entire* Congregation in mind here. We've got to try to stem these attacks on us......somehow.'

Origen's attention was fixed on Demetrius' medallion. Was Demetrius a true Fisher for the Christ, he wondered. Origen found it hard to believe. He had met Demetrius a few times before and had always puzzled about him afterwards, especially with regard to his position as pope or papa, the father of the community. This seemed to Origen utterly incongruous and ironic. True, Demetrius had something of this papa or elder quality – he reminded Origen, for instance, a little of his own father, but only in the most general of ways. But the idea of Demetrius having *spiritual* authority over him merely made him laugh. But, he argued with himself, if Clement recognizes him, then so must he.

Clement said, 'Of course, we must try to stop the attacks. But not by compromising ourselves. Christ cannot be compromised.'

'We live in a real world,' Demetrius said dismissively.

'We live in a fast disintegrating world, and there is but one thing that will hold it together – Christ.'

Demetrius tapped his foot nervously.

'Look, I've had a letter from Irenaeus'.

'Irenaeus!' Origen blurted involuntarily. He hated him! Demetrius looked at Origen contemptuously. He had not given him leave yet to speak, so Origen forced a slight, apologetic curtsy.

'Irenaeus,' Demetrius repeated, 'has advised me strongly to close the School.'

'Close the School!' Clement gasped.

'Yes! Close it. If we want to have *some* hope of curbing the animosity of the Emperor towards us.' Demetrius bent forward again. 'Clement, he thinks it is a breeding ground of demonically-inspired astrologers and Babylonian black magicians who daily consort and conspire with over-ambitious and plotting politician-soldiers. He absolutely hates it!'

'He's mad! And you, sir, should know that. There are two ways to the Christ, Demetrius, an inner one and an outer one, and our work in the School teaches how these twin paths can, without antagonism, be approached, and for those who have the necessary discipline, successfully combined. And as for Irenaeus, despite his widespread reputation as a good and devout Christian, he has as much animosity towards us in the School as the Emperor himself. I have been aware of that for some time'.

As Clement spoke Origen could not help nodding, much to the irritation of Demetrius, upon whose flabby, red face a nasty scowl had been slowly expanding. He got up with surprising agility and went over to the one small window of the study and looked out.

After a long silence he said with great emphasis, and in a deeper tone than usual, 'The path of the *Kyrios* is like a Roman road: it is to be laid out in places where everyone, and I mean *everyone*, can see and can walk upon, with maximum ease and minimum direction.'

He turned then from the window and faced Clement directly. 'We will not continue to mix ourselves up with oriental magicians, half-baked philosophers and Babylonian astrologers. We will free ourselves once and for all from all that kind of hocus-pocus and the fanciful visionaries who teach it.' After another pause he went on, 'I have made a decision.'

Clement jumped up. 'You *cannot* close the School, Demetrius,' he cried, 'you simply cannot! The School is the very heart and soul of our *Kyrios*. The entire future of the movement, not just here in Alexandria but all over the world is centred upon it.'

Demetrius was about to interrupt him when Clement lifted his hand authoritatively and said, 'Wait, please. Let me finish.'

Clement took a couple of paces deep in thought then continued, 'Look, the *Kyrios* will never be more than just one more sectarian group or one more religion among the many others in the world without this School. Please, realize this. We will be seen as no different from the rest of them. But, Demetrius, it *is* different, we *are* different! You don't need *me* to tell you that. Ultimately the *Kyrios* is not a religion at all. It is a present Being. We must simply learn to open our *inner* eye to Him. And in order to achieve this, I repeat, we do not, in the School, teach hocus-pocus, magic and the like. If you troubled yourself to attend even *one* of my lectures or workshops yourself you would soon realize the truth of that. What we teach is that the Christ can, through his sacrificial blood, purify the entire being of man. Sure, we teach meditation but that is not magic, Demetrius. It is simply naive to think so. Through meditative practices we teach how a person can lift himself up in his or her entire being, including ultimately the physical body, into His Holy Spiritual Being and how it, the Holy Spirit, then graciously bestows a divine power of transformation. He, the Christ, is a totally new kind of being, and as the new God of man and Earth, and through His Spirit living in us, in our body and our soul, we are capable of renewing *everything* in the universe. Thus the Christ is utterly new and totally different to all other gods. We have to make that crystal clear. And the School is our one, our only hope of doing so.'

As Clement spoke Demetrius' scowl slowly dissolved, and when Clement eventually stopped talking the two men stared at one another in silence for a long time. Then coming back again to his armchair Demetrius sat down heavily and motioned Clement to do likewise.

With his eyes hooded now, Demetrius began to peer down his large aquiline nose at Origen.

'What age are you?' he demanded curtly.

'Eighteen on the 11th of September next, sir,' Origen replied.

Demetrius turned again to Clement. 'You know your life is now in the utmost danger, don't you?'

'Our enemies are everywhere. Yes, I do,' Clement said.

Demetrius shuffled uneasily in his armchair. 'I have arranged,' he said in an assertive tone, 'with your former pupil, Alexander, for you to join him in Cappadocia.'

Clement closed his eyes. He could not respond. Then Demetrius went on very slowly and in the same uncompromising tone, 'Alexander now has a mature congregation there in Cappadocia, in a small new city-state near the border with Pontas, not far from the shores of the Black Sea. It is, by all accounts, a safe and undisturbed congregation.'

Clement's ashen face looked resigned. He opened his eyes but still no words came, only tears.

'Alexander, I am reliably informed,' Demetrius went on, now trying to inject an air of sympathy into his voice, 'badly needs someone to help him.'

'Cappadocia,' Clement repeated blandly.

'Yes. You must leave as soon as possible,' Demetrius concluded after a silence.

'And what about the School?' Clement sighed.

Demetrius fiddled with his medallion again, jabbed his free finger towards Origen and cleared his throat noisily. 'Er....... he can take over the running of the School.'

Clement turned to Origen.

'Origen,' he said, 'will you take over the running of the School?'

Now it was Origen's turn to close his eyes. There was to be no argument or discussion here, he knew. For although his voice was weak, Clement's question had that familiar tone to it which not only sounded out an answer, but demanded the correct one. There was only one possible response. The hand of destiny Origen never felt more firmly upon him, and the very fingers of his angel teased the words from his throat. 'I will take over the running of the School,' he announced.

Clement looked at Demetrius who now had his eyes cast downwards. 'He will be the new Master of the School, Demetrius. And the School will never have a better one, believe me.'
'Hmm. Yes, Clement. I will try and believe you. Now. When will you leave?'
'I will enquire at the port about times of ship-sailings this very day.'
'Good.' Demetrius stood up. He motioned Clement and Origen to do likewise. Demetrius then lifted his right hand in a brisk blessing. 'May your journey be safe,' he said to Clement, 'and may you continue to serve the Lord by spreading His holy Gospel. Do this through the power of the Holy Spirit, in the name of our Lord Jesus Christ. Amen.'
Turning to Origen, Demetrius continued in much the same tone, 'Come here to me again in two days' time and we can work out the details of your new position within the community.'

Without further ado Demetrius picked up a little brass bell from his desk and rang it irritably. When the negro servant appeared again Demetrius instructed curtly, 'Show my visitors to the door.'

14   FAREWELL TO MASTER CLEMENT

Only a few days later Origen had to endure one of the saddest moments of his young life when, alone with Clement, he stood at the harbour's edge as Clement prepared to board a ship bound for distant Antioch. Origen fought heroically to hold back the tears all the while as he questioned his Master and listened to him more carefully than ever as he delivered his parting words.

'Christ,' Clement said, 'is here to stay. And whether it takes one thousand, ten thousand, or one hundred-thousand years, the *Kyrios* <u>will</u> be established on the Earth. And you, my dearest of dear young friends, shall lay the foundation of this great work for the world, beginning right here in its lighthouse, Alexandria.'

'When will I see the Great Master?' Origen blurted.

'But, my friend, do you not already see Him?'

'I mean in the flesh.'

'But His flesh is the very body of our mother planet, Earth herself, is it not? – its finest fruits, its best substance, its bread and wine?' – Clement cupped Origen's face in his hands – 'its beautiful Children of the Light.'

Origen blushed. 'I shall miss *Agape* with you, Master,' he said.

Clement then embraced him warmly, gave him the Kiss of Peace, stood back and made the Sign of the Cross over him, something he had never done before. A tear slipped down Origen's face.

'And stop crying,' Clement said wiping the tear away with a tender smile. 'Practise all the spiritual exercises with the greatest degree of devotion you can muster. Grow strong in Christ.'

'Master, when will I be initiated into the Great Mysteries, like you?'

The question put Clement into deepest thought. Origen watched him carefully for a reply and never did he feel Clement's bright eyes pierce him more sharply as he answered, 'For this you must first come to know the mystery of *death* intimately. You are still too young for that. However, before this initiation or death-experience, you must first be asked a question by a certain man or woman. This must happen at the right time and in the right place. But I cannot tell you details. You can only recognise them for yourself, out of your own heart.'

'A man or woman - a question?' Origen quizzed.

'Yes, a question through a man or a woman or one who looks one. You may not know him or her, but you will know the question when you hear it. Then from there you will be led into the great initiation. This is how it works.'

'Thank you, Master. I will remember this.'

'And remember this also, my friend. The *Kyrios* will *always* have its enemies – *always*, and mighty ones. As the great Apostle Paul said, "Ultimately our fight is not against human foes, but against wickedness, even in the heavens." Whispering, dark angels move among us, forever filling empty ears, hearts, and minds with evil intent.

It is not sufficient for them that they crucified Him once - they want to crucify Him *every day*. These masters of cruelty, these black, evil beings are most active in Rome where the ancient Mysteries are utterly, utterly despised; where they worship only the Beast, and where the only love they know is the love of worldly power. So, be on your guard always. Now, farewell, my young and most dear friend.'

Clement looked forlorn and wan as he boarded the huge cargo ship with his small wooden trunk. After Antioch he had a long and dangerous overland trek, much of which was desert, to the shores of the Black Sea in the north of Cappadocia. It was unlikely, he had also said, that he would ever be able to return again to Alexandria, now that Demetrius, at last, had found the perfect excuse to get rid of him.

Origen prayed for Clement fervently as he watched the tall ship ply its way serenely through the many other incoming and outgoing, mostly smaller, vessels. It looked right to Origen that his great friend and beloved Master should be on one so proud and colourful, for its sails were dazzling black and gold, and on it's exquisitely carved prow a bright-blue eagle.

When he stopped praying Origen finally yielded fully to his tears, and they streamed down his face more freely than ever before. Never had he felt so utterly vulnerable and alone in the world as he did then, not even after the murder of his father. And yet, as he watched and cried, he felt the spirit of a harder, stronger friendship filling his emptiness. Clement may be gone physically, but he would live even more fully now in Origen's soul. Fed by the echo of Clement's Christ-spirit-words, Origen's own image of his Great Master would grow and mature all the more quickly. For anyway, what was human friendship ever but a gloomy, dying thing when compared to the fullness of the riches of spiritual friendship with the Great Master? For, through His sacrifice you were given a friendship based not on any perishable, material thing, but on a resurrected and eternally beautiful, purified body of love. This was the spiritual friendship that all true Christians must seek and value above all others.

Oh, if only he could touch Him, feel Him, kiss Him! How long must he wait! Origen raised his tear-stained face to the sky. And, 'Yes,' he heard echoing somewhere deep in his soul, 'you shall know my body. But first you must know it as a time-body. Therefore work hard, watch, wait and pray, and practise virtue *always* – and then you will see me, and in time your body and my resurrected Being will unite and we will become as one.'

Origen's saintly tears only began to ease when the mainsail of Clement's ship was but a tiny, yellow dot on the shimmering, blue, distant horizon. And when he finally managed to pull himself away from the sea he realized that only now was he setting his heart, his hands, and his face fully towards his new life; a life filled, he felt, with the greatest challenge that any man could ever have. But born of his loneliness, a new harder spirit began to take hold of him. And as he shuffled his way, still sobbing, out of the harbour, passed the busy bands of buyers and sellers, the noisy negro workmen, the piles of merchandise, the dogs, animals and ragged children, and was afterwards jostled and bumped along Canopius Way as he headed for his beloved but battered Didascaleon, he felt the new harder spirit tightening its grip with every step he took. And by the time he reached the School he had not only stopped crying, but was walking so firmly that people were getting out of his way!

By destiny he had been given a mighty task to perform, and by Christ he was going to do it, and do it right!

And it was then he knew for certain that he was never going to cry again!

15   THE BRIGHT NEW HACK

The first thing Origen did was to organise a clean-up of the Didascaleon by the students. The matron Paula helped too, but mainly in kind. Clement had given Origen his little flat in the *insulae* near the Didascaleon, so he immediately but reluctantly withdrew from Paula's patronage. But in doing so he was also very glad to get away from Paul of Antioch.

For the work on the building there was no shortage of student volunteers. Luckily no structural damage had been done, but many minor repairs had to be carried out, much of it had to be repainted, and lots of replacement furniture found. The harder spirit taking hold of Origen impelled him into hyper activity, and far sooner than he expected he was ready and eager to begin his work as new Master of the School.

Demetrius had raised his eyebrows in disbelief when, visiting him in his residence, Origen told him of the progress achieved in the short space of time since Clement's departure.

'I will start on Monday,' he said to Demetrius decisively.
Fiddling with his medallion, Demetrius slanted his large fish-eyes on him. 'You have my permission,' he said slowly, and after a short pause continued, 'And all of the money you collect in tuition fees you will give to me........directly.'
'Yes,' Origen replied.
'Good. Now, about your own salary. I will arrange...........'
'I do not want a salary,' Origen interrupted.
'Pardon?'
'I said, I do not want a salary.'
'Come, Origen. What nonsense is this? How are you to live if you do not have a salary?'
'I will not take money from you, sir. You need it more than I do. I mean, to distribute among the poor, the widows and orphans of our community. Give, if you wish, my mother and family priority. That will satisfy me.'

Demetrius was astonished! He had never heard anyone speak so naively before, and yet so honestly and with such virile determination. He sighed resignedly. He knew there would be little point in arguing. 'Look,' he said, 'if you want money then ask me.'
'Yes, I will.'
Demetrius then looked somewhat spitefully at him down his big red nose and sniffed. 'Is it true that you also take in girl students at the School?'
Origen was astounded at his ignorance! 'Yes, of course,' he replied.

'And you teach them all together, the boys with the girls in the same hall, I mean?
'Yes, we do. Neither the School itself nor the lessons could proceed without the, if I may put it so, "flower-power" of the girls.'
Demetrius looked ruffled. 'How do you come to such an idea?' he asked irritably. 'I have not heard anything like this before.'
'Why, sir, I am astonished at you! For what I say is self-evident, even from the Gospels, which I am sure you have read.... er....haven't you?'
Demetrius remained perturbed but silent.
'It's all there in the Gospel, sir, believe me,' Origen went on. 'The Great Master has taught us, by example especially, to esteem women generally - and not only in domestic or community matters, but also in the pursuit of learning, knowledge and especially wisdom. Unlike our forefathers and indeed the ancients generally, we must learn to include them in *all* of our community activities from now on if we are to become fully cognisant of the true spirit of God as revealed to us by our Great Master.'

Demetrius was fiddling nervously with his medallion as Origen continued, 'Now, this teaching regarding women was a great break with the old traditions, but a very important one, and yet another example of the great wisdom of the new Way inaugurated by the Christ. Thus, in the School the girls provide, in various ways, a perfect counterpoint to the boys. Therefore all teaching and lecturing about the Gospel of the Great Master must be gender-balanced. If this is not done it will give rise to the greatest imaginable spiritual errors and psychological damage in the future.'

Demetrius was searching continually for an appropriate tone to adopt towards Origen, something he found extremely difficult. At one level he knew he was merely interviewing the latest addition to his army of chattels, which despite the persecutions, or even because of them, was growing all the time, and thus the business of organizing the *Kyrios* continually increased also. However, on another level he was here being confronted with someone who was, despite his youth, obviously his intellectual superior by far. But Demetrius also knew that in the coming battles between the *Kyrios* and the State, those with the keenest intellects were going to be the all-important people, more important even than the virtuous, the pious or even the faithful themselves. Therefore he simply had to learn how to correctly value and manipulate these intelligent ones, and most of all turn them to profit............. for the good of the community........of course.

'There are similar schools to yours in Rome,' Demetrius puffed, 'and *they* do not allow girls!'
'Sir, with respect, they cannot be similar to ours if they disallow girls.'
Demetrius looked ruffled, but Origen continued, 'They have little real knowledge in

Rome, sir, of how to apply to the Gospel, the principles, practices and traditions of pure Greek philosophy'.

'Greek philosophy.......hmmm.' Clearing his throat noisily Demetrius demurred, 'You recognise my authority here in Alexandria, don't you?'

Origen felt a frisson down his spine. How on earth was he to answer such a question honestly! Sure, authority was important. But Demetrius...........?

'There are two kinds of authority, sir. Which one do you have?' Origen ventured, surprised yet happy with his inspiration.

Demetrius looked ruffled again. 'Name them,' he snapped.

'Spiritual and temporal.'

Demetrius sniffed and suddenly stood up. 'I have *both* of them,' he said dismissively. 'Now listen to me. Come every week at the same time and report to me personally *all* important matters concerning the School. Do you understand?'

'Yes.'

'And bring the money.'

'Yes.'

Demetrius picked up the little brass bell from his desk. Then, keeping his large fish-eyes contemptuously on Origen, teasingly he very lightly rang it. But when the slave did not appear after a minute or two Origen asked, 'May I go now?'

Demetrius then rang the bell again, very loudly, almost angrily, and when the slave appeared dismissed Origen irritably. But from his little window he could not help but continue to watch him, and as Origen disappeared down the dim, narrow street, Demetrius suddenly felt deeply envious of his firm, lean young body.

Origen enjoyed his new role, for now he could openly and freely teach about his Great Master for the first time. He liked to use the small lecture hall in the Didascaleon where, amidst the freshly-washed, gleaming white and green marble interior, from the north wall behind him, the mosaic of the serpent-conquering Christ still shone in all its splendour despite having been daubed with white paint, most of which had been removed in the clean-up.

His new task stimulated Origen tremendously! Previously all his teaching was of a secular nature, but now his primary task was to teach the Gospel. His enthusiasm indeed often bordered on the euphoric. For to instil a love of the Christ into his students, a love that would live in their hearts and strengthen them, not only for the rest of their lives on Earth, but all their future lives to come, was what he considered to be his primary and evangelical task.

As he gradually got into the habit of teaching and lecturing, and began to learn, himself, from his students, Origen also very quickly became convinced that life on Earth itself was a school, a place where human souls came to correct past errors, imperfections and sins. But to do this, souls needed to carry with them to the Earth the lessons of previous existences. Of this Origen was fully convinced and he made it an intrinsic part of his teaching. It was, however, a teaching that was very much at odds with what Christians were being taught elsewhere, particularly in Rome. A Christian doctrine was there fast evolving which held that the human soul was created anew for each incarnating human being. This Origen felt to be not only completely contrary to common sense, but he knew for a fact that it was also absolutely contrary to the basic teaching of *all* the ancient Mysteries, of which Pythagoras himself was the best known, and outstanding Initiate in the Greek world. This strange new doctrine emanating from Rome seemed to Origen a palpable and grievous error, a misguided conspiracy, a doctrine being propagated and spun, he suspected, primarily by the ever-disagreeable Ebionites whose Jewish forefathers hated the doctrine of pre-existence of souls, or reincarnation, with a vengeance, simply because it seemed to them to pander to Oriental pantheism and the like, and was therefore thoroughly displeasing to their jealous Jehovah. Nevertheless, to anyone who had even an inkling of the deeply occult nature of the soul herself, the teaching of the earthborn or earthbound soul was one that had no honesty in it at all, no logical or spiritual insight, and actually denied the majesty and cosmic beauty of the soul. Thus Origen increasingly felt it to be one of his primary duties, as a Christian teacher with a growing reputation and authority as head of the Didascaleon, to at least set his own students aright on this hugely important matter.

He hoped that in this way, and in time, the doctrine would prove to be of benefit to the entire *Kyrios*. For truth, he knew, was an unstoppable force and had a habit of spreading its branches like a tree - it simply needed time for its roots to take hold.

Ambrosius returned to the School soon after he learned, to his amusement but delight, that Origen was the new Master. He was secretly but tremendously proud of his poor, idiosyncratic friend. Now, at last, he might buy himself a new tunic!

Back at the School again with a thoroughly renewed enthusiasm for *gnosis*, Ambrosius got much and increasing pleasure as well as mental stimulation as he good-humouredly teased Origen with spiked questions about everything under the sun, but especially reincarnation. Ambrosius' knowledge of the great Valentinus had increased immensely in recent months - Origen could tell by his questions - but the intelligent and thoughtful responses Origen gave to them had the effect of endearing him to the rest of the students, most of whom soon came to recognise in him not only an adequate successor to their esteemed Clement, but clearly one who even surpassed him in lucidity of soul, depth of spirit and strength of intellect. Thus, they soon forgot about his youth altogether, his erudition and vast knowledge of scripture and philosophy casting a mantle of ageless wisdom over his entire being. Indeed the students gradually came to realize that they were in the presence of a Christ-like figure, and were, most of all, attracted by his loving, gentle nature. For Origen's entire bearing had the effect of instilling in them that pure love of freedom which was, at the heart, the very essence of the Gospel message.

In this way Origen grew in confidence. Especially in his soul and intellectual abilities, he felt his capacities growing in tandem with the challenges the new post created for him. Nevertheless, in his personality he knew there still lurked acute uncertainties and chronic conflicts which, if he was to truly build on Clement's soul and spiritual success, he knew he must resolve fully, and do so soon.

Sometimes Ambrosius came to the lectures alone, and sometimes he came with Sarah. But one evening Sarah came alone.

Ironically, on that particular evening Origen had carefully prepared a lecture, based on the important story by Moses in the Book of Genesis, about the expulsion of Adam and Eve from Paradise. He had not long commenced speaking when he saw Sarah enter the hall silently, almost mysteriously. Unusually, she was dressed entirely in black and had her *palla* draped alluringly over her head, and kept it that way, and for the entire lecture remained standing at the back of the hall.

Even from a distance Origen felt their eyes touch deeply when she entered. And

97

each time after that when he looked in her direction his customary and easy flow of words faltered, as if he were at some unfamiliar crossroads and did not know which way to turn.

He had just outlined the bones of the Mosaic story for the students when she entered. Then he continued, 'Therefore, we can see that Moses knew that before the Fall, that is, before the Expulsion, the human being was actually an undivided, bi-sexual being. Male and female were contained within the *one* body. This is clear from the story if you read it carefully. The Temptation was initiated by Lucifer, the Angel of Light – *not* Satan, as many erroneously say - Satan is actually a different angel altogether - the dark one. But after Lucifer had incited Eve, and she then offered Adam the apple of knowledge, the knowledge that is, of good and evil, and he, Adam, had bitten into it, God became very angry, so angry in fact that He fully - and by this I mean *physically* - divided them, which is another way of saying that He sent them out of the Garden altogether. And that is where we are now; that is the way we are now, my friends, outside and divided! Here, He has made us ashamed of our difference, both from one another, and especially from Him – shame is the key word the enlightened and highly initiated Moses uses in the story. He learnt it from the fleshpots of Egypt.'

But as he spoke, maddeningly Origen felt shame also; an unexpected arousal! Usually when he spoke, his thoughts flowed easily and purely; the actual flow depending upon his familiarity with his chosen subject, the purity of his thoughts upon his mood generally which, especially when speaking of the Great Master, was often prophetic, or even ecstatic. This evening, however, as he spoke he felt his entire soul constantly being dragged downwards and he had to pitch the veracity and the light of his every word against that dogged and dark force emanating from the region of his bowels. Several times he had to silently and very consciously invoke his new, hard spirit to help him, for he felt himself going quite astray. He was glad, therefore, when he heard Lukas' familiar voice rising up from the crowd of students before him.
'Master, is the Antichrist Lucifer or Satan?'
The question, like Lukas, was simple but good, and to the point.
'Satan is the Antichrist,' Origen said. 'Lucifer, as the Angel of Light, albeit a fallen one, has given us the power to separate good from evil, which is the main point of the Expulsion story. Satan merely confuses us! He is the very spirit, actually the master, of confusion. Lucifer, on the other, hand is partially redeemed, but only through the grace of the Great Sacrifice of the Christ. But even dark Satan himself will be redeemed eventually, and then *all* evil will be banished from the world soul. It is up to us – that is, to purify our soul nature.'

But Origen had to breathe deeply to keep his mind clear and keep control of himself generally as he spoke. The Paradise story was one he especially loved, but it was threatening, this evening, to take on a reality, and a truth far greater than he had ever witnessed before, far greater even than he felt he could handle. It was almost as if Lucifer himself was present!

His restless eyes followed Sarah as she moved occasionally and very slowly, almost like a vision, across the back of the hall between the two marble columns, her teeth constantly flashing at him like jets of pure, white fire. He did not usually use notes in his lectures, but he was wishing now he had some, for he had great difficulty keeping in mind the main points he wished to make.

'There are two trees in the Garden of Paradise,' he went on, a nervous flutter in his voice, 'the Tree of Knowledge and the Tree of Life. We were allowed by God to eat of the Tree of Life only.'

A young girl put up her hand.

'Yes?' Origen said.

'Why did God get angry?' she asked.

'Disobedience,' Origen replied. 'Laws are made to be obeyed. If you break them you must suffer in some way; suffer, that is, someone else's anger or wrath. Here, in this case, God's.'

A boy said emphatically, 'It was stupid of God to make a rule like that! Human beings want to know things. I want to know *everything*. Someone should punish God!'

A murmur of laugher rippled through the hall. But Origen's eyes and thoughts were continually straying towards Sarah. Deep emotion was welling up in waves through his body and clouding his mind and soul, and only with the greatest of difficulty did he manage, in the end, to finish the lecture properly.

But, maddeningly, Sarah disappeared before he could speak to her, which merely added to his growing frustration. And that night he was so totally overcome with desire for her that he masturbated several times. He raged with himself as he did so. Masturbation always made him feel ill afterwards, and for the next few days he could do very little, and even had to cancel all his lectures.

Most of these dark days he spent sitting on the huge, polished, granite steps leading up to the great, white Pharos lighthouse. For, out there he was as far from the noise and bustle of the city as he could get and, utterly alone, he let the fresh sea breeze and the shimmering azure soothe him, and instil in his soul some of those pure thoughts he was always seeking. Yet, no matter how hard he tried to keep his thoughts pure, the vision of Sarah's delicious body trembled before him like a veil, the very Veil of Isis it seemed, demanding to be lifted. Sometimes he would succeed for a while in banishing her, and his serenity would return, but ever and again the hot struggle resumed.

Oh Christ! It was the peace he wanted, the peace of Him and nothing else; the deep, deep peace which, as the Apostle Paul had said, knew no name, but was nevertheless the only thing that allowed him to have those thoughts and feelings through which he could deliver the precious, redeeming words to his beloved students in the way he wanted, in the prophetic way, the ecstatic way, the way of freedom, truth and beauty, unaffected, untainted by carnal desire.

Nevertheless in these days Origen also continually questioned himself as to whether or not he should just go ahead and take her – for she was surely offering herself to him! – there was little doubt of that – he merely had to bite her apple! But to do that would be truly to lift that shimmering veil, the veil of purest addiction; for once lifted he would have her, and have her fully and unendingly in wedlock, sacramentally prepared to give himself to her as often as she demanded, and she him. Oh, the eternal conflict, the unearthly battle for possession. And how, in the holy name of God most high, could he increase his love for his Great Master under such conditions?

He read and reread St. Paul's letters, especially the ones to Timothy and Titus in the new canon. The great Paul had not married, so why should he, Origen? Clement, he concluded, was far too soft in this regard.

On one of these days, as he sat on the great steps of the Pharos and turned over and over in his restless mind these intensely personal matters, a little ragged boy, who was begging from the sailors at the harbour's edge, spotted him in the distance. The little boy, reckoning he had found the perfect target for his begging art, wandered away from his friends near the ships and towards Origen. And due to the intense state he was in, as the little boy approached he appeared to Origen more like a cherub than a common, ragged urchin. The soiled face merely endeared him to him, and the torn clothes even had the coloured aura of wings. A yard or two from him the little boy held out his hand silently and innocently, but instead of putting something into it Origen drew the boy to him and embraced him warmly. Then they walked back slowly to the harbour, hand in hand, where Origen spent all his money on a large box of fruit, and reluctantly left the little boy as he and his numerous friends gathered round the box in an unexpected but much appreciated picnic.

After that Origen consciously decided to renounce Sarah! All the children of Alexandria were his, he decided, and he needed or wanted no more! He began praying harder and longer than ever before. He also fasted more, and even took to sleeping without a mattress on the floor. He did not inform Sarah of this decision. He felt he had no moral reason to, for, though they had many times come very close, they had never consciously or verbally exchanged terms of endearment. Each time he met her then he purposely avoided talking to her at all, or even looking at her. But it was very difficult, and moreover he knew by her behaviour that she had somehow guessed his new, inner attitude. Then sensing her awareness of his rejection, he would often feel her almost bite at him with her sharp darting looks, and as the weeks passed she began to come to him in dreams at night, haunting him, often with ugly and bestial intent.

Finally one evening, out of the greatest imaginable frustration, and from a genuine fear of going mad, when he was about to bring his hands down yet again upon his sickeningly enflamed penis, his attention was distracted by a movement in his room. He looked up, and amazingly saw the door of his room dissolve before his troubled eyes! Then in its frame a man slowly materialized. *Am I dreaming or awake?* Origen asked himself. Suddenly he felt strangely light. But no, he decided after a few moments, he was not dreaming. *But what then is this I am seeing? Is it real or imaginary; is it a vision or what?*

The man in the doorframe looked strong, slightly dark-skinned, and very well built. He was dressed in a light, black garment made of the softest, clinging material which revealed many of the rippling contours of his virile body.
'I am a messenger,' he said firmly. 'Come, touch me.'
Origen was trembling and fearful now, but nevertheless courageous. He walked across the room towards the man and touched him lightly on his face. Yes, he was real all right.

The thought of Clement and the Question suddenly struck him. The man smiled and drew Origen ever so gently by the hand across the room. But Origen quickly forgot about the Question as the man proceeded to press Origen down quite firmly upon his bed. Then, to Origen's horror, the man lifted his tunic, pulled off his underpants and began groping for his penis! Origen was soon wrestling with the man desperately, but to his utter frustration he found he could not make the slightest sound! Harder and harder he wrestled as the man, possessed of a much stronger power, easily stayed him with one huge knee on his breast while with his shoulders and hands kept Origen's legs wide apart. Never did Origen want to scream more but had to remain as mute as a sacrificial swan!

In his right hand the man then miraculously produced a gleaming, gold-handled knife with an intensely sharp, bright blue blade, and with his free hand pressing Origen's hugely enflamed penis directly down upon his stomach and thus clearly exposing his testicles, with one swift and expert movement of the knife he sliced them off! Origen experienced the most intense and exquisite pain of his life, as if he was being chopped in two with a huge machete, but it was a pain mingled also with a feeling of relief as the man stood up to release him again. The man then calmly put the knife and the testicles into a little blue bag he took from under his garment. He smiled again. 'Now,' he said triumphantly, 'you shall be called by the name of your Christ.'

After this the man walked carefully to where the door should be, stood momentarily in the empty but framed space there, lifted his hand in farewell, and quickly disappeared. The door returned.

'Now do you want to cry?' Origen heard from somewhere. Yes, he wanted to cry all right, but didn't. He struggled to his feet and looked at himself and all around the room. Surprisingly there was little blood, but the wound was intensely painful and ugly as sin. He found some soft cloth, wrapped it around himself, and spent the rest of the night whimpering, trembling violently, nursing his pain, but trying very hard not to actually cry, and amazingly he succeeded.

Luckily no lectures were planned for the next day. So, around noon, by which time the pain had eased a little, Origen dragged himself up out of his bed and hobbled all the way to a doctor, who was also a Christian friend, and who had his consulting rooms about half a mile away. Origen chose him, for he felt he could be trusted, once requested, not to speak to anyone about his strange mutilation. Although visibly astonished, the doctor did not ask any questions, as Origen also requested, and he dutifully dressed the wound and gave Origen various herbs and ointments and told him to stay in bed for a week at least. There should be no very bad side-effects apart from the obvious ones, the doctor reassured, provided Origen drank the prescribed teas and used the various ointments in the correct way over the stipulated period.

Origen obeyed! He gave notice to the School that he had contracted a very strange stomach illness and would have to remain confined to his room for some time! He reassured them that he was not very seriously ill, and tactfully refused the help of various girl students eager to look after him. He decided to keep the incident *totally* secret. No one was to know of his strange encounter with the man with the golden knife. Of course, as he lay in bed over the next week, he reflected long and deeply upon the incident. At first he could make little sense of it at all, and would hardly have continued to believe that it really happened, putting it down to some vision or lifelike dream, were it not for the all-too-obvious mark or wound that he was permanently left with.

Nevertheless, as Origen continued to muse, slowly he began to feel that there were resemblances in the incident with some important passages of scripture, passages which had often deeply puzzled him in the past, but from which he now found he could take some comfort. He thought much, for instance, about that strangest of all

102

passages in the Gospel, the one in the 19th chapter of St. Matthew, where Christ Jesus intimates to His disciples how the original asexual or bisexual condition of man is to be finally recovered through the unique power of the divine/human will which only He has made available in the world.

But there were other passages of scripture which also intrigued Origen. He pondered deeply upon what was perhaps the most dramatic of all of the Apostle Paul's various spiritual experiences, the one recounted in his second very chastising letter to the licentious Corinthians. There Paul spoke of his many visions, but, most articulately of his receiving a so-called 'thorn in his flesh' from God, implying that it was because of the Corinthians themselves, of having to suffer them, that he got this wound, and one, moreover, he would have to suffer, as well as them, until the day he died.

But perhaps the most intriguing of all the passages of scripture which Origen dwelt on during his painful recovery was that enigmatic episode in Genesis where Jacob had to struggle all night with a strange man, the same one who, as it turned out, actually gave him his new name, Israel. This man claimed to be a messenger sent from God, and Jacob had to wage a superhuman fight with him which, although he won in the end, left Jacob with a permanent wound, symptomatic, no doubt, of the great sufferings to come of the whole Israelite nation, of which he had now become, from that moment onward, their undisputed, and great new Patriarch.

Could it possibly be that he, weak Origen, was to have a similar position in the great new gathering of the Children of the Light? He could hardly fathom the thought. Whenever he tried to consider it deeply it was as if his head was about to explode. For here, one was not speaking of a mere tribe or a nation anymore, but a whole new world, a veritable transfiguration of humankind, a purely spiritual Body, a Risen One, for that was what the forming *Kyrios* of the Lord on the Earth was to be. This, Origen had no doubt, was the *final* fulfilment of the great old Covenant between God and men. All of the most ancient Mysteries and their Initiates had spoken of this time, of this great possibility, the Hebrew Bible especially. But now this revelation had been fully consummated and was written into the holy Gospel, and offered to the entire world through the Great Sacrifice of the Lord. This was nothing less than the greatest ever Event on Earth, the turning point of all time.

But how could it possibly be that he, meek, weak and shy Origen, was to become the leader of this, the most momentous happening the world had ever known? He did not know.

But if it really was to be thus, then he must consider himself merely a vessel, a tool for the Lord's work on Earth, and nothing more. For, in truth, he was no different than a thousand other men. If he was being singled out it was through God's Grace alone and had nothing to do with his own weak efforts.

With these thoughts running constantly through his mind Origen nursed his wound and in time, like Jacob, he fully accepted it. Indeed it eventually seemed to work to good effect. For, although he may have lost his deeply instinctive sexual drive, Origen soon and quite surprisingly discovered that this was not a purely physical force at all. Slowly it became obvious to him that this drive had much deeper and more powerful springs, down there in the animal soul herself, and to these he could now turn, as it were, directly, where, without any loss of faith or feeling, or indeed joy in life generally, but nonetheless neutered of the priapic appetite or interface, he found his flaming, probing *thoughts* could function far more freely than ever before. And these could now be put into the fullest and freest service of the *Kyrios*. This now was the source of all his delight and joy.

Thus, over the years, Origen developed an inordinate capacity for study, meditation and concentration. The sacred scriptures, rather than philosophy, now became his primary focus and his thoughts acquired a sword-like capacity to penetrate their secret, hidden or cabbalistic meanings. And in the process the world itself and its multifarious phenomena yielded up to him more and more of its occult secrets and mysteries. As the light, love, and inspiration from the Gospel continued to flesh out his purest thoughts and contemplations, Origen found his soul growing ever and ever more powerfully as a mighty instrument for the work of the new spirit-word of God, revealed to the world by his Christ.

17 THE ROMAN EMISSARY

In the years that followed, Origen changed and developed in many ways. Though remaining quite lean, he grew taller and ever more ascetic in manner, appearance, and outlook. His voice also changed, and in early manhood it acquired an unusually clear tone and texture that made it both light and firm, yet also possessed of the bell-like sweetness of Ammonius Saccus' voice, whose lectures in the Serapeum Origen continued to attend, his entire being continuing to be coloured by this mage's brilliant personality, philosophy, and general outlook on life.

Every moment, action and thought now was dedicated selflessly to the School and its development. Thus, apart from his already well-established reputation for wisdom and learning, Origen became equally widely known for his devotion, virtue and sanctity. And from far and wide, and despite the continued persecution of the Christians, students flocked to the School. But as the numbers increased, so did the need for organization.

As with all students, Origen's also varied in ability and potential, and in accordance with the dual nature of the St. Mark Gospel which underpinned the entire ethos of the School, Origen soon found it necessary to divide his students into two basic groups. The more advanced ones he took to himself, and taught them separately. But as well as the more usual subjects he also began to guide them into the deeper secrets of the Gospel and the spiritual disciplines implied therein for those who sought the true enlightenment and ultimately the pure, initiated intimacy with the Great Master Jesus himself. The much larger and more disparate group of students he placed in the hands of Heracles, a friend and longstanding pupil dating from the time of Paula's garden, and one who had, in recent years, made great strides in the development of his pure Christ-consciousness.

In the rare moments that Origen allowed himself for personal reflection, he usually thought of Clement, and occasionally received short but most-welcome letters from him in his exile in Cappadocia. He had arrived safely at his destination, Clement wrote, but only after he had had many hard adventures. In another letter, written when he had eventually settled down, he told of how he had developed the exacting discipline of writing, and had actually finished his first book. This was called *The Exhortation to the Greeks*, a copy of which he would send along as soon as possible. As a footnote to that letter Clement also greatly recommended the discipline of writing, to Origen himself, as a means of organizing his profound thoughts. But Origen winced when he read this! The idea of sitting down and writing all day long, or even half of it, seemed to him a totally unproductive activity when compared with the joy and fulfilment he got from teaching, or from pastoral work, to which he was also increasingly applying himself in the *Kyrios*.

Origen particularly missed the *Agape* that Clement had held in Alexandria, but ever since Clement had left Origen had made it his business to attend regularly as many of the love-feasts as possible in the different house-communities where the rite continued to be celebrated, despite the persecutions. In these years also Origen became well-known for his growing courage in the face of the ugly and ever bloodthirsty mob. And, as Clement before him had so often done, he led groups of pious and dedicated followers of the Way to the wicked yet holy sites of each of the latest martyrs where, whether butchered or burned, the followers would patiently and silently gather up the martyred bodies and, most solemnly and reverently, administer to them the last rites of the *Kyrios* and inter them amidst scenes of deepest grief in the catacombs of the western necropolis near the community-house of St. Peter, outside the city walls.

As he went from house to house and mixed in the most intimate ways with the diverse community of souls that comprised the *Kyrios* in Alexandria, Origen slowly built up a comprehensive and revealing picture of it. In this way his love for it grew immensely, and almost to the point where he wished for martyrdom himself. Yet his penetrating thought and deep concern for the community also made him realize that if *he* was not there, then who would be responsible for the deeper spiritual guidance of the community's life? For when he thought of Demetrius in this regard he merely shuddered!

In the course of these years, and from such widespread mingling with the faithful, Origen discovered many things, one of which was that there was both an official and an unofficial Council of Presbyters in the city. This in itself worried him, but when it became obvious, from the quality of his encounters with individuals from both sides, that the deeper spiritual knowledge and wisdom of the Gospel very obviously lay with the unofficial, and, also by far, the largest group, he was worried all the more. It was Demetrius, of course, who was behind all this and who had approved, if not actually appointed, the so-called 'official' group – this indeed was how it had come to acquire any status at all, any status, that is, different from the presbyters in general. And so, like Clement before him, Origen now began to question, in a very basic manner, the validity and origin of Demetrius' authority, for it seemed to him that Demetrius, despite his good intentions, had the capacity to do great, if not the greatest, possible damage to the fragile flower of the *Kyrios*.

One day Origen received an unexpected summons from Demetrius. An important visitor wished to meet him, Demetrius said in a note delivered to Origen in the middle of a lecture in the Didascaleon. He was to come as soon as possible.

Recently Origen had been meeting with many important people, not only from

Alexandria, but from all over the Empire; men often occupying high places in the army, the civil service or the commercial world, who were avidly seeking, amidst the turmoil and decadence that everywhere surrounded them, for a good, or even the best possible education for their sons and daughters. Many of these, especially the more wealthy ones, were so concerned about their children that they often attempted to bribe Origen if he had to refuse them for one or other reason, reasons which were often purely logistical. For, as the years passed he found he had to restrict the numbers coming to the School in some way.

Others also sought him out; wealthy matrons hungry for some kind of spiritual enlightenment in the great melting pot of the Alexandrian *gnosis*. Some, he felt, may eventually become followers of the Way, and he tried to encourage them. Others, like the politicians for instance, who also came, he had less time for, for more often than not they were merely seeking to know which way the intellectual wind was blowing.

But no matter who they were Origen studied and patiently listened to them, trying always to discern what goodness was in their motives, if any, but also trying to help in some way. Yes, he was popular all right. But this was the first summons he had received from Demetrius on his special, official papyrus, which had stamped on the top Demetrius' regal-style monogram in bright purple ink. This obviously was a sign from Demetrius, a sign on the one hand of their developing professional relationship, in which Demetrius came increasingly to accept and grudgingly respect Origen's position within the *Kyrios*; but it was also a hint, without having to spell it out, that he should act immediately.

Origen decided to curtail the lecture and he set off straightaway towards Demetrius' *insulae* in the Brochium.

When Origen entered Demetrius' dark study he saw him sitting stiffly in his old, red, high-backed armchair, conversing with a man to his left who was seated on a plain, wooden chair. The man was well-built, middle-aged and of Latin complexion. He was wearing a white toga which had a conspicuous, gold-embroidered hem – obviously a man of some importance.

'Thank you for coming so promptly, Origen,' Demetrius said. 'This is Julianus. He has come all the way from Rome - especially to meet *you*!'
Julianus stood up to greet Origen. He did so silently and formally, by placing his right hand on Origen's right shoulder. Origen returned the gesture after which Demetrius motioned to a stool on his right upon which Origen sat down.

'Julianus has been sent by the pope of Rome, Zephyrinus. He is in fact his private secretary,' Demetrius informed.

'I am truly honoured,' Origen said, bowing slightly.

'We hear much about you in Rome,' Julianus proffered, with a practised, perfunctory smile onto his russet, Latin lips.

'Thank you,' Origen said. 'I hope it's not all bad!'

The tease extracted an involuntary laugh from Julianus. 'You have some fine young people in your congregation,' he said, addressing Demetrius.

Demetrius looked down his big red nose at Origen. 'I am continually amazed at the pace of his development,' he said.

'Is your patriarch, Zephyrinus, well?' Origen asked Julianus.

'Patriarch? We never use the term. We simply call him pope, *the* pope, the Holy Father, actually. Yes, he is quite well, considering his very advanced age.'

'And the faithful?' Demetrius interjected.

'Oh, suffering, like yours,' Julianus replied, stifling a yawn. 'But before we proceed I must deliver some good, in fact some *excellent* news that I bear from Rome.'

'Good news is exceeding rare these dark days, Julianus,' Origen said. 'I am all ears.'

'Mmmm. Well, the first thing is that the Caledonians have become so troublesome in Britannia that the Emperor himself has decided to go there to sort things out – at the head of the biggest army he can muster of course.'

'Ah! Now this *is* good news,' Origen said. 'To be as far away from *him* as possible is surely a recipe for real peace.'

'The Emperor is a brave man, Origen. He need not go personally to Britannia.'

'The Emperor is a greedy man, Julianus, and he should stay in Britannia!'

Demetrius grunted disapprovingly, but Origen merely added, 'He is no friend of ours.'

'Well,' Julianus demurred, 'I did not come here to argue with you about our Emperor. He has a difficult and important job to do, keeping the peace.'

'Yes. But surely not by allowing the mob to tear the bodies of our innocent Christians apart like wild animals any time they like, for their entertainment?'

'Yes. All right. All right. But please, let me come to the point. It is this. Before the Emperor left on his campaign, Zephyrinus had a personal visit from one of his top aides who told him that Severus had........wait for it............. withdrawn the Edict against us!'

'Praise be to God on high,' Demetrius mumbled and blessed himself.

'He has found a better scapegoat in the Caledonians, I suppose,' Origen suggested sarcastically.

Julianus pinned Origen with his piercing black eyes. 'We must be most grateful for this concession.'

'We are,' Demetrius emphatically declared, nodding, 'we are,' and searched Origen for an equally appropriate response.

'Yes,' Origen echoed mechanically, 'we are.'

Demetrius fiddled with his medallion. 'But when will we be *religio licita* Julianus, when? That is what I would like to know.'

'That will come too, Demetrius, believe me, that will come. These things take time. In the meantime we are growing at an *enormous* rate in Rome.'

'Enormous?' Origen queried.

'Yes. We are opening our doors wide, particularly to the *lapsi*, especially now that the Edict is lifted. Soon we will have more followers than even that despicable, pagan bull-god, Mithras, who, as you probably well know has been gaining hugely in popularity for decades all over the Empire, and especially in our highly valued army.'

'Do you impose any conditions on the *lapsi*?' Origen asked. 'I mean, surely so many of them are just cowards and hypocrites of the first degree. On the one hand they tried to benefit from the real bread of life of the *Kyrios* and then, just because the Emperor decided to oppress us for some evil reason they threw it all away and joined the latest fashionable or formally approved sect, like the Mithras one?'

'Oh, come now, Origen. Let us not be so, so......pie in the sky about this. All right, some of the *lapsi* were bad fellows, I grant you, but is not the message of the Gospel *forgiveness* above all else? We are *growing* Origen, and fast, and *that* is the important thing.'

'Are you sure, Julianus, that you have your priorities right? Is not quality more important than quantity here, especially in matters such as this? After all, we are not merchants trying to sell merchandise at the cheapest price, are we? Julianus, I, more than anything else, am concerned about preserving the core values and ideals of the *Kyrios*. Preserving these for *all* the faithful is more important to me than mere numbers.'

'And what is important to me and to Zephyrinus is a strong *Kyrios*, Origen, one which is all-inclusive, catholic and universal, like the Lord himself.'

'I don't deny that that is important either.'

'If we want the *Kyrios* to be universal it must be strong. If we want it to be strong it must be unified. If we want it to be unified it must be orthodox. All these terms are mutually reinforcing.'

Sensing a clear if understated line of argument, Origen asked bluntly, 'What are you implying?'

Julianus appeared jolted. He took a long, slow breath through his narrow nostrils and appeared suddenly sour. 'Look, in recent years in Rome the *Kyrios* has grown, as I said, enormously. But this has also to do with the fact that many other cults and pagan religious groups of all sorts are looking into the Gospel and are deeply attracted by it. In one way this is good, but in another way the whole thing has given rise to a....a veritable witches brew of....of.......'

'Beliefs?' Demetrius prompted.

'Yes, all right, beliefs, if you like. But so much of it is just sickening, so alien to the true message. Flagellants, Stylites, snake-worshippers, devil-worshippers, you name

it – and all claiming to be Christian. It's monstrous! We simply have to sort all this out someway. Now, Pope Zephyrinus has a plan......'
'It's the same here in Alexandria,' Origen interrupted
'It's worse in Rome, Origen, believe me. The Gnosis is spreading like wildfire all over the Empire. And we simply have to stamp it out.'
Origen shuffled and cleared his throat noisily. 'Julianus, have you read Tertullian?'
Julianus slanted his eyes sharply on him. 'My friend, has not *everyone* read Tertullian?'
Origen glanced impishly at Demetrius, whose anxious face categorically declared that he had *not* read Tertullian! Had Demetrius ever read *anything*, Origen wondered? But he continued to address Julianus, 'Tertullian is a very learned and wise man, is he not?'
'Yes,' Julianius agreed with slight hesitation. 'But why........'
'But why is Tertullian so concerned? He is more than concerned Julianus - he is deeply annoyed with this open-arms policy of Rome towards the *lapsi*. He has written extensively about it. And yet, on the other hand he finds it difficult and extremely ironic, to say the least, how some powerful people in the *Kyrios* in Rome seem to demonize many others simply because they want to follow the inner path with diligence, dedication and true devotion. This is all *very* ambivalent, Julianus. Something is wrong in Rome, something is wrong with the way you..........'
'There is *nothing* wrong with Rome,' Julianus said sharply, asserting his seniority now in a very autocratic tone, 'and as for Tertullian, if you ask me he has far too many ideas. He reads too much Greek philosophy.' Julianus looked at Demetrius who smiled and said feebly, 'There has to be but one path.'
'Heretics must be rooted out of our midst, once and for all,' Julianus announced menacingly.
'Is this why you wanted to see me?' Origen asked after a pause.
Julianus looked him in the eye again and said slowly and solemnly, 'We are, with the lifting of this current Edict, entering a great new phase in the development of the *Kyrios*. Rome wishes to nurture this growth.'
'And so does Alexandria. It............' But Julianus lifted his right hand authoritatively for silence. After a short pause he went on, 'I did not come here to argue with you, young man. I have come to deliver an important *request* from Rome. We are aware that your School here in Alexandria teaches many, many things. And we are justly concerned that what you teach does not deviate from the true message and meaning of the Gospel. We want you to test *everything*, and I mean everything you teach against this new revelation and teach *nothing* that will injure the peaceable growth of our young and tender movement, our new world religion. You, young man, are extremely well-known throughout the *Kyrios*, even though you have not, I am told, written one word as yet. However, your part, your voice will be crucial, central to this whole new development. This much is obvious to me, now that I have met you. However, I want you to think most carefully of what I have just said. For that

in fact is what I came here to say to you. And that also is what our Holy Father in Rome wants you to know.'

As Origen made his way home after this meeting he felt his head reeling again like in the old days. He had actually thought that he had put an end to all that confusion by now. But he obviously hadn't! He did not want to think about Julianus, for he did not know *what* to think about him, yet somehow it seemed he simply had to think about him. The *Kyrios* a new world religion? Was there not enough religion in the world already? Did He not come to end all that....all that life-denying, freedom-denying Law? Granted, it may have been necessary for the Jews, for the preparation of the ground upon which He had to walk. But was not His *Kyrios* something entirely new and different in the world, a present Spirit, a real Being living in the heart of mankind? Did He not say as much Himself? The Law was given by Moses, but, as St. John said in his Gospel, Grace and Truth was given by Christ. Did not a new religion merely mean more, or even a new, Law?

Origen did not like the sound of all this! And the more he tried to deal with his thoughts in this regard the more he heard those post-scripted words of Clement's letter rise up in his soul, the words that had advised him to write himself, not only in order to clarify and strengthen his own thinking, but to preserve it, so that the pure and magical spirit of truth contained in the Gospel would not get lost in a mad rush for a merely worldly kind of power.

And over the next few days, as the after-image of Julianus faded from Origen's soul, this advice of his old Master Clement was all that was left of his meeting with the Roman cleric.

18 AGAPE – THE LOVE FEAST

Origen's growing responsibilities and reputation did not prevent him from keeping a distanced but careful eye on the growth of his various but much-loved brothers, especially John, the youngest. He, therefore, eagerly looked forward to those occasions when, taking time out of his busy schedule, he paid visits to his mother in the old family home in Rhakotis, the Egyptian quarter of the city.

Here a great joy and pride was felt by all; where, after a meal together, at which Origen always both teased and challenged his various brothers, accumulating, in the process, much knowledge regarding their own lives and the life of youths generally in the city, his mother would request that she be left alone with him for a while. The boys would all then reluctantly but obediently withdraw, the younger ones to play with friends out on the street, the older ones to read or study in the little library, the others simply to amuse themselves quietly in their bedrooms.

No one, of course, was more proud of Origen than Miriam herself. For he made her feel so strong! Towards her, Origen grew increasingly, if quietly, respectful. Despite her petite form which totally belied the seven sons she had given birth to, through an almost indefinable quality of character, Origen glimpsed in her aspects of the Great Mother herself, and often inwardly mused on this while outwardly discussing mundane or domestic topics, such as the boys' education, the behaviour of neighbours, and matters of finance. Demetrius, she assured him, gave money to her any time she needed. And recently, she said, he had even made it possible for her to hire, for one day a week, a slave-girl from a better-off nearby neighbour, to help her with the many tasks of motherhood.

During one such meeting, their quiet exchanges were interrupted by a gentle knock on the front door of the house.

Miriam went out of the dining-room and returned a few moments later with an old man who looked familiar to Origen but whom he could not immediately place.
'Son,' Miriam said, 'this is Christophorus. He wishes to speak to you.'
The old man was small, slightly stooped and carried a gold-tipped, black walking-stick. His weathered, walnut face was serious but serene.
'Shall I leave you alone?' Miriam asked.
'No, Mother, please stay,' Origen said and motioned the old man to be seated. As he did so Origen suddenly remembered where he had seen him before.
'You are Christophorus, a member of presbyter Matthew's house-community in the district near the Serapeum?'
The old man smiled in acknowledgement.
'Yes,' Origen went on, 'I go there occasionally for *Agape*.'

'Yes, you are right. But I think perhaps I know you better than you know me, Origen Adamantius,' Christophorus suggested with an air of mystery.

Origen sensed in the old man an unusual degree of psychic and spiritual awareness which also helped explain how he knew where Origen was, for he had not told anyone he was visiting his mother.

'Age brings the fruit of much insight into the great mysteries of life, Christophorus,' Origen suggested, 'Perhaps you even know me better than I know myself!'

But the old man shook his head. 'Oh, no. Only *you* can know yourself, Origen.'

'Guided, you would surely say, by the Gospel of the Great Master.'

'Yes, of course. I know nothing without Him.'

'But you do know a lot Christophorus.'

'The more I know, the less I am - the smaller, the weaker I become.'

'Mmm. This is the plant-nature of our life on Earth, is it not? Born but to blossom and die. But He, the Flower of Humanity, grows in you Christophorus. I can sense it. You possess the seed of a new world in you - the Master Being of wisdom and knowledge. I see it.'

'Thank you, Origen Adamantius. But you too have much knowledge and wisdom. Indeed, you are more favoured than most in the great new outpouring, this Pentecostal expansion of the feminine soul, inaugurated by our Great Master.'

'Yes, my joy in Him grows with each new day. Each dawn a new leaf appears on my tree of life, thanks to Him. Yet, know this Christophorus. I still await His purest touch, His sweetest kiss, His deepest gesture of love. My knowledge is incomplete, Christophorus, it is immature, whereas yours, I can see, is rich with ripeness.'

In the old man's face Origen saw all the sculpted beauty and serenity of an ancient Greek temple.

'Why have you sought me out, Christophorus?' he asked eventually.

'I am part of the inner circle of Matthew's house-community. We wish you to join us,' Christophorus answered.

Origen was shocked and delighted! Blissfully he looked at his mother who had been silently but eagerly following the conversation. Now she appeared holy, otherworldly.

'Your mother is the necessary witness in the congregation to the delivery of this important invitation, Origen,' Christophorus revealed.

'Thank you, Christophorus, and thank you, mother. I am overjoyed.'

'We look forward then with the greatest of joy to receiving you...... next Sunday.'

The old man stood up. 'The peace of God be with you and your family.' Then bowing slightly he added, 'My apologies for interrupting your precious time together.'

Miriam smiled, and showed the old man to the door where, as he was parting, he gave her the Kiss of Peace.

It was Spring, and the following Sunday morning, as Origen made his way towards Matthew's house where he had been on numerous occasions before, the gleaming streets of Alexandria were remarkably clean. The air too was fresh and full of the sweet scent of flowers. For, everywhere in Alexandria flowers were cultivated with great enthusiasm and dedication and, especially at this time of the year, grew abundantly because of the temperate climate of the city. Origen sucked in the air greedily and was so happy he felt that in his very breathing he was partaking in a kind of holy communion with his Great Master.

Matthew's house was near the ship canal that linked Lake Mareotis with the Port of Eunostus. Perched at the foot of the summit upon which the great temple of Serapis, the Serapeum, looked down with power and majesty over the whole city, Matthew's house was a modest *domus* with its own small but pleasant garden.

As he went through its ornamented, black, wrought-iron gates, never did Origen feel the contrast between Matthew's *domus* and the Serapeum more sharply. For, despite its obvious cultural and religious value to Alexandria, the Serapeum's formal structure suddenly appeared arrogant to him, almost inhuman, compared with the warmth and simplicity, yet deep spirituality to be found in Matthew's *domus*.

Ever since Clement had left, Origen had felt homeless. Apart from the fact that he was living on his own and no longer enjoyed the closeness of either his family, his old friends, or Clement himself, his sense of homelessness had much to do with not attending any one of the *Agape* in the city on an on-going basis, as he used to with Clement. The School therefore was his real community. But this was so varied and professional he felt a growing need for the deeper, spiritual companionship to be found in an intimate, small group. Being invited to the inner circle of Matthew's *Agape* seemed therefore like the ideal solution.

Origen had been carrying out a kind of private investigation of the *Agape*, going from one to the other, compiling, one could say, a kind of mental history of it. It really began with the Evangelist Mark. For, ever since he had arrived in the city from Rome in the middle of the first century, bringing with him both Peter's Gospel and his own, the *Kyrios* community in Alexandria had grown in a very special way, quite differently, Origen came to realize, from Christian communities in most other parts of the Empire. This was easily understood when one considered the unique, Gnostic nature of Alexandrian life; its hugely eclectic religious ethos. For this was a fervent, volatile, even chaotic mix.

However, it was in just such an atmosphere that the Gospel could actually find the fertile soil it needed in order to germinate, root and grow. The Gnosis, in a sense, prepared the ground, in that it cultivated that special nuance of temperament in man which remains receptive to the purely esoteric or even magical, as opposed to the mechanical or atomistic view of the world. And in Alexandria, because of its history, the Gnosis was a particularly learned one in this regard. Thus, when St. Mark arrived with his Gospel, it found fertile soil because Mark's, more than any of the other Gospels, had the unique ability to foster the esoteric side of the overall Gospel message. It genuinely and deeply addressed both sides of the Christ Mystery, the inner and the outer, the spiritual and the physical, the historical and the archetypal. Because of this, the growth of the *Kyrios* in Alexandria had been entirely individualistic and organic, absorbing into itself, on the one hand, what was best about the Gnosis generally, while, on the other hand, through the work of deeply intelligent and penetrative minds - like Origen's and Clement's especially - rejecting what was obviously antithetical to the Lord's revelation.

In effect, and because of its strident efforts to keep the deep inwardness of Christianity alive, the forms and structures of the *Kyrios* that had evolved in Alexandria were not hierarchical. For such forms, it was instinctively felt, militated against the free-flowing Spirit of the new Christ-God of man, an esoteric perception of whom, it was clearly understood, was made much more amenable to individuals through social forms and bodies that were spherical and consensual as opposed to hierarchical or pyramidal, which latter forms had far more to do with the old ways than with the new, which was the Way of the freedom-proclaiming Lord of love.

This egalitarianism was in fact the basis of the developing social forms in the *Kyrios* of Alexandria, at least until Demetrius appeared on the scene. Basically it functioned around the celebration of the *Agape* at the various house-communities on the Sabbath, the house-community being the basic unit of the *Kyrios*. The *Agape* was broken into two basic parts, the second for the baptized only, and this latter had an inner circle formed out of the baptized members of the particular house-community. These circles usually met after the first two parts were completed and this meeting represented the heart of the entire *Kyrios*.

Most of the established house-communities had evolved such a circle whose number was fixed at twelve, a number which the Lord Himself had stipulated in line with the ancient esoteric teaching regarding the cosmic Temple. This wisdom-teaching always held that the fullest being of man living on the Earth below, was a reflection of the starry world above him, and that if he was to be fully understood, man must be regarded as a composite being made up of twelve basic parts, types and divisions.

One became a member of this inner circle, again in accordance with instructions received from the Lord Himself, that is, by invitation only. There was no other qualification whatsoever. Outside of it, however, in Alexandria, a larger, single, very informal but nonetheless powerful circle grew up over the decades, known as the

Council of Presbyters, whose concern was the broader, more practical, public or pastoral work of the community. But this circle, as far as Origen could make out, was something quite different from what Demetrius regarded as the Council of Presbyters. Since finding out these inner workings of the *Kyrios*, Origen had been eager to find out more, but that was not possible, he gradually came to realize, until certain questions were asked of one, otherwise the delicate spirit of a perfectly ordered and angelically balanced form was in danger of being defiled. Although simple and easily understood by anyone willing to do so, steps into the *Kyrios* were carefully guided spiritually, even angelically, which basically meant that nothing was ever forced.

Now, however, Origen was being invited to take such a new step. He had always, in his heart, been a man of the *Kyrios*; now he was about to turn this into a very concrete reality.

Presbyter Matthew greeted him warmly at the entrance to the *atrium* where the meal was held. It was already full of people; men, women and children of all ages. They stood, sat, on chairs or couches, or some even on mats and cushions on the floor. An expectant murmur of lively but quiet conversation permeated the *atrium*. Origen was one of the last to arrive.

The form of the *Agape* was similar in most house-communities. Thus, after ringing a bell, Matthew came forward, stood on a slightly raised platform and after an opening prayer formally but joyfully welcomed everyone. Then, after more prayers, time was given for the reading of various notices of interest and concern to both Matthew's own house-community and the community at large. Then a passage of Mark's Gospel was solemnly read. After this, many hymns and psalms of praise to God were joyfully sung by all. Matthew then blessed bread and breaking it distributed it among the congregation while quietly uttering the words, 'The Body of the Lord.' A helper came alongside him with a single glass of light, sweet red wine, for each one, who, as they took and sipped, Matthew said, 'The Blood of the Lord.' All this was done in a mood of quiet, informal reverence.

When the distribution was completed people began freely conversing again for a while. Then after another bell-ring, after which more hymns were sung, Matthew rang the bell a final time, read a final prayer and then requested that each one give to his neighbour the Kiss of Peace. Then the inner circle came forward from the Congregation (eleven people if the presbyter was one of them himself, which Matthew was – paradoxically the presbyter was not necessarily one of the Twelve, his role being considered, primarily, a public rather than an inner one in the congregation). The eleven stood together with Matthew, as the Congregation left. Origen, however, stayed precisely where he was, which was near the *atrium* entrance and there he waited and watched for a sign.

When he was the only one left, Matthew extended his open hands and said, 'Come Origen. Join us.'
Origen came forward nervously and the Twelve then formed a circle about him. There were eight men and four women, mostly much older than himself, some very old. After a short silence, Christophorus, the one who had issued the invitation to Origen while he was with his mother, spoke, 'My dear brothers and sisters, most of you will probably know this young man. His name is Origen Adamantius. He has been a devotee of the Lord here in Alexandria since his birth, at which time, also here, he was baptized with water by presbyter Clement, whom you also know, but who is unfortunately now no longer with us, since his enforced exile. Origen has been invited to join our inner circle. Should any of you wish to give voice to any reason why he should not join us at this time, please say so now.'

After a short silent pause Christophorus unrolled a small scroll he had been holding and read, 'Origen Adamantius, do you fully accept the Christ Jesus as your Lord and heavenly Master, and the fully incarnated Son of God most High?'
'Yes, I do,' Origen said.
'And will you follow and uphold his Holy Gospel unto the death?'
'Yes, I will.'

Then Christophorus read the Verse of Acceptance: 'In the name of our Lord Christ Jesus, Son of the Living God, God Himself incarnate, and our Redeemer and Risen Saviour, we receive you into fullest fellowship and communion with Him. Amen.'

Then each one pointed his or her right index finger at Origen and began chanting in chorus, 'Christ in you, Christ in you.' Then pointing to themselves they similarly chanted, 'Christ in me, Christ in me.' Joining hands they then came forward and encircling Origen tightly, repeated, 'Christ in us, Christ in us.' Following this, each one in turn silently placed their hands on Origen's head, while he, spontaneously but quite correctly chanted, 'Christ in me, Christ in me.'

After this Christophorus approached Origen and gave him the Kiss of Peace. 'Welcome to our brother-and-sisterhood,' he said warmly.

In the weeks and months that followed this ceremony, and his intimacy with the inner circle grew, Origen also became more and more familiar with their manner and form of approaching the Lord, which was essentially based on a rich, orally transmitted tradition which had a direct link, through St. Mark and St. Peter, with the Lord himself. Thus, Origen became acquainted with sayings, disciplines, and rituals cultivated both within the small group itself, such as the Christ-in-me forming circle, and others which he had to cultivate individually. In the time since the Lord's original twelve, a rich, oral and spiritually-bonding culture had developed in the Gnostic *Kyrios* and the circles of twelve had become increasingly united both psychologically and psychically, creating by their work a kind of 'inner net' through which not only individuals within the twelves could communicate with one another psychically, but often complete circles with others also, and over great distances. The efficacy of such spiritual networking depended upon the maturity and degree of development within any group, but by virtue of the overall culture, Origen grew more and more certain that sooner or later he was going to be fully initiated into the ancient, Great Mysteries of the world which had found their fulfilment two hundred years before on the Hill of Golgotha, an initiation that Clement himself had assured him he would eventually receive.

After the first few meetings of the inner circle *Agape*, Origen became aware that Christophorus was no longer among them. Enquiring about this he was told that for each new member received, one, usually the most advanced spiritually, moved on to another circle. He was also told that this was an instruction received directly from the Lord Himself, through Mary Magdalene, regarding the running and development of the *Kyrios*. This was, the Lord had instructed her, the fundamental way or method by which His *Kyrios*, His spiritual soul-body, should grow out into the world. Origen immediately understood the sense behind this; nevertheless he was somewhat disappointed that he never saw Christophorus again.

After his reception into the inner circle Origen felt a marvellous inflow of energy. He now began to discover the truest and deepest secrets of the *Agape*. For it was within this circle that the great alchemical transformation of life on Earth inaugurated by the blood-sacrifice of the Christ could not only be observed, but actively participated in. The outer part of the *Agape*, for the general congregation, was based on a simple sharing of bread and wine. But a portion of these substances was always held back, and in a simple but profound ceremony, carried out when only the twelve were left, the leader of the twelve consecrated these substances in a sacred Cup around which they gathered in deepest veneration. Then, after the consecration, the leader asked the Risen One to indwell the simple substances. And, in this most holy of all acts, accompanied inwardly by the fervent prayer and deep meditation of all those present, it was not unusual for the Lord Himself to become visible to some among them as they ate and drank from His Cup.

In this way Origen's vision of and closeness to the Lord deepened considerably, in a short space of time. Sometimes the energy he felt after an inner circle meeting was so strong that he feared it would unbalance him! But it never did! Rather what he experienced, and in a lasting way, was a wonderful deepening of his breath, a fiery inflow that seemed to be actually clearing him out inside, as if his very soul was being set aflame, or washed, even baptized. It was a lustral feeling whereby, apart from the bread and wine, pure air now seemed sufficient for supplying all his strength, becoming his very food. He began then to wonder, was this the feeling, which was a real and sustainable vigour for life, which the ignorant were dissipating and abusing, or what was being simply dubbed 'magic' by others, the totally uninitiated, who observing its effects were often led into hostility because they sensed here a power beyond themselves they did not understand, and therefore feared?

But if it was magic then it was magic of the purest kind, the white magic of Christ, the very breath of His Holy Spirit pouring into the soul of each follower. This, for Origen, soon became his very purest nourishment. For how easily could he now fill himself with the wonderful parting gift of the Lord, His peace, a thing so beautiful and profound it had, like Paul had written, no name.

Concomitant with this experience, Origen's insights into the Gospel increased in manifold ways and the inspirations he received during his lectures were such that not only did he not need notes any more, but he felt an urge to increase his teaching and lecturing so that an ever greater amount of his inflowing stream of insights could be channelled and shared with others, especially those whom he now felt needed his wisdom more than he did himself. For a titanic strength was fuelling him into action!

Understandably, he felt the need to clearly mark this change, this great stepping stone in his life. So he tonsured his head in the Oriental fashion and also took to wearing, all the year round, a long, black, hooded cowl instead of his usual knee-length tunics. However, he continued to wear the red cord around his waist as he always did since his youth, and came to increasingly identify this as a sign of his blood-link with the Christ.

Soon Origen became a unique and familiar figure on the streets of Alexandria; tall, austere, a formidable man of God, feared by some, loved by many, but respected by all, the living sign and symbol of the *Kyrios* in Alexandria.

19   A REUNION

As Julianus of Rome had predicted, the persecutions against the *Kyrios* in Alexandria soon began to abate. A collective sigh of relief went out from the mouths of the faithful as the soldiers now were seen, at last, to act on their behalf. Any time now that the soldiers observed hate being stirred up against the Christians, whether by Simon the Stylite, one of his acolytes, or anyone else, the soldiers, acting on instructions from their *Legatus*, immediately apprehended the troublemakers. These were then either severely cautioned or else simply thrown into prison for a while. But if they continued to stir up the mob after their release, Christian citizens now had the right and freedom to bring them before a *praetor* in the Senate, who, also acting upon instructions from Rome were invariably favourable to the Christians in their judgements. And in this way the persecutions finally ceased altogether, and another period of blessed peace was ushered in for the *Kyrios*.

As the years passed Origen became so devoted to the School that he rarely gave any time at all to his personal, social life. Ambrosius continued to attend his lectures, but Origen had little contact with him outside of the lecture hall.   However, observing him even at a distance and having the odd few words with him, Origen could not help but notice a marked change creeping over Ambrosius as time went by.   No longer did he possess the flippancy and joviality of his youth.   Perhaps, Origen thought, that his own more earnest role in life called forth a different attitude from Ambrosius, or maybe it was that the increasing power of his lectures was having a serious and profound effect on him.   But even if that was the case, Origen suspected that more personal factors were also involved.

Eventually he became eager to find out.   So, one evening after a lecture, he approached Ambrosius and invited him to come to his apartment, and over a simple meal of bread, fruit and grape-juice (Origen by now had also included abstinence from wine among his numerous austerities) the old friends chatted away for hours and caught up with one another's varied and busy lives.

'And how does it go with Valentinus?' Origen asked. 'As far as I remember, you were studying him deeply a few years ago.'
The more serious Ambrosius, Origen immediately noted, was also more circumspect. Ambrosius knitted his brow and thought hard for a while. Eventually he said, 'Yes. He is, or was I should say, very interesting. But I do not read him anymore.'
'Why, pray? He is such wise man,' Origen teased.
'Well.........for a start he seems to believe in the one nature of the Christ.'
'And......?' Origen prodded
'Well......I............I just came to suspect a.......a.... fault-line in there somewhere.

120

'How do you mean? Come.'

'Oh, Origen, I don't know. You tell me, what do *you* believe?'

'You mean, I suppose, was He God or man, angel or seraphim, a ghost, or even a phantom, like some of the Gnostics believe?'

'Yes.'

'Well, I can tell you, I do not believe He was a ghost. Far from it.'

'Yes, but what was he, is he, Origen. Tell me, *what?*'

Origen went very silent for a few moments. Then he said, 'My dear Ambrosius. Listen. He was a Son to his heavenly Father, an Angel to the choirs of Angels, a man to us men, and what is more, he is the very soul and spirit of our planet, our Mother Earth. Now what more do you want?'

Ambrosius looked thoughtful, but remained silent. Origen continued, 'But yet, are not all these mere definitions? The Great Master, Ambrosius, is beautiful, so beautiful - He is the very Spirit of Beauty and Imagination. Is this not sufficient for you to embrace Him wholeheartedly, to believe in Him without question?'

'Oh, Origen, yes, yes. But believe, you say, believe. And my whole path is to do with *gnosis*, knowledge. I want to *know.*'

'Yes, of course. Knowledge, as much as belief, is important. But you do not need to know, Ambrosius, in order to believe. Remember that. It is important. Your intellect is a bit like your hair, it's a wavy thing, with lots, millions of different strands. Now, go out into the wind, say of the busy market place, and what happens? Your hair gets all knotted up, doesn't it? Too many impressions, sensations, thoughts and ideas and you end up knowing nothing, believing nothing, even doing nothing!'

'It's not that I don't believe, Origen, it's just that.......'

'Ambrosius, have you learned to pray yet?'

Ambrosius smiled. 'Yes,' he said, 'a little.'

'Excellent! Prayer is the comb, the brush that gets rid of all those knots, Amrbosius. Use it as often as you can, and like a beautiful woman's, your hair, your soul - for that is what we talk about - it will shine. Now, that shine is achieved by faith and it comes through prayer, meditation and contemplation. No other way. Not reading, or studying, or thinking, although these too are necessary pursuits if we wish to fully know the Lord. But these are all head activities and you can ultimately only know the Lord through your heart. This is the vessel of faith, and faith is the vital ingredient.'

'Origen,' Ambrosius said after a while, 'you have changed so much since you became Master of the School. Your thoughts run so much deeper, so much finer. I just can't hear enough of you.'

'Ambrosius, my good friend, how nice it is to talk to you again after all this time. We must renew our friendship. But, please, do not flatter me too much. I have my faults also.'

'Yes, maybe you do. But still, I want to hear more from you Origen, much more. You can answer my many questions, I know you can, even questions I still do not know of.'

'The Lord will answer *all* who call upon him.'

They were sitting opposite one another reclining on low couches with a table between them. Ambrosius looked up at the ceiling and with shining eyes exclaimed, 'Origen, you should write books. Become really, really famous!'

'But I am already famous!' Origen laughed.

'I mean for a thousand, two thousand, nay, ten thousand years. I feel you have it in you to ....to become more famous than.....than....Plato!'

'Plato!'

'Yes. Plato!'

Origen sat up. There was a puzzled look on his normally serene face, 'More famous than Plato............Is such a thing possible, Ambrosius, do you think?'

'Hey, I can tell by the look in your eyes, I can still give you good ideas, my friend.'

Origen sighed and falling back on his couch said, 'I do not have the time to write books, Ambrosius. It's as simple as that. Time!'

'You *have* to write books,' Ambrosius insisted. 'You simply have to. Think of the future generations. In your lectures we are only hearing a fraction of your wisdom. We need to get more of it, and we need to preserve it. Quills are the magic wands that can do this, papyrus the magic carpets that can carry us to the heights, the towers of your wisdom'.

Origen took an apple and uncharacteristically bit greedily into it. Then he went very silent.

Eventually he asked, 'How is your beautiful sister, Sarah, these days?'

'Ah, yes, my learned friend. I knew you would ask that one. She used to talk of you a lot, but not anymore. She said you went all funny on her; couldn't make you out at all anymore she said; said she thought that either an angel or a devil or some kind of a yolk got hold of you.........er... somewhere. However, she hasn't lost interest in the Christ, you will be glad to know. She is a true seeker. But she is kept quite busy nowadays with other things.'

'Other things?' Origen queried.

After a short pause Ambrosius blurted, 'Origen, dammit, she got married!'

'Married!'

'Yes. And to Philemon of all people! You remember him, the initiate of the Eleusinian Mysteries, no less. And now also a senator to boot. Sometimes I suspect that that's actually why she married him, just to find out more about the Eleusinian Mysteries.'

'Is she happy?' Origen asked, subduing a strange stirring of his old, instinctual desires which the hard-earned unction of his mature solitude had almost put entirely to rest.

'I think so.'

After a pause Origen asked melancholically, 'Is she still beautiful?'

'No, not as much as when you knew her, Origen. Rare orchids like her bloom but for a day.'

Origen chewed pensively on his apple.

Ambrosius asked, 'Origen, is marriage an impediment to knowing God?

'For a few, yes.'

'A chosen few, eh?'

'Ambrosius, the Hand of God works in very strange ways, and the better you know Him the stranger He works. Nevertheless, the nearer you come to Him the happier you will be, one way or the other, whether in or out of marriage.'

Origen stood up suddenly and came over to Ambrosius. Unexpectedly he gave him the Kiss of Peace. Ambrosius became uncharacteristically weak and innocent-looking, like a little boy, but also frightened. Origen asked, 'Ambrosius, my dearest friend, something has happened to you. I know. What is it?'

Ambrosius then laid his head on Origen's breast and started to weep, softly at first, but then bitterly. Between sobs Origen heard him say, 'My father committed suicide last year, Origen. I should've told you. But I was so ashamed.'

Soothing him Origen said, 'Yes, the Hand of Destiny works in strange ways all right. I am so sorry to hear this, Ambrosius, believe me. I will pray for your father this very evening. But all these things hold some meaning for us. Of this I am certain. All of life has a purpose.' After another while he asked, 'And the business?'

Ambrosius dried his face and sighing said, 'Oh, I carry it on. But my heart is not in it any more, Origen. I do it, actually, mostly for my mother's sake.'

'But is not that a good reason?'

'Yes. I will carry it on.'

'Give my kindest greetings to Sarah when next you see her,' Origen said much later as he bid farewell to Ambrosius at his door.

20   A TRIP TO ROME

One cold, damp, winter morning in Britannia, just south of the border with Caledonia, while inspecting an *auxilia*, newly recruited there from the wild indigenous population to repair a huge breach in Hadrian's wall near the eastern shoreline, the Emperor Septimius Severus received a deadly poisoned arrow in his left thigh. It was fired from the finely carved bow of a painted, Pictish warrior, a colourful party of whom swooped down from the hills behind the breach with no warning whatsoever as Severus paraded proudly among the neatly formed lines of his newly-uniformed men. Nine of them died instantly from similar arrows. Severus, however, who had the strength of a hippopotamus, fought the poison like he would the most savage barbarian in the Empire, and in the throes of such a lone battle he was carried ceremoniously on a palanquin all the way to Eboracum where, however, he eventually lost his will to fight, and died on the 4th February 211AD.

Severus' sons, Caracalla and Geta then ascended their father's throne as co-regents of his ever-tottering empire. Like the animal after which he was nicknamed, the most vicious of the wild cats of Africa, the caracal, Caracalla's savage disposition, long held in check by his father's superior authority, now found its fullest release. The first thing he did was to murder his brother so that he could have complete freedom in the exercise of his evil propensities. And in order to be sure of no further opposition from those who even tentatively appeared to support his brother during the short co-regency, he simply murdered them all! – some say up to 20,000 men and women.

The Roman Empire had always depended for its success on the might and power of its army, but never was this more evident than during the reign of Caracalla. However, becoming increasingly aware of *its* growing power, the army too pressed for higher and ever higher rewards. Caracalla, in his unceasing efforts to appease them, exhausted Italia with his extortions and then turned his monstrous gaze upon the provinces where, in order merely to increase the number of his taxable subjects - and thus his revenue - he granted Roman citizenship to all and sundry.

Inevitably, therefore, the position of the *Kyrios* in Rome and in the Empire generally was once more put under severest threat. Caracalla did not actually issue edicts against the Christians, but his bestial shadow loomed large over them, and they knew only too well how the passions of this latest evil Emperor could be kindled into a blaze of purest hatred on the flimsiest possible pretext. So, once more, they held their collective breaths.

In Alexandria, Demetrius became increasingly anxious. Each new report he received from Rome merely made him more nervous. Julianus of course kept him well informed, but from his own, highly suspect perspective only; one which he was expert at keeping from the discerning ears of old Zephyrinus, the longstanding, saintly, undisputed, and legitimate pope of Rome. But in the turmoil caused there by Caracalla's murderous regime things were not only rapidly changing for the worse, but Julianus, and all shrewd observers, could easily see how the heart of the Empire was being slowly ripped apart. For, evil, greed, and bestiality were the order of the day, especially among the so-called leaders.

But what was most worrying Julianus was how those dreaded Gnostics and not the *Kyrios* seemed to be making the most moral capital out of the entire situation! One of them even wanted to become pope, of all things! This irked and angered Julianus to his wits' end, for he considered himself to be a most-righteous follower of the Lord Jesus, and certainly did not want to be associated with any of those Gnostics, their questionable antics and starry-eyed ideas. Indeed, he could barely handle his indignation at all, and finding himself caught up in this frothy tide of Caracalla's deranged rulership, his own wild menagerie of dreaming beasts began to awake also. These he then let loose upon the twin problems of how, on the one hand, to deal with the Gnostics, and, on the other, how to win more souls for the *Kyrios*, of which latter he considered himself a kind of self-styled, and self-appointed guardian. Julianus, in fact, was one of those sorts of individuals who once placed in powerful positions immediately display symptoms of megalomania. And in his appointment by Zephyrinus as his private secretary, Julianus' fuse was well and truly lit!

It was the beast Caracalla's total misunderstanding of the moral meaning to the masses of religion, together with Julianus' own hatred of the Gnostics and their particular brand of wild, oriental dreaming that soon made him want nothing less than a totally new world-order. This he envisioned as emerging out of the social debris Caracalla – after he got the, by now almost inevitable, assassin's chop - was sure to leave behind him. Julianus' new order was to be one built entirely on the back of the *Kyrios*, with Roman state law as its foundation, and the pope of Rome himself as the sole and fully legitimised ruler.

Such a scenario, Julianus reckoned, was entirely possible, given the monumental growth the movement was currently experiencing. If this growth continued, and he firmly believed it would, once the *Kyrios* got its act together, then, by simply forging a true and lasting orthodoxy, binding throughout the entire jurisdiction, which basically meant getting rid of the Gnostics, Julianus could have himself such a universal state! He saw it as being populated by a new kind of citizen moulded by his Christian orthodoxy, a thing which was to be fully state-sanctioned and legally enforced. Such Christian laws would breed a passive piety among the populace, would be guarded and defended by a uniformed army of ecclesiastics and clerics who, as well as being righteous and pious, would be more powerful and militant than any of the present army when put to the test, precisely because the Cross of the one true God was on its side! But all these hopes were now being severely threatened.

And matters were brought to a head by an upstart who went by the name of Callistus.

Callistus, who was an avowed Gnostic, was outraging Julianus by shamelessly canvassing the faithful of Rome for the position of pope! Julianus was absolutely adamant that the scholar Hippolytus, and no one else, should be the new pope, once old Zephyrinus died which would be very soon. In his book, *The Refutation of all Heresies*, Hippolytus, Julianus said to all who cared to listen to him, had marked himself out as the only possible candidate for the job of the pope of the capital city of their Empire.

Although Demetrius in Alexandria had in his own way the welfare of the *Kyrios* at heart, he was neither a clever nor an independently-minded man. He relied heavily on Julianus' reports from Rome to guide his every action in Alexandria, and the last thing he wanted was to appear to be out of step with the latest developments in the Roman *Kyrios*. Julianus' reports were welcome, therefore, but often highly disturbing also, and this was especially the case when it came to questions about how to deal with the increasingly thorny problem of the Gnostics. Julianus himself seemed to be very clear on such matters. But, living in the hotbed of Gnosticism, as Demetrius was, he was unable to form such cut-and-dried attitudes as those of Julianus.

For, although he was not, as far as Demetrius knew, a member of any of the well-known Gnostic groups, was not Origen himself a kind of Gnostic? What indeed was the precise definition of a Gnostic anyway? In his rare reflective moments such questions occupied Demetrius, but he never got very far with them; it all seemed so hopelessly complicated. But, if Origen of all people, who nowadays was regarded as one of the most important voices in the whole of the movement, displayed Gnostic tendencies, well then what in the name of God did Julianus mean by orthodoxy, a word which he never tired of using in his missives? Indeed, 'we must forge an orthodoxy at all costs' was a kind of mantric battle-cry of Julianus. Demetrius agreed wholeheartedly, but the problem was, what exactly was meant by this word? Demetrius had, in one of his own letters to Julianus, asked this vital question, but the reply he eventually received was not helpful: Julianus said simply, that it was the opposite of heresy!

Matters got much worse for Demetrius when Julianus wrote to say that Zephyrinus was now on his deathbed and that, accordingly, the politics of the Roman *Kyrios* was hotting-up tremendously and he, therefore, needed Demetrius' full support in certain matters. He outlined the problems connected with the Gnostic Callistus.

126

Demetrius, understandably, was confused by all this. For one thing, he had long known of both Callistus and Zephyrinus, as well as Hippolytus, and he knew also for a fact that Callistus was highly regarded by Zephyrinus. So what was he to do, and who was he to listen to now?

Demetrius decided on a drastic action! He would send Origen himself to Rome and get a first-hand account of how matters stood there. For although, like Clement his master, Origen displayed Gnostic tendencies, at least Demetrius could trust him to deliver an objective, honest and intelligent report, and in an important diplomatic mission such as this one, honesty was the highest virtue one looked for in the chosen candidate.

Origen for his part was delighted with the assignment and was eager to go immediately. If he was to bring back the best possible report, he said, he must get there before Zephyrinus died. So he made plans straightaway. He gave over the running of the Didascaleon to his trusted right-hand man, Heracles, who by now was not only a member of an inner circle of the *Kyrios*, but had also developed into an astute teacher and organizer.

Thus, less than a month later, Origen found himself in Rome where he spent three of the most interesting, educative, and valuable weeks of his entire life. His knowledge not only of history, art, and architecture blossomed as he walked the streets and absorbed the atmosphere and the many wonders of the ancient city, but in his numerous encounters and conversations with the ecclesiastics and influential people of the *Kyrios*, as well as with the ordinary members of the many house-communities, his knowledge and love of the *Kyrios* deepened immensely also.

Julianus had courteously assigned to him, for the duration of his stay, a bright young man called Titus, whose enthusiasm for Rome, his birthplace, and all things Roman, coupled with his great and obvious love of the Lord was such a potent cocktail that sometimes Origen thought it threatened to explode inside him, and do him intestinal damage! But as well as being enthusiastic, Titus was also perceptive and articulate, and in their many and long conversations Origen gathered much valuable information about the state of affairs in Rome of which, however, the more he heard the more concerned he became.

Although Origen at first detected reluctance in Titus to talk about some matters, as the days passed Titus became increasingly free in disclosing his opinions on various subjects of particular interest to Origen.

They were walking slowly along the avenue leading away from the Temple of the Divine Claudius and towards the Aqueduct of Nero, Origen having fully satisfied his curiosity about the so-called god, Claudius. It was near midday and very hot. Titus was sweating profusely but this did not dampen his enthusiasm one iota. He mopped his brow continually with a red kerchief.

Origen was pressing him on questions regarding possible candidates for the new pope.

'I am all in favour of Callistus,' Titus said, 'despite what Julianus says.'

'But are you not supposed to believe what Julianus believes?' Origen asked, slightly teasing.

'I am,' Titus nervously confessed, 'so please don't tell him what I say to you.'

'All right,' Origen agreed, 'do not worry.'

'The whole city is madly in favour of Callistus,' Titus went on with renewed enthusiasm. 'He would make a wonderful pope. Even Zephyrinus, I believe, wants him, although Julianus will not say so. Zephyrinus has not made any public announcement on the matter.'

'Ah, then he must be a wise man.'

'He's over ninety. Of course he is wise!' Titus said with a winning smile, his blue eyes sparkling.

'And Julianus?' Origen prodded. 'Is he wise?'

'Oh, I do not know, sir. His mind functions like the army, as far as I can see; his thoughts are all cut, dried and drilled up, in uniform, neat straight lines, his answers to every problem filed away and labelled somewhere in his brain, and his entire soul responsive only to quick, sharp catch-phrases. Maybe he is wise in a mechanical kind of way.'

'He is orthodox,' Origen prompted.

'Is he? Well, then I must be a heretic,' Titus replied nonchalantly.

'Oh, but that is surely dangerous, is it not?'

'Not if Callistus gets to be pope it's not, no way.'

'Do you know Hippolytus?'

'Everyone knows Hippolytus!'

'Yes, but I mean personally.'

'Yes, I've met him once or twice. He is very influential, but that's mainly because he writes books. The people, the faithful, don't like him at all.'

'Why?'

'He's too much like Julianus; dull, dry, regimented. Callistus is a free man, a free thinker, or I should really say a free *spirit*.'

'He was a slave, I believe, before he became a Christian.'

'Oh, yes. And a common criminal too. But his criminality means nothing when you compare it to the likes of our current Emperor, Caracalla, and his henchmen. Compared to these, Callistus is a veritable saint.'

'You have a free mind yourself, young Titus, I can tell.'

'Thank you, sir. I'll take it as a compliment.'

'Freedom is good, the province, the prerogative of youth. But it is also very difficult

to maintain. It can even be dangerous at times.'
'Dangerous?'
'Yes. It tends to frighten some people.'
'Frighten people!'
'Yes. The fact as much as the concept. Humans are very strange beings, Titus - you may have noticed. They mostly prefer the dark of their servile passions to the light of their pure freedom, when it comes down to it. Or to put it another way, they mostly prefer to be goaded, or led, or told what to do, rather than act freely. Slavery, in whatever form, is a very hard thing to shake off. But we, Titus, have the Great Master, and he has given us the means to be free. He has shown us the Way to it. We merely have to follow, and if we do, and gain, we have a duty to share our gains with others also.'

They walked through the elegant marble columns that marked the boundary of the Temple's grounds and out onto the paved, narrow street which ran alongside the towering aqueduct walls in the shadow of which they now took some welcome refuge from the blazing sun.

After enjoying the cool, silently for a while, Titus said, 'You know, sir, working for Julianus I sometimes get the opportunity to listen in to very learned debates about the Lord.' Origen observed that Titus' enthusiasm had wilted somewhat. He looked perplexed.
'And.....?' Origen prodded.
'It can be so horribly confusing at times.'
'Knowledge is always confusing, Titus, and that is because experts will always disagree. But faith in, and love of, the Great Master is easy. You should remember that.'
'I have faith and I have love, I hope, sir. But still, when I listen to them argue, say about whether or not His, the Lord's, heavenly Father was greater than He Himself, I get confused, I even get annoyed sometimes.'
At this Origen laughed out loud. 'I smell the blood of a Gnostic.'
'Do you understand the Trinity?' Titus asked unperturbed.
Origen waited a few moments before replying.
'The problem of the Trinity, Titus, cannot be solved without recourse to what I have to call "initiation knowledge". Now, that is a very different kind of thing to mere theology, which is what your learned friends are usually engaged in, I suspect. When compared to the spiritual facts of initiation knowledge, theology often seems like so much hot, clerical air.'
Titus demurred. 'I have heard much about you, sir. Are you not also a theologian?'
It was an unexpected question! Strange, Origen thought, he had never considered it before.
'I am a teacher,' he said at length.

'Of initiation knowledge?' Titus questioned with a frown.

'Yes, all right, you can say that. In my School we are deeply aware of the value and importance of all the ancient mystery wisdom of the world, especially as this came into play in that marvellous and revolutionary new development in human evolution, that of the emergence of pure, independent thinking in the early Greek philosophers, many of whom were actually initiates of the ancient mystery religions.'

'Like Pythagoras?'

'Indeed.'

'And did he not believe in reincarnation?'

'Well done, Titus! I can see you are a learned young man also.'

'I like reading Greek philosophy in my spare time, if that's what you mean.'

'Yes. This surely is good for you. Develop your independent thought. But I must also say that you should not let such pastimes interfere with your duties as a Christian – I mean prayer, fasting, giving alms, helping your brothers and sisters - you know, all of what you are being taught in the *Kyrios*.'

'I have spoken to Julianus about reincarnation, you know.'

And...?'

'He nearly went mad! He exploded into a terrible rage at the mere mention of the word.'

'Yes I can well believe it.'

'Do you believe in reincarnation?'

'Oh...well......yes.........there is much in this ancient doctrine, you know, one of the most important and basic ones of the old mysteries actually, especially as they have come down to us out of the vast and deeply spiritual Orient. However, it is not easy to figure out *exactly* how it all works, and I have to admit that as yet I cannot be precise on such matters either.'

'Julianus likes precision in all things. Maybe that's why he got angry!'

'I would find it very difficult to explain the *precise* reasons for Julianus' rage, which nevertheless does not prevent me from understanding it, in a certain fashion. A concept such as reincarnation goes very deep, you know, just because it is so ancient. It obviously touched some buried, raw and troubled nerve in Julianus. Some people are afraid of certain thoughts in the same way as others are afraid of well, say.........mice, or even leaves – taboos, phobias, that kind of thing – all these have a spiritual origin. The human mind is a very strange thing, Titus. And that's why people like Julianus are so fixed on theology, which is supposed to make all spiritual matters crystal clear in words. But such a thing is impossible. The spirit can never be put into a written word-formula. It can only be in one's self, in one's heart. I'm not criticising theology *per se* by the way. The job of the theologian is to put our *thoughts* regarding Christ into a clear and teachable order. Fine! But the job of the philosopher is to ask questions that go deeper, that get beyond the mind, that get into the *heart*, in other words, which is a different, but I would say, even more necessary, task than mere theology.'

'Are you a philosopher then?
'A Christian one, maybe.'

After a long pause Titus asked, 'Sir, do you believe in eternal damnation?'
'No, definitely not! This is a preposterous notion which some people with twisted minds are trying to foist onto our *Kyrios* for reasons impossible to figure out. And that, I can tell you Titus, is something that makes *me* very angry.'
'I cannot imagine you being angry, sir.'
'Oh, everyone, without exception, has some anger in them, Titus. Your are, I hope, familiar with the scene in the New Testament where even the Lord himself gets angry.'
'You mean where he drives the dealers and moneylenders out of the Temple?'
'Yes, exactly.'
'Strange one that, sir. For, is not anger a sin?'
'No, Titus, not in itself. It very easily becomes one however, if and when it is *abused*. It then becomes a raging fire and the sin spreads like one. Then it becomes the deadliest sin of them all, because war itself is often nothing less than one man's abused or ill-controlled anger infecting a thousand or a million or a billion others. And is not war *the* most evil thing in our world?'
'The work of Satan!'
'Yes, surely.'
'Then he should stay in Hell.'
'Ah, my young friend, I can see too that you have a sense of humour, which is also very important. But no, he will not stay in Hell – Satan will be healed of his sins by the blessed Lord, whose divine love and forgiveness knows no bounds, whether on Earth, in heaven or in Hell itself.'

Titus stopped walking suddenly in order to breath in these words of Origen who noticed also how he had closed his eyes and was nodding his head in agreement. But when he opened his eyes again Titus looked distraught. Origen gazed at him sympathetically, encouraging him to speak out whatever was troubling him.
'I.........I.........really don't know if I should say this to you, sir, but I feel I must tell *someone*, for I have not spoken about it to a soul, yet.'
'Titus, my young friend, please put your complete trust in me.'
'Yes, sir, I will. It is this............one day, about a month ago, as I was passing Julianus' office, the door was ajar, and unintentionally I glanced inside. I was astonished to see him speaking in hushed tones to one of Caracalla's most notorious henchmen - a high-ranking officer in the army – Romulus, by name, an absolute brute of the highest order. I was utterly horrified! What could Julianus possibly have to do with or say to such a beast? I simply had to try to find out more. So I stood as close as I could to the door and listened carefully. I could not make out everything

they said, far from it. Lots of it I simply could not understand at all – but I did recognise the names of various people being mentioned, people in the army, the senate and from other sections of Roman society, but yet other names I knew nothing of. Nevertheless the more I listened the more I felt that they were actually in league or planning something. In fact the whole tone of the conversation was one of absolute conspiracy. But I simply could not understand! However, as Romulus was leaving I heard Julianus say one thing to him that I will never forget. He said, between his teeth with great and obvious anger, that if Callistus becomes the pope of Rome he personally would start one of the bloodiest wars the Empire has ever seen, and it would be against those infernal Gnostics – 'I will get rid of the bastards once and for all,' he hissed. And Romulus was grunting in approval like a happy pig as he left.'

After a long silence Origen sighed and said, 'Thank you, Titus. Thank you. I appreciate you telling me this. I assure you of my strictest confidence.'
'It is not right, sir, is it?'
'Absolutely not! I'm afraid you are confirming my very worst suspicions about what is going on behind the scenes here in Rome.'

After a pause Titus asked, 'What is your pope in Alexandria like?'
'Oh, you mean old doddering Demetrius. He is not so bad. He has the best interests of the *Kyrios* at heart.'
'Will you become the pope of Alexandria, sir?'
'Ah, Titus, my friend, I am not even a presbyter yet. And I fear Demetrius has little interest in ever making me one either.'
'Why?'
'Why? A good question! But the simple answer, I suppose, from his point of view anyway, is that it would be safest to keep me out altogether of the ecclesiastical side of things. Still, we shall have to wait and see.'

In the days that followed, apart from when speaking with Titus, Origen kept his silence in Rome as far as possible. He asked many questions, of course, and listened and observed attentively. He spoke with Hippolytus, Callistus and other important people, and even had a short interview with the ailing Zephyrinus himself who, in the course of their few short words, confirmed his preference for Callistus as his successor. But the nearer it came to Origen's time for departure from Rome the more he realized how active Julianus was in his efforts to resist Callistus who was nothing but a common criminal in Julianus' eyes, and one whom he obviously hated. But, Origen argued with himself, is it not laudable that those very ones whom the Lord came to save, the criminals, the poor, the despised, are qualifying themselves for the highest offices in the *Kyrios*? Is this in fact not the best possible proof of how good His teaching is, and how well it is working?

On the way back from Rome Origen paced the deck of his ship at every spare moment and turned these thoughts over and over in his mind. He did not like one bit what he had found out in Rome. How was he to combat this ignorance, fear and narrow-mindedness he saw entering the *Kyrios* there? How was he to preserve the pure, deep and majestic wisdom that was embodied in his Risen Lord, the Great Master, the vision of whom was daily expanding ever more powerfully in his soul? Confronted with this growing and dogmatic militancy he had perceived among an influential but powerful few in Rome, who seemed to be bent on turning the entire movement into a kind of spiritual machine, how was he to ensure that the simple purity of the faith he practised and the deep truth of the *gnosis* he possessed, be not only strengthened but passed on to all the future generations?

No! They did not know Him! *That* was the problem. They thought they did. Their knowledge, their *gnosis* was as thin as the papyrus they wanted to pin His great majesty, wisdom and beauty onto. They did not know this fabulous Friend of the Heart that had been breathed into all mankind. They were blinded by their love of power. Yes, that was it! Power! For all they seemed to care about, all they seemed to want was neat, learn-by-rote formulas. This was the essence of their programme for orthodoxy. All right, Origen argued to himself, theological formulas may have a part to play in the *Kyrios*, but they should never become either its foundation or its heartbeat. For, mere written formulas, learned by rote, dogmas, or articles of faith could never contain or impart the highest, initiating wisdom that the Great Master was the very embodiment of. Such methods smacked far too much of a return to the old idea of Law which the Risen One had overcome, had finally fulfilled. From now on there was, as He said Himself, only one law, and that was the great new *Law of Love*. This law could not be written in words – it must be lived in the heart. The new law was thus the law of the heart. There was no need for any other. And, as for dogmas and written formulas - had not the *Kyrios* recently acquired, after much heated controversy and heart-searching, the cannon of the Gospels and the basic exposition of the New Testament? And there was simply no need to add to this. Anyway, the belief that you could pin the wisdom of the Lord down into the mere matter of printed words was the very antithesis of that individual freedom and intimate spiritual friendship which was the heart of His promise to all mankind.

And the more he thought about it, the more the truth of the matter seemed to be that Julianus and his like in Rome were dead-set against allowing any knowledge whatsoever of either the Mysteries or the ancient art of initiation to gain a hold in the expanding, administrative or teaching structure of the *Kyrios*. They were badly prejudiced and blinkered in this regard, truly a pitiable state, born no doubt of the cruelty and spiritual ignorance that was the hallmark, that lay at the very heart, of their bloody Empire. But if they succeeded in their designs, they would take away nothing less than the soul, the very kernel of spiritual truth in the *Kyrios*, the pure white magic of Him. Thus, in their hatred of the Gnostics and their determination to get rid of them, they were, in Rome, in the greatest possible danger of throwing out the most beautiful baby in the world with the slightly soiled, Gnostic bathwater!

As Origen paced the deck of the shining, white cargo vessel he had procured a return passage on, he often tried to banish these troubling thoughts and lose himself instead in quiet contemplation. And, as the great, red, noisy sails billowed above his head and the sounds of the sea and the shipmates and the creaking vessel itself melded into one pleasing, pulsating mantra, he would sometimes think he heard a single, sighing voice weaving through it all. It was a lonesome voice that receded if he strained to listen, but came when least expected. He tried then to make out, was it male or female, human or divine, was it indeed himself or God? He thought of Clement and the Bath-Khol. He thought of the Voice of Conscience, of the Great Master of Love, and of how He came upon the waters and of how He was yet again coming, He said, on the clouds. Often at such moments, as the sea sprayed about Origen's face and heaved and swelled beneath his feet, its smell was like the smell of his God, filling his nostrils; the pure, fresh breeze His very breath. Origen was then consumed with sweetest ecstasy, and it was then also he found himself yearning once again to kiss His feet, kiss him like Mary, his truest lover.

But a kiss as sweet as that was not of this world Origen realized; a kiss like that could mean nothing less than death. But before this death in Him could become a reality there was so much to do, so many conflicts to solve in order to ensure the survival of His temporal body on the planet Earth, the *Kyrios*. For the harvest, as He had said Himself was great, but the labourers were few.

A few days later, as that soaring symbol of the light of Hellas, the Pharos, came into view once more, a powerful thought struck Origen, so strong he almost fell to the ground. It suddenly seemed to him that there was only one possible way he could deal with all these recurring conflicts and difficulties, difficulties concerning the true understanding of the Lord, difficulties which he had always sensed, even from the very beginning, but which his trip to Rome had thrown into starkest possible relief; and that was to try to invoke the mighty magic power of the Word himself.

There was no question about it any more. He would simply have to start writing books!

21   THE BIG DECISION

Origen was delighted with the way Heracles managed the School in his absence. When he went to inspect it, early on the first morning after his return from Rome when no one was yet around, the entire atmosphere exuded an air of freshness and cleanliness; the various halls, rooms and corridors were swept and tidy with lots of cut, fresh flowers in elegant vases adorning carefully selected spaces. The mosaics too on the floors and walls shone with exceptional splendour and the students themselves, when he saw them later in the morning, all looked wonderfully happy as they greeted him and joyfully welcomed him back.

A few days later Origen decided on a little remembrance celebration of his trip to Rome and invited Heracles, Ambrosius and one of his oldest friends, Lukas, to a simple meal in his apartment after the day's activities at the School were over. He cancelled his usual evening lecture.

The four friends almost filled Origen's small dining-room, and because he had not enough couches to accommodate them singly, he removed the two already in the room and spread mattresses on the floor instead. There they reclined and ate off a large embroidered tablecloth he had spread on the floor and upon which he had placed various bowls of fruit, nuts and nougats, plates of bread and pastries, as well as a small *amphora* of red, Arabian wine and some decorated, terracotta cups.

'We are eager to hear more about Rome,' Heracles said, after Origen had thanked him once again for the valuable work done in his absence. Heracles, who had grown into a most trustworthy aide, was a little older than Origen; he had become tall, bearded and dark-complexioned. He wore his black hair long, the way Origen himself used to before he tonsured it after his reception into the inner circle.
'I have informed Demetrius of all the salient points,' Origen said non-committally.
'But you can tell *us* the truth,' Ambrosius joked.
'Oh, I told him the truth, too Ambrosius, have no fear.'
'There are all kinds of rumours going round, Origen,' Heracles suggested with a frown. 'Are we to expect a heave against the Gnostics?'
'If we are, then Ambrosius better watch out,' Origen jibed, staring at Ambrosius.
'I am not a Gnostic, Origen,' Ambrosius asserted.
'Then join a house-community of the *Kyrios* and prove it,' Origen suggested.
'I already have!'
'Really?' Origen was genuinely surprised. 'Whose? Where? Pray, tell me more.'
'The house-community of Josephus, the Ebionite, in the Brochium.'
'Josephus! Well, congratulations. I am truly delighted to hear this. But, please, don't call Josephus an Ebionite. He can't be an Ebionite if he hosts a house-

community of our *Kyrios*.'
'Oh, sorry! I forgot. Well, he *was* an Ebionite, is that it, eh?'
'Yes, more or less. I know Josephus well. His parents were, probably still are, fanatical Jewish Ebionites. They wanted us not only to retain that disgusting and savage practice, the circumcision, but also the Mosaic Law, the Talmud, the Torah, the Mishna, the whole kedozzel! They wanted to keep it *all* going, full blast! We would never, in a thousand million years, become anything more than yet another Jewish sect if *they* had their way! They absolutely hate Paul, you know. But Josephus read St. Paul when he was quite young. It was I myself who actually recommended him to do so. And, as I knew he would, he saw the light of the Risen One shining clearly through every word of Paul's, and soon after that Josephus became a true Christian.'

'Origen,' Lukas said tentatively, after a pause, 'I have heard of some people who have been barred from house-communities because they also attend the ceremonies of Serapis up in the Serapeum. And I have also heard of others being barred because they were members of some other Gnostic groups in the city. Is this right?'
'No, definitely not, Lukas! It is not good at all that people are banned from house-communities, for any reason. There is a place for everyone in the *Kyrios* - pagans, Gentiles, Jews, prostitutes, Gnostics, sinners, criminals, tax-collectors, you name it. It's really a question of the degree of one's awareness, one's consciousness of or nearness to the holy Vessel – that's what counts, that is, the ability to *see* the Lord Himself. Anyone, absolutely anyone without exception can become attached to a house-community and start out along this wonderful and momentous journey and as such they are to be regarded as members of the *Kyrios*. However, in order to be able to attend the *Agape* they must first have received *some* instruction in the Gospel. There are no other rules that I know of. Where did you hear all this? I have not heard of such banning before.'

Lukas hesitantly ran his hand through his honey-gold curls. His clear, green eyes looked puzzled. 'Can't remember. Oh! I think Markus told me, and he............he also said eunuchs were not allowed!'
'Eunuchs!' Origen went pale as a ghost.
After an uneasy silence Heracles said with uncharacteristic grimness, 'There are all kinds of rumours going around, Origen.'
Origen sighed deeply and said, 'Heracles, there are all kinds of people inspired by evil spirits going around also. And they are dead-set on destroying the good work of the Lord on Earth.'

After this they all ate and drank in silence for a while.

'I have heard, Origen,' Ambrosius said eventually, 'that that beast Caracalla intends to........to "visit" us soon.'

Origen shot up from his mattress. 'Ambrosius, wherever have you heard this from?'
'From Alexandros, my contact in the Senate. It's on very good authority.'
'Then truly this is bad news. I must inform Demetrius straightaway. Have you any more details?'
'No. But I can get you them. Alexandros is very well connected.'
'Then do, please.' After a pause Origen continued, 'You know, my friends, I learnt a lot while in Rome. Actually, I went through a kind of awakening. I have come to believe that our movement, our entire movement, is entering a very critical phase right now. All the way home on the ship I tried to evaluate our position here in Alexandria in relation to these changes.   And more and more I realized that Alexandria has a very special task to perform for the world *Kyrios*. This place, where the light of Hellas has been kept burning brightly amidst the increasing and terrible brutality and darkness that Rome has brought down upon the world, I believe is being chosen by God as a sanctuary where the light of his Word can also be protected and remain alive. Thus, destiny is calling us. I feel that here we have the profound duty and task to preserve for the entire *Kyrios* and for all future generations, what is fast being lost elsewhere, and that is the Gospel that Peter received directly from the Lord and which he brought across to Rome over 150 years ago. And remember, that the Lord Himself regarded Peter as the strongest and most able-bodied of His twelve disciples.'

Origen went on, 'Now, Peter in turn passed on his Gospel to Mark when he arrived in Rome some time later. And there, in Rome, Peter and Mark established the *Kyrios* which steadily grew through the cultivation of their most precious Gospel. For they possessed, as well as the more open and public Gospel, the deepest, most profoundly esoteric part of the Great Master's teaching, the inner magical part. Mark came to Alexandria because he knew only too well the great danger that lurked for the Gospel in the belly of Rome. He brought the whole of the Gospel with him. And we still have Mark's secret Gospel carefully preserved here in our *Kyrios*; it is revealed to the initiated. But I believe they have virtually lost all this inner teaching in Rome, truly the most important part of the entire Gospel. And they are losing it not least because ignorant beasts like Caracalla, who could never, in a thousand years, know anything of the true Mysteries of God, are prowling like greedy wolves among our flock ready to devour it for their own bestial and purely materialistic purposes at the opportune moment.'
After a pause Origen continued, 'So, my friends, with all of this weighing heavily on my mind I have decided on a plan.'

Ambrosius' mouth dropped. He was intuitively and excitedly anticipating Origen's words.
'Yes, Ambrosius,' Origen said responding to him, 'there is so much error to be

countered, so much work to be done. We have to set down once and for all the basics concerning the straight and narrow path to the Lord's great Door. Amidst all the growing confusion, turmoil and persecution, the unending speculations and fantasising, the angelologies, theologies and codologies, someone simply must try to put the record straight! I can, as yet, see no one doing this properly, my friends, I simply do not. Some, like say Tertullian, are trying their best, but the work to be done is vast, simply vast. My mind boggles. I have for a long time turned such thoughts over in my head but have been put off acting by the sheer magnitude of what seems to be required. But my visit to Rome has brought home to me the urgency of the matter.'

'Origen,' Ambrosius interrupted, 'you are, you are........'

'Yes, my friend, my good friend, Ambrosius, I have, at last, decided that I will write.'

Ambrosius put down his cup and crawled across his mattress to Origen where he enthusiastically hugged and kissed him. 'I thought you would never say it,' he said, beside himself with joy. After a while he asked, 'But will you find the time?'

Origen too was overjoyed with Ambrosius' display of affection. He said modestly, 'Oh, I shall get up earlier or something, Ambrosius!'

'But you already get up far too early!'

'Well then, I shall go to bed later!' Origen laughed.

'This is excellent,' Heracles said. 'What will your first work be about?'

'That is a good question, Heracles.' Origen threw himself back on his mattress. 'There is simply so much to do. I hardly know where to start.'

'When will you start Origen?' Lukas interjected timidly.

'Believe it or not, Lukas, I have just this very morning begun something. Once I made the decision, I simply could not wait to get going. I have begun a book that will be based on the Old Testament. In it I will lay the foundation for a complete understanding of how the Hebrew Bible everywhere speaks of the coming to the Earth of our Blessed Lord, our Great Master. I shall use every already-known translation into Greek of the Hebrew Bible and shall actively seek out others, and as well as interpreting the sacred scripture in this way from the Christ-centred viewpoint, I will write it in such a fashion that every word in every known translation can be checked one against the other so that the reader can truly *decide for himself* the real meaning of the sacred text. My friends, be aware of this: I am *not* writing a new scripture, a new theology, a new law, or anything of that sort. No! I am simply going to make Christians aware of their most sacred heritage.'

'Bravo!' Ambrosius cried. 'This is truly fantastic news. But, pray, Origen, tell us – such a monumental work – surely it will take you a long time?'

'Yes, I believe it will. But while working on this fundamental book, I have decided that I will also write other, easier ones, in between. I will, for instance, also soon begin a basic statement of Christian values for all newcomers to the Way – I will call

it *First Principles*.'
'Yes, yes, this is most urgently needed,' Ambrosius excitedly agreed.
'I will also write a tract against that arch-enemy of ours, the pagan Celsus, and put the people of the *Kyrios* right, regarding his preposterous defamations once and for all. I will also write a commentary on St. John's Gospel, on St. Paul's letters, on the old prophets. I will write a......a....'
'Hey, hey, Origen, by the sound of this you will have no time for sleeping at all,' Ambrosius interjected.

Origen took a piece of nougat and bit deeply into it. 'I will write, Ambrosius,' he continued with determination. 'I will write out the Way of the Lord for the whole world clearly to see; I will write it, and I will keep writing it until it will shine as clearly as the sun in our Egyptian sky shines by day or the light from our majestic Pharos shines by night; I will write and write until they burn me or butcher me like all the other blessed martyrs before me. Ambrosius, I will die writing! As long as I can speak, nay not even speak, but *think*, and hold a quill in my hand, I will proclaim the Word of the Lord.'

In the long silence that followed, Origen's riveting words sank deeply into the minds and hearts of his friends. A serene sense of timelessness descended upon them and the room. It was a sense strangely magnified by those perennial but nondescript noises the dwellers in every town and city the world over are familiar with: children playing somewhere on a street, dogs barking in nearby yards, foghorns of distant ships returning from or setting off on long sea-voyages. And, as the friends ate, stimulated in their various ways by Origen's words, great, even heroic visions of challenges seemed to rise up before them as representatives and guardians of the *Kyrios* here in this ancient city; a *Kyrios*, they had little doubt anymore, was spiritually led by this inspired and saintly man in their midst.

Eventually Ambrosius broke the silence. 'The world awaits your voice, Origen,' he said prophetically, 'and I fervently believe it will resound with it for thousands and thousands of years to come.'

They spoke little more after this and all left quietly in a mood of almost holy expectation.

Amidst the on-going and often vicious political intrigues of the Empire, as well as the mounting pressure from Rome against the Gnostics, the need of the *Kyrios*, to not only appear but, to actually become a united body, grew ever more urgent. For how else could they possibly survive the attacks against them by the like of Caracalla? More important for some, however, was the question of *religio licita*. How else could they achieve this unless they presented themselves as an ordered, unified body? Rome demanded order! Indeed, was this not the very bedrock of all its thinking and acting, of all its law? For in deepest truth its civilization consisted of little else, apart from its roads and monuments and of course the army upon which the whole strange structure rested.

The Roman governor of the recently created and strategically vital province of Arabia, Maximus by name, was particularly worried. For one thing he considered himself to be, and indeed actually was, comparatively speaking, an honest, law-abiding if high-ranking citizen. More than this however, whether by taste, temperament or pure aesthetic sensibility, he had a gut dislike for the rampant hedonism and grossly indulgent sensuality that was everywhere on the increase among the populace, not only in Arabia, but all over, and especially, of course, in Rome itself.

Maximus was not a puritan by any means, but he instinctively realized that that species of hypocrisy which, through a thin disguise of religious legitimacy, gave free rein to the populace to gorge themselves as often and as much as they liked in the vilest forms of animal and sensual indulgence, would, in time, become nothing less than the very downfall of the Empire. The so-called religions which promoted such rituals were misnamed in Maximus' mind. He had a better, a more refined idea of religion, though he could not articulate it very clearly. It was simply that the hereditary disposition he received from his own mother and father informed him of what it was *not*! He was totally unhappy, for instance, with the idea of God as an erect phallus or some equally suspect object, and his unease spurred him to cast the net of his active and inquiring mind far and wide in an effort to find answers.

Maximus wanted to be honest. That much was very clear. And he felt he was doing all right. But something deep down inside him told him that in order to remain honest he must either address or even embrace this new thing called Christianity. This was not to say that he was not *genuinely* interested in it either. For he actually was! But he was also thoroughly confused as to who or what Christians were, or who or what this singular god was that they purported to, and really did by all accounts, so strongly believe in – no one he ever spoke to on the matter, whether bishop, presbyter, deacon or simple layman, satisfied him. Half of the time they seemed to him to absolutely contradict one another, often about even the most basic points of their system, if that was what it was.

Maximus was also an astute politician. And, like Demetrius in Alexandria, he wanted at all costs to be on the right side of Rome – he honestly wanted to keep his job! He had heard Origen's name mentioned often in the various conversations he had had with members of the *Kyrios* and decided, in the end, that the only way to solve his dilemma was to talk to Origen himself. If anyone could set him right on these tricky, doctrinal, yet fast becoming political matters, then this man sounded as if he could. So Maximus took the bull by the horns. He sent instructions to the governor of Egypt to, in turn, instruct Demetrius of Alexandria to send his famous Origen to him, at the first available opportunity. He had full authority to make such a demand, for all the men concerned were Roman citizens answerable to him, by law of the Emperor.

In this way Origen, in the autumn of the year 213AD, journeyed by ship down the Red Sea, disembarked at Aden and took a caravan to the hilly city of Al Nisub situated high above the Gulf. There he was greeted by the governor Maximus at the entrance to his superbly appointed residence.

And so, after a days' rest, over the following few days, Origen expounded his Christian doctrines and elaborated his various and philosophically informed views, which in response to Maximus' questions were mostly concerned with the Holy Trinity. Maximus, whose watery eyes were so large and receptive they seemed to Origen to be doing twice the work of his ears, was mostly satisfied with Origen's responses. Indeed, Maximus was so happy near the end of the visit that in the penultimate and final conversations he had a scribe appointed to record all of Origen's answers.

During his stay in Al Nisub it was the habit of Origen to take a relaxing walk through the narrow, rambling streets of the hilly town after his last conversation of the day with Maximus. One evening, after such a walk, as he was nearing his accommodation which overlooked the jostling, ever-crowded main street, he picked out from among the approaching mass a small figure, a stooped old man, carrying a walking stick, face to the ground. As the man drew nearer Origen began to think that he knew him. And when, at a few yards distance, the old man lifted his sad eyes and met Origen's, Origen was astonished. For although the face was much more worn and older than he had known it before, it was undoubtedly that of Christophorus.

Origen's heart thumped wildly in his breast! For in this face he had seen such a profound and chaste beauty and from its mouth had come the most significant words

141

ever spoken to him. Now, however, it was a face so shrunk it could almost be a death-mask.

'Christophorus!' Origen cried.

The face remained corpse-like but, as white lightening momentarily reflects with a dazzling brilliance upon the face of a still dark pool, flashing from Christophorus' eternal soul through the windows of his haunting eyes, Origen caught a glimpse of purest recognition.

They did not speak, but people by now were complaining, pushing and shoving to get past, for no one ever blocked the street by conversation. Origen, however, was about to speak when the old man lifted his left, trembling hand, and in a weak and tired voice Origen heard the strange words chanted, 'Whom does this vessel serve?'

Though puzzled, Origen was about to respond, but in an instant Christophorus had moved on. Origen stretched out his hand after him, but like a drop of water falling back into the eternal ocean, Christophorus suddenly disappeared into the seething mass of humanity.

For a long time after this, the tall, austere figure of Origen could be seen battling against the flow of the jostling crowd, stretching his long neck this way and that, scanning the heads, pushing in pursuit of his vanished brother-in-Christ, hoping forlornly to catch one last glimpse of him, wishing he could hear him speak just one more time, but all in vain, for he never again either heard or saw him in this earthly life.

Christophorus' parting words, however, echoed clear as a golden bell in Origen's ears for months afterwards and, in time, they actually became a kind of mantric focus for all his thoughts and meditations. *Whom does this vessel serve?* For, though very puzzling, wherever or whenever he heard them echo, they seemed to challenge him to the very depths of his being, why he could not say. On the one hand, they seemed to act like fire in his soul, giving him spirit-energy for all his inner and outer striving, yet also they seemed a resting point, a paradox, a riddle and a great mystery.

As more time passed and the words matured through meditation and reflection, Origen gradually came to realize that Christophorus had uttered a kind of eternal question. He seemed to have given voice to the very essence of the great Quest, the perennial one for God, a *quest*-ion indeed, a summons, an offering and a resolution, all rolled into one. How strange that such few words could prove so powerful, and the more he considered them the more Origen realized that they could have no other meaning, source or cause except that of the Christ Himself. These words were not just food for thought, they were the logoic nourishment of the very soul, uttered through the mouth of Christophorus, but now acting in Origen's own soul with a life of their own, a veritable being, driving him further and further along his way, and drawing him into ever more profound Christ-centred inspirations, psychic and spiritual experiences.

And then one day all of this synchronistic activity seemed to culminate in the unexpected and unannounced visit of a mighty strange personality.

It happened in the middle of the day, at the end of a class lesson at the Didascaleon. Origen's young class assistant, Jude, approached Origen and whispered in his ear that a very strange but important-looking man wished to speak to him. He was, she said, waiting for him in the library.

When Origen entered the library he saw, standing with his back to him, a tall man wearing a purple turban and a long, brightly-coloured robe, which was richly patterned in arabesques of semi-precious stones. Even from a distance he exuded whiffs of exotic perfumes and expensive incense. When he turned, Origen saw a neatly-bearded face with shiny skin the colour of orange-gold, sharply-pointed features, and eyes fixed and firm, yet lively as two ancient cedars.

Origen immediately recognised a Babylonian magician!

'Yes,' the man said in a crisp, clear voice, as if hearing Origen's thoughts, and approached him with measured steps, a strong hand extended, 'I am Sneferu from Babylon. I am attached to the royal household.'

Origen greeted him cautiously and motioned him to sit down. But, 'No,' Sneferu said firmly, with a polite, polished smile, 'I must not stay. However, I have an important message for you. Please listen most carefully.'

Origen was well aware of the kind of knowledge that these Babylonian magicians cultivated. It was a rich and ancient wisdom, so old, he believed, it stretched back to the time of Plato's Atlantis and beyond. Based on the Zodiac and the mystic art of astrology, which the Babylonians had turned into a real science, it was truly a rich and astounding Gnosis, probably the richest in the world.

It suddenly flashed across Origen's mind of how St. Luke had spoken in his Gospel of these mages, and of their prediction of the birth of the Christ, and of how some of them had actually journeyed great distances to worship Him at His nativity, bringing with them the symbolic gifts of gold, frankincense, and myrrh.

'I have come to warn you,' Sneferu said. 'I am a member of the Order of the Naziens.

We know and deeply cultivate the richly significant wisdom of the Christ and we remember continually His Great Sacrifice. Now, however, our charts have shown us that exactly two months from today, that is, on the 12th June, a most significant alignment of the planets will take place. It is an alignment which augurs acute danger for you. We have known of your activities for a long time and as a great servant of the Christ we deemed it most important that you should be aware of this danger. We do not know precisely what will happen to you but we advise that you be on your guard.'

Sneferu did not say anything else but looked deeply into Origen's eyes for a long time. Eventually Origen nodded. 'Thank you,' he said. 'The 12th of June.'
'Yes. And this is also what we call a day of initiation.'
'Thank you,' Origen repeated, 'I will try and remember this.'

Sneferu bowed courteously, swished passed Origen, and vanished from the Didascaleon quite as suddenly as he had appeared a short time before.

23 THE INITIATE

The Emperor Caracalla surrounded himself with an entourage of learned sycophants whose only other qualification, apart from their learning, was the wickedness of their minds and tongues. These men's delight in life, their great and constant game in fact, was to outdo one another in inciting their mad master, Caracalla, into ever more vicious modes and methods of killing. They even kept scores and often argued zealously among themselves as to which of them *really* should take the credit for his latest atrocity. For their evil game they actually had a carefully devised points system based on Roman law with a scale of heinousness at its centre.

One of these so-called advisors had a speciality – Alexandria – and took every opportunity to inform Caracalla of the exotic pleasures to be had there. Alexandria was a place Caracalla had never actually been to since ascending the throne. He had, on a number of occasions, been tempted, and said he would go there, and even once made concrete plans, but had called off the visit at the last moment when some more immediate pleasure attracted him. But feeling exceptionally bored one wet afternoon, upon a whim he ordered the captain of his personal ship to organise a cohort of the army as quickly as possible. He wanted, he said, to at last honour the citizens of Alexandria with a visit, and have some fun as well, of course. It was to be a surprise visit.

Caracalla was insane.

He arrived in Alexandria on the 1st June 216AD, having made sure that at least some people knew of his arrival a few days in advance. But in fact, as it turned out, he was greeted with a surprising degree of pomp and splendour in view of the short notice anybody had. The streets were strewn with flowers, lined on each side with rows of brightly burning torches, and everywhere costly incense burned and sweetened the hot, still, summer air.

For, some on-the-make senators, on hearing the news, had sprung into action! And with an eye to winning the much sought-after favour of their Emperor, apart from the flowers and incense, they also quickly assembled fifty of the most voluptuous and intelligent *hetaira* in the city. The *hetaira* were the top of the three grades of prostitutes in Alexandria; a highly sophisticated and cultured class of beautiful young women, formed, in equal measure, through the delights of the mind as well as the flesh, but most especially, taught how to please educated and often very world-weary men.

These fifty chosen beauties, who were to be reserved for Caracalla's exclusive use and pleasure for the entire duration of his visit, were given a crash course in how to please him and in the process were made very aware that his tastes were about as varied as they were hard to satisfy. Understandably they felt daunted, but nevertheless honoured, and looked forward with great anticipation to seeing him.

For a while all went well. However, after a few days, when the initial burst of excitement had died down, a rumour, fanned by the forked tongue of one of Caracalla's cleverest, and most vicious aides, came to his supersensitive ears. It appeared that some people in the city were actually calling him Geticus instead of Caracalla! This pseudo-title was hugely satirical, even mocking, for it expressly implied that Caracalla had gained the imperial throne at the expense of his murdered brother, Geta.

Upon hearing this, Caracalla flew into one of the worst rages in imperial history! How dare these pompous Alexandrians say, even think, such a thing of their Emperor! 'Make them pay,' a squeaky little devil's voice whispered in one of his ears. 'Make them pay like they'll never, ever forget.'

Caracalla was thus incited to go on a totally unrestrained rampage of violence in Alexandria. He began indulging his vengeful, lustful anger by inviting 'for an entertainment' as many of the citizens as could be crammed into the amphitheatre. The stage of this he had divided, for the occasion, into two halves. Caracalla had instructed that the 'entertainment' was to be kept absolutely secret. Thus, when the audience arrived, although they saw that the stage on one side was richly bedecked with flowers, cushions and draperies, and that the other side was quite bare except for a large, raised white marble slab, that looked like an altar, no one knew what to expect.

Soon, however, the excitement began to mount when Caracalla's fifty, beautiful, mouth-watering *hetaira* arrived. They were all very scantily clad, and were made to stand on the bare side of the stage. Caracalla himself then arrived with due pomp and splendour and immediately went among the girls and played with and teased them for a while, picking his unforbidden fruits like a god, a juicy one here, an even juicier one there, and sending them to the other, adorned part of the stage. Eventually, when exactly half of the *hetaira* had been sent across, Caracalla moved among them and began slapping and stripping them playfully, while he encouraged them to do the same to him. The other half remained silently standing.

Soon, however, a cordon of soldiers arrived out of the blue and marched menacingly onto the stage. They squarely faced the standing girls, forming a thick, impenetrable wall between the two sections.

Suddenly a wave of fear, sharp as a steel-tipped lance, ran through the standing girls.

Some of them started to cry. Then a small, select group of Caracalla's soldiers and gladiators eagerly emerged from this walled formation, sadistically wielding clean, silver machetes that glinted ominously in the bright sunlight. The girls started screaming frantically. Their cries, however, were not heard by their nearby colleagues, for a special group of plain-clothed soldiers planted in the audience had already got the crowd cheering as wildly as at a bullfight, even before the first decisive moves were made.

With their free hand these thick-muscled, war-hardened soldiers and gladiators then slowly began stripping the beauties; and when they had them all totally naked, one by one they were pulled by their hair to the raised, white, marble platform specially positioned for the purpose, and there, no doubt fancying themselves sacrificing priests of the latest satanic, government-approved cult, viciously hacked Caracalla's lovelies to pieces.

Now, this 'entertainment', this evil spectacle continued all the increasingly hot afternoon – on one side of the stage the monstrous massacre, on the opposite side Caracalla cavorting and having sex, also on a specially raised platform in full view of the audience, with as many of the remaining twenty-five girls as he could manage, none of whom could either see what was happening near them, nor wanted to if they could, the feral screaming of their colleagues but a stimulating addition to the already wildly cheering and clapping crowd. For *all* now in the amphitheatre were becoming increasingly maddened, and screamed for more and more of what was on offer on both sides, as a swirling, evil spirit in their midst took total possession of them.

As if to suggest that he neither knew nor even cared about the difference between hell, heaven and earth, at the end of his orgy Caracalla had a valet publicly bathe him and brush his hair. He then carefully donned a pure silk robe of royal blue, came forward and stood in full view of the entire audience. He raised his hand and addressed them directly, 'Dear citizens of Alexandria,' he said wearily, 'please, when you get home, do think carefully about calling me nicknames again.'

A cheer of 'Caracalla' went up from the excited, blooded crowd and Caracalla's brute face registered a rare thing for him, a genuine if one-sided smile. But, when the cheering died down again and sexually bloated and self-satisfied Caracalla was walking slowly away, he heard a lone young voice cry out from somewhere the obnoxious nickname, 'Geticus.' Caracalla stopped dead, his head bent to the ground. Now the coldest, angriest, darkest shadow imaginable fell across his face. Every gut and sinew, every tissue of his body tightened into a feral knot of fury, and he strode off the stage in the vice-grip of a totally demonic hatred. Who had shouted? Who? 'It was the voice, sir, of an insolent, dirty-arsed boy!' one of his henchmen coldly advised.

Caracalla immediately gathered all his generals together and between his sharp teeth hissed instructions at them to keep back in the amphitheatre every male below the age of twenty-one. The rest of the Guard was to be instantly deployed to search every street and house in the entire city and collect up all the other young men to be found there of the same age. Thus, in a relatively short time, some fifteen thousand young men, the very flower of Alexandria's youth, which included most of Origen's best and brightest students at the Didascaleon, were rounded up like beasts and assembled outside the city walls. Caracalla then took up a secure lookout post in the Temple of Serapis above the city, and from there, amid scenes of unimaginable horror, he directed his soldiers and gladiators in the massacre of these young boys, carried out in groups of fifty at a time. It was one of his bloodiest orgies ever.

Over the next days he aimed his venom at other aspects of the city and its life and culture which irked him. In the midst of this sickening orgy, the evil fumes of which the entire city was now totally soaked in and would be for a long time to come, Origen, of course, feared greatly for his precious and beloved School, the one institution which he knew offered some long-term hope for those people who could retain even a modicum of goodwill in their hearts amidst the fumes of such furious hatred. He remained in the School all the time, night and day, harbouring the strange hope that he might protect it in this meek way. But he instructed all his students to stay away from the School for the entire duration of Caracalla's visit.

One eerie afternoon, all alone in the library of the School, trying hard to study and meditate but failing every time, at a moment when he began to feel that maybe Caracalla had miraculously overlooked the School, he heard a commotion erupting outside on the street. He froze, fearing that the terrible moment had come at last. He remained seated and began to pray.

The library door was ajar. Outside, on the marble floor of the corridor Origen heard a single person enter the building. The heavy footsteps echoed eerily as he listened with almost super-sensible intensity. In the distance he heard a voice issuing indistinct instruction to others outside. Then the footsteps drew closer. The owner of these was obviously surveying the entire interior of the building. He took a few more steps, slowed down, stood still, then a few more steps, stopped again. Gradually the footsteps approached Origen's slightly opened door. Origen's eyes were transfixed upon it. And then he saw it move. Inch by inch it opened until, finally there, filling its frame was the squat, egg-shaped figure of Caracalla, his brute, yellow face sick with hatred and anger.

'Who are you?' Caracalla demanded.

148

'Origen.'
'What are you?'
'A teacher.'
'Huh. Where do you teach?'
'Here. This is my School, the Didascaleon'.
Caracalla looked about him and sniffed the air like an animal.
'What do you teach?' he hissed.
'About the Christ.'

Caracalla then came towards Origen menacingly. 'So you are one of these believers in the Christ then, eh,' he sneered.
'Yes.'
Face to face with him now, Origen got the whiff of what could easily have been ten sweaty dragons in heat. With a horribly distorted grimace Caracalla reached out his scarred hand and reefed Origen's red cord from his waist hissing, 'Fuck your Christ.' Then he walked away and began lashing the stacked shelves of the library with the red cord, 'And fuck your School too.'

Origen made for the door.
'Wait!' Caracalla snapped.
Origen turned.
'Do you know who I am?' Caracalla demanded.
'Yes, of course.'
'WHO? SAY IT!'
'Why, your Excellency, you are the Imperial Emperor, Caracalla.'
Caracalla spun into a mad, hellish laughter. Menacingly he came towards Origen again. 'No, you stupid Christian fool,' he growled, 'you are wrong. I am not Caracalla.'

No, Origen thought, perhaps you are not. For these eyes he was staring at were not those of a man but of a mad beast.
'Who are you?' Origen asked, trembling.
'Why, Satan of course. I am Satan. Don't you recognise me?'

With his head swirling, Origen ran out onto the street and fought his way desperately through the crowd that was gathering outside the School. Growing increasingly restive, they were sensing some excitement in the offing. Origen was near the back of the crowd when he heard Caracalla shout orders to some of his Guard soldiers outside who soon began to enter the building. Then Origen's heart sank to its lowest point ever!

Oh, these soldiers! They knew how to do everything: burn cities, butcher young

149

girls, crucify old men, wreck beautiful, marble halls! Not long afterwards Origen watched with horror as smoke began to pour from the windows of his beloved School.

Enormous emotions were engulfing him now, emotions so mixed, so potent and so powerful he was almost numbed by them. Satan! Who was he? Where was he now? All those devilish vices Origen thought he had conquered - fear, hatred, doubt, anger, resentment – these all now teamed into his head like a hornets nest suddenly kicked into activity, and he hardly knew what to do. Heroically he began to fight, but with himself, and with the only weapons he had, his long-cultivated Christian virtues of hope, forgiveness, fortitude, and most of all love!

But were these weapons strong enough *for Satan*? Soon the bright orange flames were leaping through the windows. They reflected on Origen's face which he held heroically towards them firm as marble; they danced the *danse macabre* in his eyes, eyes that were fiercely resisting tears, but when the flames eventually broke through the roof he felt his forced heroism fading and he could look no longer. He was about to walk away when something seemed to pull him back, an invisible hand. Riveting his eyes one more time, deeper than ever now into the heightening flames, he felt himself being drawn into them, almost as if a part of him was burning with them.

Oh, burn away all my sins, he prayed; burn away my hatred, the last shreds of my evil! Burn. Oh, can you teach me now to forgive, Lord, to forgive, forgive, forgive?

Praying wildly thus, Origen suddenly saw something quite miraculous! There before his tortured eyes, in slender, graceful, dancing capitals of fire, he plainly saw written the word:

YES

And it struck him then like a thunderbolt that today was the 12th of June! Immediately the mysterious figure of Sneferu, the Babylonian magician, came before him. His predictions were stunningly accurate. And what had he also said? - That today was a day of initiation? Yes. That was it.

Mesmerized, Origen continued to watch the flames. Surely this was the very hand of God speaking? But could he live up to this word? Could he really forgive this unspeakable evil he was witnessing?

Oh God, he cried, what are we – animals, spirits, or devils? And slowly he became consumed by the greatest of all those beasts that lurk in every man's soul, the beast of doubt, the one that tests his faith in God to the very limits of his endurance.

And as the letters faded all Origen could do was close his eyes and sink his reeling head upon his breast. One thing alone now was not in doubt, one thing alone was certain: if evil was ever to be defeated it certainly would not be achieved by this weak and wretched man, Origen.

He turned. Nothing now, not even another miracle could make him look for a second longer.

He began wandering away from the crowd. Now he had done with men. He wanted never to see another one of them again. All day he walked and knew not nor cared not where, but later, in the twilight, when he found himself among the deserted streets near the harbour, he went way out to the Pharos, sat by it with his head sunk low upon his breast, and later still, as night drew on, he wandered in the dark woods near Eleusis. All this time he was fighting with his thoughts and feelings, with his God, his angel, with himself, sunk in utter despair and anguish. But fight! he kept counselling himself, keep fighting. He must not, *he must not* give in to hatred. He must *try* to understand. Love your enemies, he kept saying, thinking, hearing. No, no. Yes, yes. Love. Nothing else. Love and forgive. Even the Devil? Yes, even him.

But the fear, hatred, and anger would keep stirring up in him like lurking, writhing beasts. *Yes, yes, yes* he kept hearing, *love without condition or not at all. This is my rule, my only law; this is why I died.* And suddenly there before him stood a huge, shining, golden crucifix, flaming up out of his darkness, like a sphinx come to life out of the dead desert sands, a sordid figure begging him from the Cross to understand, to forgive. Then to each side of the crucifix he saw sprout a small black cross, and the more he looked the more the total vision grew; it grew and glowed mightily, utterly filling his mind and imagination until his very soul was drawn away, far, far away into another world, the hellish world of the Hill of Golgotha.

But his earthly feet continued to walk, and they carried him to the outskirts of the city towards the great wall. At the frayed edges of his vision, now his whole life flashed before him, crumbling, fading, reforming; his many lives, past ones, even ones to come, a strange kaleidoscope of memory, prophetic vision and imagination, all pressed together and all shot through with this shining golden crucifix and the black crosses on the green hill.

Only half consciously, he went through the great pillars that marked the Gate of the Moon, and then way out beyond the city walls where his physical eyes saw the huge summer moon herself setting on the crisp, razor-edge of the vast, empty, Egyptian desert. His soul sank down with her but he kept on walking, following her, farther and farther out into the desert. And as her afterglow disappeared and the sand turned blue, indigo, and finally black, there was nothing left on the canvas of his soul except the Hill of Golgotha. Nothing could remove this from his mind's eye. Clearer and clearer the crosses became, until they spoke so loud he fell to his knees before them; the great archetypal images burning white hot into his soul, branding him, to the very depths of his being, a Christ, and bringing him into an uncanny awareness of the great power, austere truth and tragic beauty of his saintly, martyr's calling.

He clung to the Crucifix, and then hung upon it. 'Ah, you Christ', he sighed 'what exquisite power and pain, what sacrifice, what utterly divine and everlasting love'. Origen knew in his bones then that this was the greatest Event ever, the death of the God on Golgotha, forgiving mankind his awfulness, his bestiality, his unbelievable savagery; this, his wickedest crime ever, and He, the God, saying simply and gently before He died, 'Forgive them Father, for they know not what they do.'

Hanging and falling, dying and rising, all night long Origen wandered over this black desert canvas. Sometimes he lifted his head up and wiped the blood of his passion upon the glittering stars above, and like a Veronica, they gave him some little respite, some small comfort, for he saw in this starry beauty nothing less than his Celestial Mother, the very embodiment of his cosmic homeland. Here below there was only blackness, wickedness, but up there was the true, white, milky body, the beautiful Spirit of his beloved Great Master, his Mother and Father, all Three contained in the One great white Cosmic Spirit of Love. Here below there was naught but destruction and black death, as His simple Cross, better than any other picture nature or artist could ever paint, so well, so perfectly illustrated for all mankind.

The stars glistened over the desert more brightly than Origen had ever seen them before. And truly they soothed him, even began to speak to him, for he heard delicate sounds, whispers, songs of comfort and of confirmation, brief snatches of the Music of the Spheres, albeit played as a requiem. Once he even opened his mouth to lick them!

But then he began to cry.
He fell a final time to the cold sand and could not get up. He started banging it with his fists. And still the crosses loomed before his inner eye. He writhed and pounded and screamed, his face buried in the sand, choking. And eventually, after many more hours of torture, quite suddenly and totally unexpectedly he let go, and went into a deep, long sleep.

In the morning, as the sun began to rise over the horizon, Origen awoke with it as if from death. At first he did not recognise the desert, for, bathed in the first golden rays of the rising sun it looked so pure, clean and lovely he felt he could almost be in paradise. He also felt light as a feather, tingling and trembling in every tissue, as if he had wings. He began pinching his body all over to see if he really was awake or even alive, for this new self-awareness was so calm, sweet and ethereal he was genuinely quite unsure of the new status of his overall being. He felt as if he was returning from a great Gnostic festival, as if he had overnight imbibed nothing less than ambrosia, the pure, sweet, draught of the gods, the draught of highest wisdom and knowledge. It was truly as if he had gone through a Damascus-type initiation and had been made into a new man. He was full of a tremendous sense of relief, of spiritual power, warmth and worldly potential.

He stood up and felt like a giant, a god even. 'Jesus Christ,' he said to himself, 'this surely is going to take some getting used to!'

He looked about him with utter amazement, for the desert now seemed not to be just dry, brown sand anymore but a marvellous, multicoloured carpet of tiny, glittering jewels. The new light within, he now felt was streaming out from his eyes, so that it seemed to penetrate everything he looked at, revealing amazing, cosmic secrets about forms and figures mere surfaces could never show. Everything, absolutely everything was suddenly new and utterly alive! This so-called dead desert was not dead at all! Even the still morning air, touching Origen's waving hand as he caressed it in wonder, had the quality of an ethereal body or being. This air you could kiss! And he actually did! He was filled with a boundless joy. It was no fleeting joy however, it was one he knew could last forever, so pure and strong it was. This was a death-defeating joy!

Thus a powerful, new, magical spirit had entered Origen. Now he knew for certain that in loving this insignificant sand and air, this pure blue sky, this sunlight, he was loving the Great Master Himself, His real Body. Life would never be the same again. Now, at last, Origen knew what those old Hibernians meant when they called Him, out of the vast depths of their most ancient and sacred Gnosis, the Lord of the Elements. There was no need for temples or schools made of stones anymore – for if you opened your eyes you saw Him *everywhere*.

Truly Origen was re-born.

And what was more he had forgiven the Devil!

24   THE GNOSTIC PAPAL CRISIS

After his morning bath in his own specially built bath-house in Rome, on the 8th April 217AD, while Caracalla was cooling himself in the bath's *frigidarium*, he was stabbed, by a hooded figure, from behind, but precisely through the heart, exactly thirteen times with an elegant eight-inch, richly-jewelled dagger. The hand that held the dagger was cold and old, but inspired and strong; that of Martialis, one of Caracalla's valets, but a terribly angry and righteous one.

Martialis was angry because, quite unknown to Caracalla, he was a most devoted follower of the god Mithras whose keen, if often cruel, sense of justice greatly appealed to him, and because of this he could no longer stomach the murderous, godless and insane rule of Carcacalla. The assassination was not his own idea, however. It was that of Macrinus, Caracalla's praetorian prefect, who, inspired by a pathological love of power got deeply into the ear of Martialis and did not let him be until the murder was accomplished. Macrinus then, instantly and boldly, declared himself to the citizens of Rome as the new Emperor. And, in the turmoil that followed, the citizens did not object. For, the truth was that they found little in their mad Caracalla to love or remember apart from his questionable entertainments and the beautiful and luxurious bath-house he built for them. And so the more sober and sane Macrinus quickly became acknowledged as the undisputed new Emperor.

Macrinus, as it turned out, was an associate of Julianus, and like Julianus he had great personal and political plans for the Empire. Thus, Julianus was greatly excited by these latest developments, for he felt certain he could manipulate both Macrinus and this latest round of anarchy to the direct and long-term advantage of the *Kyrios*. However, to Julianus' chagrin the Emperor Macrinus, after only a few months, began to be severely criticized by the soldiers who felt he was being far too strict with them. Macrinus was in fact a very bad politician. For instance, he banned the soldiers, supposedly for some oracular reason, but in truth for purely economic ones, from eating meat on Fridays. He had no idea. And of course even the *thought* of losing such a valuable perk as their ration of meat was, for the soldiers, like waving a red rag at a bull. But that was only one of many other similar sanctions imposed by Macrinus, whose dull sense of political reality caused him almost to put economy before breathing! So, getting fed up with his steady stream of penny-pinching by-laws, true to form, the soldiers began fishing around for a suitable alternative to him as their Commander-in-Chief. They eventually got their eye on a fifteen-year-old orphaned boy of high military parentage, actually a cousin of Caracalla's.

This boy seemed like a good prospect for many reasons; the chief of these was his youth - he could be easily manipulated. Another thing in his favour was that he already believed himself to be a god anyway, or at least the son of one, and that

154

surely was a help to any aspirant to the throne of Rome. They boy's name was Heliogabalus. This was obviously not his birth name but one given to him, he said, personally by the god; it was the same name actually as the god himself, a Syrian sun-god whose penchant for bloody sacrifices attracted the boy to him like magic, almost from his birth. Apart from all this, it must also be said that the boy was extraordinarily beautiful.

Heliogabalus readily agreed to the soldier's cleverly concocted suggestion that he should become the next Emperor, especially when they told him that this was actually prophesised by no less an authority than the Sibylline Oracles! The demonically precocious Heliogabalus didn't bother checking the Oracles, of course, for it seemed perfectly natural to him that what the generals said was true. And so the proclamation was duly made with at least half of the army generals' approval. Half was enough.

Needless to say Macrinus, was infuriated and instantly mobilized the other half of the army. Soon a great battle took place on the borders of Syria and Phoenicia, but Macrinus lost, and in this way Heliogabalus became the new, sole, and legitimate Emperor of the Romans.

Heliogabalus' reign, however, was also very short - just three years - at the end of which he too was assassinated. During this time he displayed no interest whatsoever in his citizens but spent every moment of his time and as much coin as he could extract from the masses on devising ever more extravagant and vicious public sacrifices to his gluttonous and blood-sucking god.

If Caracalla was insane, Heliogabalus was doubly so. Many observers said his debaucheries in every respect outdid those of Caracalla's.

To add to the confusion, in the middle of all this, old Pope Zephyrinus eventually (and probably very gladly) took his leave of this evil, troubled world, and the turmoil already rife in the civic life of the populace now extended to the more sober and shielded life of the Christian *Kyrios* also. The upshot of it was that Callistus, the arch-Gnostic, to the terrible rage of Julianus, got himself declared, and let it be said, in a very democratic way, pope of Rome. Predictably, Julianus denounced this election result in the vilest terms possible and did so in every circle, civic, religious, mercantile or other, that he was allowed into. Furthermore, he encouraged his learned Christian associate, Hippolytus, to declare himself, on assurance of the support of a few influential people in the army mainly, to be the true pope of Rome. Hippolytus duly obliged, and thus Rome now had two popes, one Gnostic, and one not Gnostic, both nonetheless vehement and vociferous in their claim to be both legitimate and Christian.

During this turmoil Demetrius sent Origen away altogether from the city of Alexandria, to Caesarea in Palestine. Demetrius hoped that matters might be easier for him to handle and direct, in his city, if he did not have to try to understand or regularly take into account Origen's often suspicious views and opinions on important-sounding matters of doctrine which Rome anyway always wanted to dictate.

In recent years, Origen had, in Demetrius' opinion become ever more heterodox in his views. Origen listened to others all right, and paid close attention to what emanated from Rome, but he always came to his own conclusions in the end. It was as if he had some special knowledge or insight all of his own. Even the way he looked was different, drawing upon himself nowadays the airs of some ancient Greek sage, but one whose eyes, Demetrius often felt, were not any more those of a man but of an eagle. In short, Origen made Demetrius very uncomfortable, whether in his presence or not. Anyway, there was nothing for Origen to actually *do* in Alexandria, with the School now but a black cinder of charcoal, and unlikely ever to be anything else again. So Demetrius concocted some flimsy excuse and sent him away.

Origen, not one for disobeying orders and certainly disinclined to risk creating a schism in the *Kyrios*, which, by objecting to this act of Demetrius, he felt he could easily do, in Alexandria at least, went away quietly. He believed that, at the appropriate time, hopefully not too distant, matters would settle down again, and he would be able to return to his beloved city and continue his work for the *Kyrios* there, even re-establish the School. However, as soon as he found his bearings in Caesarea he started up a new School there and quickly gained a large following. Indeed his reputation continued to grow enormously both inside and outside the *Kyrios*. Learned people everywhere were now saying that he was in fact more than a Christian, that he was a great Initiate, far greater even than his old Master, Clement. Origen, on these very esoteric matters, wisely said nothing and actually disliked speaking of himself in personal terms at all. Nevertheless, both his Christian vision and his manner of expressing it became ever more impressive, penetrating and inspiring. His charged, Christ-filled, light-filled personality was clearly discernable by all.

By now Origen had published his great work, *Contra Celsus* against the vociferous arch-pagan Celsus, in which Origen totally demolished that scholar's influential objections to Christianity by countering them with his own wide-ranging learning, both philosophical and doctrinal, but most of all with his penetrating insight into all things spiritual whether Christian or otherwise.

In Caesarea, Origen found a safe refuge in the warm, hospitable household of the virgin Juliana, a young and beautiful woman of sound faith and growing wisdom who had been instructed initially in the way of the Christ by the Ebionite Symmachus whose translation of the Hebrew Bible was one of those that Origen was using in his great work of elucidation of the Scriptures, which he would eventually call the *Hexapla*, a book upon which he worked almost every day. Most lovingly cared for by Juliana, Origen was able to devote himself more diligently than ever to his writing, but he still felt there was so vast an amount to be done that he was often very frustrated with the slow rate of his output.

Ambrosius, who sorely missed Origen in Alexandria, became less and less interested in his import and distribution business, and when his mother died of a heart attack at the height of Caracalla's murderous visit to the city, he felt little impetus to continue with it at all. So he sold all his stock and his beautiful *domus* and moved to Caesarea, primarily in order to be near Origen whose daily lectures at his new school fructified his growing faith in Christ to such an extent that he took little or no interest in the extraordinarily beautiful women of Palestine! With this Origen was very impressed.

Ambrosius provided Origen with the money for renting a modest building which housed his new school, a place which, though it lacked the marble and mosaic grandeur of the Didascaleon, Origen, nevertheless, loved dearly. Its most precious characteristic was a small but beautiful garden, the centrepiece of which was a rectangular lotus pool where Origen often sat in the quiet of the evening with some of his closest friends and students.

On one such evening in July he was in the company of Ambrosius, Juliana, and Gregory.

Gregory, who as well as being one of his newest and brightest students ever, also had an uncanny clairvoyant capability. This latter Origen viewed with a due measure of circumspection while not denying its often practical usefulness. Gregory for his part quite literally adored Origen and often saw his head bathed in a golden nimbus so bright it sometimes prevented him from looking at him at all, thinking that he might be committing a dreadful sin by doing so – for Gregory believed one was not allowed to look upon the face of a god. He was only seventeen.

Gregory was sitting on the grass near Origen's feet, looking towards the pool. 'Who am I, Gregory?' Origen asked with a loving glint in his eye.

Gregory turned his dreamy face to Origen with closed eyes he said, 'The sunlight of God, Master.'

'Open your eyes Gregory.'

Gregory opened his eyes.

'Where am I?' Origen asked.

Gregory placed his hands upon his heart. Origen said, 'Keep your eyes, your physical eyes open Gregory. See as much of the Earth as you possibly can. Imbue it with the sweet, golden light of your open, inner eye. Then you will know Him all the better. For everything, *everything* in the Earth, on our Earth *is* the body of our Lord. It is not a planet anymore. It is a Being. He has sacrificed Himself into it, united Himself fully with it – Corpus Christi - fertilizing its most precious fruits, like you, with the love-drops of his divine soul-blood.'

Origen was sitting on a small stone throne, his favourite garden chair, a little apart from Juliana and Ambrosius who were at the top of the pool on an old wooden bench. In front of them, upon the dark backdrop of the water, the peach-white lotuses gleamed as lovely as a constellation of stars. The sun itself was dipping towards the horizon casting long shadows across much of the garden.

Juliana, who was tall and slender and wore a lovely bright-green tunic, sat with her long legs crossed beneath it and her sparkling blue eyes fixed firmly upon Origen. Her small oval face surrounded by the neat bun of her fine black hair always reminded him of a bird's egg resting in its nest. Her voice, too, was bird-like, clear, and sweet as a little prayer-bell.

'He is your only master, then?' she queried.

'He is the Master of all Masters, Juliana. He is also an invisible Presence among us; invisible for most that is, but He can be seen, believe me. Think: what is sight anyway, but an absence of dark? But He is all light, pure Light. Look, Juliana, you have to learn to see in a new way, see through the dark shadow. I see, I feel Him more in you than I do in myself.'

Juliana gave him a puzzled smile. But Origen continued, 'John the Baptist said it best – "as He grows, I must diminish". Juliana, I see a vast countenance arising out of the physical matter of the world. And it is *His* face. Before this I am nothing, but He, It is all. I have come to know, to believe that matter's substance rests entirely upon its ability to *reflect*, and nothing else. Matter of itself doesn't exist at all. They are absolutely right in the Orient when they talk about *maya*. Think about water. It is the most common and revealing form of matter. You know, the earth is ninety percent water; so too with our bodies. All of this merely reflects His spirit. But the reflection is not Him. The Earth is but His magic mirror. For, He is all soul-light, the etheric flame that is the light of the life in this water. Therefore, we must learn to dissolve our bodies like ice dissolves before such a flame. That is just another way of saying that we must die in order to be, to rise with, Him; we must melt into Him to truly know Him in His Risen sense, His essence. That is the secret of His Light, His Life, His Way and His Breath, but most importantly of all, His Love.'

As Origen spoke he sat perfectly still, projecting his every word with care, clarity and precision, his entire body concealed beneath his large black cowl, with only his shaven head visible. Even his hands were rarely seen, for he mostly kept them within the opposite sleeves of his cowl.

After a long pause Ambrosius said slowly, but with a brightness in his face that bespoke a deep inspiration: 'We must die to our *lower* self.'

'Absolutely right, Ambrosius. Well done! We are not just one single self. We are at the very least a duality – for if we think about if for five minutes we will realize the sense in the statement that we have a lower animal being as well as a higher spiritual one. St. Paul has spoken of this at length in his first letter to the Corinthians. Now our truest self must be our higher one, our spirit self. And this part of us is to our lower animal body as that lotus there is to the sediment at the bottom of the dark pool from which its long root rises up and makes the blossoms possible, here in the sun. Now, all of you, when after your time of preparation in the *Kyrios* – for that is what the *Kyrios* is, a *preparation* - you become initiated into the Great Mysteries you will know that this higher self I speak of is none other than the Christ in me, the Christ in you. The Initiates have always known this, all down the ages. Paul, too, was a great, in fact one of the very first, Christian Initiates. He says what I have just said in his letters to the Galatians and the Colossians. Zarathustra is another, more ancient example. He spoke of the coming of the Christ to the Persians in his great religion of light, the Ahura Mazda. But a turning point has come in the great mystery/wisdom tradition of the world in that the Christ, the God, at the Baptism of John in the Jordan entered into a purely human body, that is, into the body of the Master we call Jesus of Nazareth. This God-infused being then suffered and died as a man. This was the great turning point of time: the death of the Godman on the Cross of Golgotha. Since then the secret of life is to learn to share in that death. In learning about this death, in and through the Gospel, in sharing in it in this way, we come to know also of the new life, the resurrected life, we come to share in the immortal, the eternal life of the Angels, and the Gods.'

Gregory had his eyes closed again and his face was shining like a star. 'The Temple Master,' he whispered, 'please, speak of the Temple.'
'Only if you open your eyes, Gregory.'
Gregory opened his eyes, looked hesitantly at Origen for a moment then back down at the lotus flowers again.

'Yes, Gregory, a new Temple is being built. But it is one that will be far more beautiful and contain far more wisdom and truth than Solomon's ever did, or indeed any temple that was ever constructed of blocks of stone, or by the hands of men. The new Temple is the ethereal Temple of the Imagination, invisible to physical eyes but, none the less, real and all the more enduring precisely because of that. The *Kyrios* is but the outer sign of this grand new Temple. Nevertheless, it is an entirely new, an inner kind of structure and one of which He, Our Lord, is both the Master Builder and the Grand Hierophant or Initiator of all the aspirants who come to it and wish to be part of it. He is the measure of all masters, spiritual or physical, and ultimately we need no other. He is the King of Initiates. *Kyrios* – He is the Lord of our spirit and lives in the temple of our bodies which we can fashion through His power into an etheric body, a risen body, a grand new temple. This great new structure will, He says in His Gospel, last forever. There is no more need for temples of stone, for man-made structures. The Spirit has come down to us – Immanuel - one of His glorious Names. The instructions on how to build this new, inner Temple are given in the Gospel of Mark – most especially in his secret Gospel. Mark, who together with Ormus, a priest of the ancient mysteries of Memphis-Misraim, Christianized these ancient Egyptian rites and gave them to the *Kyrios* in Alexandria where we still preserve them within the inner circles. That is all you need to know of the Temple at the moment, Gregory. The Great Master will ensure that you will find out in time what is necessary for you to know for your own initiation. And this is sure to happen, provided you follow the precepts taught to you within the *Kyrios*. You must be patient at all costs.'

As he was speaking, Ambrosius got up and was listening standing by the pool, his head bent sideways and his eyes resting on the same peach-pink lotus flower as Gregory's. Ambrosius lifted his eyes and with uncharacteristic seriousness asked, 'Will *I* ever be initiated, Origen?'
'You must accept the reality of the Master, first, Ambrosius.'
'The Great Master?
'The Masters.'

Juliana was biting her lip. After a long silence she said ecstatically, 'Master, I will follow you, and you alone.'
'But, sweet Juliana, I have already said I am nothing.'
'Will you not be my Master then?'
'Oh yes! But your Master Servant, Juliana, your Master *Servant*. My only wish is for you, for all of you, to share in His beautiful Body. You are all part of the *Kyrios*. That is enough for the present. The *Kyrios*, remember, means for us not just Lord, but the *Body of the Lord*. I will work for you all to be fully, inseparably joined to this, now, and for all time. For this I wish, I hope

I am prepared to die! You see my friends, the great question is not anymore how to live, but how to die so that we may be re-born.'

Now Gregory was secretly weeping. As Origen spoke he let the sweet, hot tears roll down his cheek, luxuriating in them; little burning rivers of love, boring into his soft, young body, his Master's body, Origen's body, a soul-brother, a soul-friend for life, nay, for ever and for ever and for ever.

Origen stood up.
'And now I must bid you farewell, friends. The sun has set. Time is moving on, and I have still much work to do before nightfall.'

He went out of the garden swiftly, leaving all three friends to muse upon his words by the pool. Ambrosius, however, after a few moments, bolted in pursuit of him.
'May I walk with you to your *domus*?' he asked when he caught up with him.
'Yes, of course, Ambrosius,' Origen replied.

Juliana's *domus* was about ten minutes walk away, just off a side-street at the back of the city's main bathhouse, the activity surrounding which often both bemused and disturbed Origen. His room, however, despite this, was mostly quiet.

'How is your writing going?' Ambrosius asked.
'I wish you could see into my head, Ambrosius. It's like a secret library full of books, or a hidden heap of creative ants all waiting impatiently to be seen.'
'Yes. I think I get the drift of your thoughts. You have to squeeze and scratch each word out slowly with your blunt, ever-snapping quill onto the rough, resistant papyrus, and by the time one little word is properly written down a thousand other, better ones have come and gone forever.'
'Yes,' Origen laughed, 'you understand. It's quite maddening at times.'
'The whole blessed business is so damn slow!'
'Precisely!'
'Origen, I have the solution.'
'Really?'
'Yes. I will place my *entire* fortune at your disposal.'
Origen stopped dead in the street. He turned to Ambrosius. 'Pardon?' he enquired.
'You heard me. I will place my entire fortune at your disposal. I don't know what else to do with it! I have given up the women; I am not a pleasure-seeker anymore; I want knowledge and you have it. So it is perfectly obvious to me that

I should place my fortune at your disposal.'
'What do you mean precisely, Ambrosius? How will placing your fortune at my disposal further the spread of my knowledge?'
'Like this. You can have as many stenographers and calligraphers as you need. Then rather than the laborious business of writing yourself, you can *dictate* all your books, catch all those elusive, beautiful words immediately they pop into your beautiful mind. Furthermore, apart from the School building here which I am already paying for, I will rent you another large room or even a villa somewhere, somewhere very pleasant, perhaps in the garden of one of those beautiful Greek temples over there behind the amphitheatre, and this will be your..........well.....your own publishing house!'

Origen was now questioning Ambrosius deeply with his wide-open eyes, but an irrepressible excitement was stirring in him. Ambrosius had the face of a happy child.
'I mean it, Origen,' he said, turning suddenly serious again, 'every single word.'
Origen placed his hand on Ambrosius' shoulder then embraced him. 'My friend,' he said, 'my good friend, how blessed I am.'
'No, Origen. How blessed *I* am.'
'I will dedicate all my work to you,' Origen said. 'This is the most wonderful news I have ever had.'
'Good' Ambrosius said, 'so it is settled. I will get to work on the project straightaway.'

They walked off again slowly.
'Yes,' Origen said, giving vent at last to the full fire of his excitement. 'Yes, yes, yes.' He stabbed the air with his fists. 'Yes. I will say *everything*. I will now be able to say everything that needs to be said. I will leave nothing out. Absolutely nothing.'
'And I will see to it that your books get as wide a distribution as possible. I will send them all over the Empire, and far beyond.'
'Good. Fantastic! Oh, Ambrosius, you are an angel.'
'No. Not quite, Origen. Not yet.'

They passed under an archway and out onto the main, paved street of Caesarea that led down towards the docks. The street was deserted but for a few straggling people conversing here and there at corners.
After a long silence during which they both pondered in different ways the exciting new venture, Ambrosius said, 'The *Kyrios* here holds you in the very highest esteem Origen.'
'Yes.'
'Unlike in Alexandria.'

162

'Demetrius is becoming an increasingly slippery fish to play, Ambrosius.'
'You bet! So will you stay here?'
'Yes. But only until Demetrius allows me, or calls me back again. Alexandria is my home. I have no wish to live anywhere else.'

After a short pause Ambrosius said, 'Origen, I have been speaking with Pope Theoctistus here recently.'
'Ambrosius! Really? Pope Theoctistus. You do get around, don't you?'
'Yes. Blame it on my sanguine temperament!' he said facetiously. 'But look. Theoctistus now knows I am a good friend of yours. He was delighted when I told him. And he has asked me to ask you to address the entire congregation here to mark the anniversary of Stephen's, our first martyr's, death.
'What! Me! Address the *entire congregation*?'
'Yes, including himself, Pope Theoctistus, and all the archbishops, presbyters, deacons, inner circles, a kind of Christian convention you could say, or what the Jews call *ecclesia*.'
'This is most unusual, Ambrosius.'
'Yes, I know. But I can tell you that Theoctistus has issued the invitation most sincerely. He is an inspired man in his own way, Origen. And if you agree he will definitely convene such a large, unprecedented gathering! I know he has a huge estimation of you and has no doubt whatsoever that your words will instil a great new and powerful life into the *Kyrios* here. Will you do this?'
'But, of course,' Origen said, overcoming at last the hesitancy of his innate modesty, 'of course. It will be my great pleasure.'
'Good. I will convey this to Pope Theoctistus, tomorrow.'

25   THE FIRST EVER CHRISTIAN CONVENTION

Pope Theoctistus' idea of a festive gathering to commemorate the death of Stephen was his own brainchild designed to stir up enthusiasm and instil fervour into the life of his particular branch of the new, momentum-gathering social movement, the *Kyrios*, in Caesarea-Palestina. And if the great Origen addressed the gathering, Pope Theoctistus was certain it would be a milestone in the development not only of the Christian community in Caesarea, but all over as well.

Origen, for his part, had never actually addressed such a large gathering before. For virtually everybody of note in the whole of the Christian community of the Roman province of Arabia and some from even farther afield turned up in the amphitheatre on the appointed December day. There they first heard a variety of speeches and witnessed a number of ordinations and other suitable spectacles, but when the time came for the world-famous Origen to speak all was hushed as he delivered to them a long portion of his legendary and undeniable wisdom.

Origen had resolved to speak his mind openly, and he did so, and on many and very varied subjects. But the centrepiece of his homily was a stunning and sustained eulogy on the redemptive power of the Christian virtues which he declared to be the foundation of the great new Way to God and compared to which the innumerable extant systems and philosophies of the pagans and others paled into insignificance. He laid the greatest possible emphasis on the spiritual values of humility, modesty and chastity. He received a standing ovation at the end and there was little doubt that the entire congregation had received, as Theoctistus had so deeply wished for, a strong draught of spiritual nourishment.

This event was so unusual, however, that word of it soon spread abroad. Far and wide people of every class and cult began to speak of it. And while most of the talk was approving, not all of it was! For in Rome especially, some of them were not only displeased; they were positively outraged. For what, these people argued, if matters went on in this way, with any old pope in any old city calling a great gathering, festive or otherwise, any time he felt like it – what on Earth would the end result of all that be? Spiritual anarchy!

Julianus, who was actually the prime mover of this kind of gossip in Rome, was particularly angry because this event in Caesarea occurred at a time when he was just about beginning to succeed, albeit by stooping to increasingly ruthless and cold-blooded methods, to steer things back in his favour in the Roman *Kyrios*. The most grievous of these acts was his authorization of the murder of Callistus, the popular Gnostic who had managed to get himself elected pope of Rome.

Julianus actually had Pope Callistus suffocated in his sleep by a common, street thug, upon a promised payment of a few denarii.

With Callistus out of the way, Julianus' favoured candidate, Hippolytus, then became the sole pope of Rome. And beginning really with this murder, in Gnostic Rome, with the evil Empire itself as the true source and foundation of its inspiration, the standard was set for what was eventually to become one of the most powerful, ersatz religious institutions in the world, one which was to be built up, army-like, over hundreds of years out of the substance of fear, fraud, hatred and superstition, as well as wholesale murder and bloodshed, and all on the back of the purest and most innocent victim who ever walked the face of the Earth, his murder on the Cross the veritable apotheosis of their unfathomable hypocrisy and cruelty.

Julianus, however, could know nothing of such things. He was about as far from a seer as you could possibly get! Power, far more than religion, was his creed, and he was gaining it rapidly. His vision at last was beginning to materialize and this tickled him to the pit of his bowels and he was a thoroughly happy man. Moreover, the new Emperor, as fate would have it, also worked in his favour.

For, Alexander Severus, the teenager who succeeded Heliogabalus, could not have been more unlike his predecessor. Due, no doubt, to his sweet temperament, but also very much to do with the excellent education he received from his mother, Julia Mamaea, Alexander Severus turned out to be a cultivated, thoroughly moral and caring young man who not only included the reading of Plato, Cicero, and Virgil in his leisure pursuits, but who also, despite remaining essentially a pagan in his religious beliefs, looked with great sympathy and favour towards Christianity. For his intelligence and purely moral vision clearly showed to him that in the Christian Way there was available to the citizens at large at least one sure way for them out of the decadent swamp they were being daily dragged deeper into, through being given nothing but fraud, vice and debauchery as example by most of their leaders.

Alexander Severus was not, of course, aware of what conspiring Julianus had in mind. And neither was his mother. Taking full advantage of this latest respite for the Christian *Kyrios,* Julianus worked day and night for the strengthening of its position within the militaristic orthodoxy of Rome, and at the same time became ever more active in his determination to rid himself of the dreaded Gnostics, once and for all.

Thus, after hearing of the strange event in Caesarea, he lost no time in writing to Demetrius. Soon after receiving his letter Demetrius sent a special envoy to Caesarea-Palestina armed with one of the most strongly-worded letters that he had written in his clerical career so far. In it he castigated all the clergy, even the pope himself in Caesarea for allowing themselves to be addressed by a layman, of all things! This, he said, was unheard of in the *Kyrios*. He ordered them to send Origen back immediately to Alexandria.

Without objection, and secretly glad of his summons, while puzzling greatly over the strange logic that Demetrius used in it, Origen returned to Alexandria. Of course, given the great ambiguity, irrationality and even suspect morality of Demetrius' words, Origen kept thinking that they and the actions they were inciting Demetrius into, could have no other possible origin than Rome.

26   THE PUBLISHING COMPANY

Ambrosius and Gregory came back with Origen to Alexandria.

Origen was reluctant to visit Demetrius at first and put it off for as long as possible. Eventually, however, he received an official, strongly-worded 'invitation', which he duly honoured a few days afterwards. But when he arrived at Demetrius' residence, Origen found him changed in many ways, not just in attitude, but in appearance also. For one thing, he seemed fatter and had acquired some kind of a stomach ailment, for he belched continually, and often quite rudely, Origen thought. He was also far more fidgety and arrogant than usual.

'What will you do in Alexandria?' Demetrius enquired, tapping his fat little pink-slippered foot.
'Write! I have been writing a lot lately,' Origen informed.
'So I have heard,' Demetrius said grudgingly. 'And what, pray, are you writing about?'
'Oh, you know, the Way, the Way of our Lord,' Origen said with an affected air of flippancy. For how, he wondered, could he possibly give this strange man any idea whatsoever of what he intended by his writing, which was essentially to instil in his readers a feeling for the wonderful magic of the Christ that lived so abundantly in his heart? Demetrius seemed to have no openness whatsoever to this white magic.
'How many books have you written so far?' Demetrius snapped.
'Thirty-five.'
'Thirty-five!' Demetrius repeated. Now he looked angry.
'Yes,' Origen confirmed. 'But, believe it or not, I haven't really started yet. However, now that I will not be able to lecture here in Alexandria, since we do not have a proper School anymore, I will be devoting far more of my time to writing.........er.....unless, that is, you have..... plans for me............'
'I would.....'
'Anyway,' Origen interrupted, 'whatever other duties you *may* wish to put upon me, I will, I am afraid, always *have* to give priority to my writing from now on.'
'What are these books about, what are their titles?' Demetrius demanded.
'*Miscellanies, Contra Celsus, The Commentary on St. John's Gospel, The Hexapla* – I'm still working on this last one, but I have also published numerous of my homilies on...'
'All right, all right,' Demetrius interrupted, 'now, listen. Give me a copy of *everything* you have written so far and *everything* you write from now on.'
Then Demetrius stood up abruptly and took his little bell from his desk, 'And continue to visit me at least once a....a.......'

'Month?' Origen suggested hopefully.
'No, no, every......every ....two weeks.'
'All right then,' Origen agreed reluctantly.

Not far from the southern city wall in Alexandria, in a beautiful, quiet, open, but hilly area where the aqueduct went majestically over the wall to the Nile ship canal and the port of Lake Mareotis beneath, Ambrosius bought a modest but lovely villa. Here, together with Origen and Gregory he lived, all three wholeheartedly dedicating themselves to the pursuit of study and mediation; a monastic kind of life certainly, but one also that was never lacking in interesting work for them to do. The work was in fact the very essence of Alexandrian life and culture, what made it famous throughout the world even long before Origen's time, and that was the written word, the literary arts generally, or more particularly the pursuit of knowledge or *gnosis*, which in Origen's case actually meant the mass production of books.

This work was carried out in two of the largest rooms of the villa. In one of these, each day for a set number of hours, Origen paced up and down with his hands behind his back and his head held high in the air like a bird's, and dictated in a divinely inspired flow of philosophically formed words and sentences to as many as seven stenographers at the same time. The results of his inspirations were immediately brought, sheet by sheet, into the adjoining room where an even larger number of copyists and others were continually engaged upon the task of editing and turning these single sheets into full-length, easily readable and beautifully finished manuscript scroll books. In this way Origen's output far exceeded any other known writer of the time, and all due entirely to the generosity of Ambrosius to whom Origen kept his word by dedicating many of the titles to him.

In this way over the years, the villa became a small but industrious Christian community in which the three founders ordered their day according to a simple but very strict 'rule'. This, Origen gladly wrote down, upon request from Ambrosius and Gregory, soon after little domestic difficulties made it obvious that if the general purpose of their striving and sharing was not to suffer unduly, the three of them, living and sleeping together under the same roof, needed something to keep them from quarrelling over trifles. This 'rule' was an instant success and apart from allocating responsibilities for various domestic chores it basically broke their day up into three parts – work, study and meditation, but with the three aspects interpenetrating one another rather than having to be carried out in strictly alternating blocks.

Not long after they had settled down into this productive routine, Ambrosius made the enlightened suggestion that they invite the virgin Herias to join them. Origen and Gregory readily agreed, and from the moment of her arrival, Herias, whose natural sense of order, combined with the almost magical lightness of touch with which she accomplished and directed the domestic affairs, graced and enriched the household atmosphere immensely. Herias, who had been a very young student at the Didascaleon even during Clement's time, but afterwards also under Origen, always carried a deep love of the School in her heart. But after it was burnt she was most distressed and was always seeking ways of dedicating herself to her most gracious and loving Lord Jesus. Therefore, the invitation from Origen came like an angelic answer to a long-standing prayer.

Origen's literary production continued to grow. And Ambrosius, using his expert, commercial knowledge, was able to sell the books to virtually every known library, as well as to important book-buyers and collectors all over the Empire. Most of the profits were ploughed back into the business, into increasing the quality of production, and procuring for the books an ever-widening distribution. However, Origen made sure that Demetrius received a fair percentage of the profits for sharing among the needy of the *Kyrios*, not only in Alexandria but wherever there was a known and legitimate need.

Demetrius never read any of the books Origen wrote and presented to him as requested, but he was growing ever more painfully aware that the negative missives he was constantly receiving from Rome about Origen increased proportionately to both the production of the books themselves and the revenue received from their sales. Thus, the receiving of these sums of money from Origen, while always welcomed by Demetrius, meant that he found it increasingly difficult to relate to him, or to know what exactly to do about him.

Origen's fame, however, continued to grow rapidly. He now received letters of praise and commendation for his work from all over the Empire, and from people of all walks of life, both inside and outside the *Kyrios*. Many now regarded him as more authoritative and knowledgeable than any of the ancient Greek philosophers, even Plato himself. Each new book from him was awaited with huge and widespread anticipation. He became a household name and was known from the lowest to the most exalted members of society. Although many people remarked upon his almost Herculean capacity for work and his frighteningly austere lifestyle, which was also legendary, and many others, who knew him personally, spoke about the strange look of otherworldliness that often fell across his face when speaking, no one doubted his virtuousness, his saintly capacity for love and self-sacrifice, and his total dedication to service in the name of His Risen Lord.

The Emperor's mother, Julia Mamaea read everything Origen wrote and became so fascinated with him that she personally sent for him. She said in her letter that he had evoked so many questions in her soul that she felt the seams of it might burst if her questions were not answered, and she knew of no other solution to her growing problem than to actually meet and talk to him in the flesh. Such an invitation could not be refused. And so in the spring of the year 227AD Origen set sail for distant Antioch. In their beautiful summer palace, where Julia lived with the young Emperor, Alexander Severus for that part of the year, over a period of a full month, Origen instructed her, often in the presence of the Emperor himself who also listened most attentively, in the ways of his Great Master, the Lord Jesus Christ.

Julia loved Origen deeply and insisted that he be with her for far more time than he considered healthy or wise. She soaked in everything he said, with a lust that actually perturbed Origen in the beginning, but he eventually managed to transform her enthusiasm into a restrained and dignified capacity for spiritual love and faith, and he was certain, even before he left – eager as he was to return to his beloved work in Alexandria – that he had won another most faithful and good servant-soul for the Lord.

27   THE LYRE OF ORPHEUS

Around the community in their villa in Alexandria a little school of sorts emerged over the years. Some of the old pupils of the Didascaleon would come occasionally and sit with Origen in the garden where he would converse with them and answer questions.

Herias, who loved him dearly, but who was also slightly afraid of him, was particularly interested in his attitude to women.

'Master,' she asked one evening out of the blue in the garden, as a number of them were relaxing after a long and fulfilling day's work, 'they call us the weaker sex. Is that true?'
Herias had the lithe, little body of a sprite and her mind worked like lightening.
'We are all weak, dearest Herias,' Origen replied, 'in the eyes of God, that is.'
'I suppose she speaks of natural, traditional, male prejudice, or some such thing,' Ambrosius proffered, looking up, reluctantly, from wet proofs of the latest book by Origen.
'Yes, Ambrosius. But I propose that we do not suppose anything. Better ask her, don't you think? Herias, what do you mean by weak?'
A coy smile brightened up Herias' pale young face, but as she failed to find words Origen prompted, 'Physical or spiritual?'
'I suppose, Master, I would need to really know the difference between the physical and the spiritual to answer that,' she replied.
'Dearest Herias! If anyone knows the difference between the physical and the spiritual, you do. Perhaps it is simply that you have not got the words to express it?'
After a short pause he continued, 'Gregory, can you tell sweet Herias the difference between the physical and the spiritual?'
Gregory was sitting, dreamily, near his Master's feet with his face turned towards the setting sun.
'I think, Master, it is to do with what we mean by the soul. If we know what soul is, we know that it goes down into the physical body, and up into the spiritual body.'
'That, Gregory, is very good. Except I would have to ask you to define exactly what you mean by a spiritual *body* - this, on the surface of it at least, is a bit of a contradiction in terms, is it not?'
'Yes, Master. It is. I agree. I....'
'Nevertheless, Gregory, despite this difficulty of terminology, what you say is quite true. "The key to the universe is the soul" – from the great master Pythagoras! And the soul is feminine. This gives the physical body, to which it is most intimately attached, an overall feminine quality does it not, whatever the

171

gender? Mother Earth is the mother to, the mother of, all our bodies. Our Father in heaven, however, who, let it be said, holds the key to *all the generations*, that is, the seed of man - he is pure *spirit* as St. John says. We have to learn to distinguish clearly between the different parts of the Holy Trinity, of body, soul and spirit. That is the basis of all Gnosis. And that is why we call Christ, who, although He was filled with the most beautiful sophianic soul-nature imaginable, appeared on Earth as a male, the sign of the spirit, or the divine and most Holy Spirit of His Father God. That is also the reason why He did not include women in his twelve, initially. We must remember that the Lord was always speaking and acting out of archetypes or in archetypal tone-pictures or words, as well as in ordinary ones, of course. This was His great and magical characteristic. He lived in *both* spheres at the same time! However, out of this awareness, we can ask that just because the Lord did something, must we slavishly do the same? No! Definitely not! Often quite the opposite can be the correct way. Do you see? So if we allow these archetypes to guide us, we can acquire the freedom to order the world according to our human, which is also our soul, nature, quite as much as to the higher spiritual nature. We must learn to discern the true spirit and to balance our life on Earth accordingly. We must overcome our weaker, lower nature, certainly. But to say that the male human being is stronger simply because he is nearer, *archetypally*, to the spirit is to get it........well, all a bit mixed up really, don't you think? Inwardly, in our deepest nature we have all come from the same Father Spirit and as such are all equally strong or equally weak.'

Herias drank in all his words and said nothing, but her smile had widened and sweetened.

After a long pause Ambrosius said dryly, 'Pity we don't have a stenographer here, we could've caught all that, Origen. So much of your wisdom escapes into the flipping ether!'
'Oh, come, Ambrosius. How can you be so sure that sweet Herias cannot repeat everything I said, word for word? In any event, just look at her. Can you not see all her petals shining like rays of the sun? It doesn't really matter whether she can remember what I said or not. I have pollinated her little flower with my words, and look, you can almost see it growing before your very eyes!'

All eyes turned upon Herias whose smile had faded but whose face now shone quite magically, catching as it did the last red rays of the dying sun. She closed her eyes.
'Your voice to her is as the lyre of Orpheus, Master,' Gregory suggested quietly after glancing momentarily at Herias.
'Thank you, Gregory,' Origen replied, 'but look upon her yourself again. Look

away from the sun and look upon the loveliness, the flower of your soul. Look in fact upon the very embodiment of the difference between words and pictures. Believe me, Gregory, here is a picture, a soul of one who, unlike the great tragic hero of the Orphic Greeks, Eurydice, will *not* die. She, us, we have been freed from Lucifer's snare by the Great Master. Gregory, look upon this soul as your eternal companion in purest, sweetest, spiritual love.'

Gregory looked again at Herias and tried to follow his Master's advice. *Yes*, he said to himself, *she is beautiful, and I will love her chastely, and always.*

The following year Ambrosius busied himself feverishly by providing a grand new extension to the villa, necessitated by the ever-expanding publishing enterprise. But also more people wanted to join the community, so that by the time the extension – which was almost as big as the villa itself – was completed, the community had grown from the founding three to over fifteen, which included both men and women. Some of the copyists and stenographers also wanted to join, something which greatly warmed Origen, for most of these were pure professionals who, at the beginning of their work for him, had little interest in Christianity.

As the community expanded, the wish was often expressed to Origen that it should become a house-community of the *Kyrios*. But Origen repeatedly replied that this was not possible and the reason was that he could not celebrate the *Agape*, for he was not a presbyter.
'But why are you not a presbyter?' Ambrosius exploded one day in utter frustration. He could not understand this.
But Origen merely smiled calmly at him and said cryptically, 'Why, because of the big D, Ambrosius, who else?'
'Demetrius?'
'Yes.'
'Oh, hang him, hang him,' Ambrosius retorted loudly.
'Of course, I know you do not mean that, Ambrosius.'
Ambrosius shrugged. But Origen went on consolingly, 'I'm afraid I cannot do anything about it.'
'You could ask him to ordain you' Ambrosius responded and added, 'No, no, you could *tell* him to ordain you.'
'I could, I suppose. But I have a secret policy towards Demetrius, Ambrosius, and I will confide it to you right now: I do not ask him anything, ever. I *give* to him only. I know of no other way to deal with him, actually. The most important thing for me – and ironically I feel it is the same for Demetrius – is the *unity* of the *Kyrios*. I would prefer to die rather than cause a split in it here – in fact I feel I would die if there were a split in it here.'

173

But Ambrosius went away thoroughly unhappy from the conversation, and more and more he began to feel that Demetrius was little more than a thorn in the side of the *Kyrios* in Alexandria.

28 THE HERETIC!

Under the leadership of Pope Hippolytus, the *Kyrios* in Rome hotted-up its campaign against the Gnostics. Both Julianus and Hippolytus, by employing a small army of spies in various quarters of society, by minute observation of the overall situation in Rome themselves, as well as by meticulously trawling the various written works against the Gnostics by the now deceased Irenaeus and others, over a period of six months compiled a formidable blacklist of all the groups and cults in the city which were from now on to be considered, by all baptized members of the *Kyrios* there, to be either pagan, Gnostic or just plain heretical, and definitely *not* orthodox, catholic Christian. Moreover, Julianus was firmly fixed upon foisting this list not only upon the Roman *Kyrios*, but on every branch of it throughout the Empire. His ultimate goal was to make the list nothing less than binding everywhere by the 'canon' force of Roman law, something he felt he could do once Christianity was made *religio licita*.

But, of course, there were difficulties. And of all the different Gnostic groupings he had to contend with, the ones who followed Valentinus were the most difficult to handle. Valentinus was on Julianus' list basically because he was one of the greatest supporters of the initiations and the initiates of the old Mystery religions of whom, in his time, there were many in the *Kyrios* but even more nowadays.

Although all through most of the 2nd century, Valentinus was regarded as one of the great Christian teachers of his day, as the polarization between paganism and Christianity increased he began to fall out of favour with some people, especially those who actively disparaged the old initiation wisdom. These latter types saw in the ancient wisdom a threat to the creation and enforcement of a clear, concrete, orthodoxy and authority within the *Kyrios* generally, the propagation of which they deemed possible only through intellectually worked out, written, and widely published formulas. Julianus was, of course, foremost among these types in Rome, those who increasingly saw the *Kyrios* in purely black-and-white terms, as little more than an institution which took upon itself the role of the defence of a God whom they naively considered to be hopelessly locked into a kind of eternal warfare with his absolute opposite, the Devil, and therefore needed someone to defend him on Earth. The Valentinians, on the other hand, and those of a similar persuasion, had a much more reasonable, if eclectic, approach and were all for keeping the greatest possible number of colours flowing through the thinking heart and the general teaching life of the *Kyrios*. These types were fiercely suspicious of enforced creeds and the like, but most of all they wanted the *Kyrios* to keep on board the principle of initiation, which stemmed from the ancient mystery religions.

Origen's mind was more wide-ranging and his soul more colourful than most in this regard, and he was recognised and liked precisely because of this, his all-embracing yet deeply Christian eclecticism. His writings were full of the most clever and subtle arguments for keeping the ancient spirit of initiation alive in the *Kyrios*, while, at the same time, he unceasingly pointed, mainly with the uneducated masses in mind who were flocking to the *Kyrios*, to the authority of the sacred scriptures, and especially to the richness and depth of spiritual meaning contained in the Gospel and Book of Revelation of the great Christian Initiate, St. John the Evangelist, whose initiation sign was that of the Eagle. Thus, when a well-known follower of Valentinus, Candidus by name, who was also recognised by many as an authoritative Christian teacher, came to prominence in Athens for promoting a doctrine which was particularly favoured by Julianus and the Romans generally – the doctrine that salvation and damnation are predeterminate – Julianus was put into quite a quandary; on the one hand, he wanted to oust the Valentinians altogether, while on the other, he saw in their controversial doctrine one of the linchpins of the orthodoxy he wished to forge for the entire *Kyrios*. *So what was he to do?*

He watched the controversy raging in Athens with a keen eye and a keener ear and particularly when it was suggested, by some important people, that only the great Origen himself could answer one such as Candidus, he followed every syllable of it. Julianus reluctantly supported the idea that Origen should go to Athens to debate publicly with Candidus and, when Origen agreed to this, Julianus decided he would have to attend the debate himself.

Thus, in the early summer of 229 AD Origen set sail for Athens on yet another important mission for the *Kyrios*. However, he decided to take some extra time from out of his gruelling work schedule in order to visit his many friends in Caesarea-Palestina. Pope Theoctistus was especially delighted to see him and expressed a deep wish to accompany him to Athens to hear the important debate, a wish, however, he knew would not be fulfilled. For he was far too overworked as it was!
'This debate will set a new standard, a whole new line of doctrine in the entire *Kyrios*, Origen,' he confided to Origen one evening. 'I am certain of it. Candidus is one of the greatest Christian minds alive, you know.'

Origen actually knew very little of Candidus except that, by all accounts, he seemed to believe some things which Origen found not only hard to swallow, but even quite obnoxious.

'Does he speak well?' Origen enquired.

'He is a trained and well-practised orator, Origen. You are going to meet your match.'

'I feel nervous already, Theoctistus. But I wish only to say what inspires me by the Holy Spirit.'

'I have little doubt that that indeed will happen, Origen.' But after a pause Pope Theoctistus continued, 'Origen, I am appalled that Demetrius has not ordained you yet. Why is this? It is a quite preposterous situation. You need at least the authority of a presbyter when debating before such a large and influential gathering of the clergy and laity as will undoubtedly be there in Athens. Anyway, was Demetrius not upset precisely because you addressed us here as a mere layman the last time. What is he up to?'

'I am not sure,' Origen replied timidly.

After another long and ponderous pause Theoctistus said, 'Origen will you accept ordination from me?'

Origen was taken aback! He was not expecting this.

'At the very least, you would have much greater confidence because of it,' Theoctistus pressed adding, 'and Demetrius will not be able to complain so easily this time.'

Almost involuntarily Origen found his head nodding.

'Good. I will arrange it straightaway,' Theoctistus said embracing him warmly.

'Thank you, Theoctistus, thank you.'

Thus it was, that for three long days in the first week of August, both in the full heat of the sun and in the relative shade and cool of the evening, in the amphitheatre just below the Parthenon in Athens, presbyter Origen faced the great Valentinian, Candidus, and debated with him before a packed and enthusiastic audience on various matters of doctrine, theology, and philosophy relating to the ordering, management, direction and teaching of the great new movement that was daily gaining in strength and numbers throughout the Empire, the Christian *Kyrios*.

Most of the debate was taken up on relatively minor matters concerning what was and was not permissible at the *Agape*; matters of dress codes were also debated, protocol regarding ordinations, what constituted good Christian manners, and so on. More heat entered into the debate, however, which was often accompanied by loud cheering and clapping, mostly for Origen, when questions such as the use of images and incense in house-communities, the wearing of ornaments and jewellery generally by both laity and clergy, but especially by women, came up. But there were two questions, which the organizers of the debate very prudently and cleverly kept until the final session, at which there was the fullest possible attention and utter silence as each man spoke his mind. The first of these questions was to do with the matter of predestination, and the second with reincarnation.

The Valentinians like most of the Gnostics were dualists, meaning they could never fathom the idea of God being responsible for evil in the world, and thus they believed in the absolute and irredeemable existence of the Devil, an idea which Candidus expounded with great articulation and to not a little clapping from a certain section of the audience which, of course, included Julianus and the group of sycophants he had brought with him from Rome for the occasion. Julianus, however, was disappointed that he could not get the audience worked up very much on his side, despite repeated attempts.

When Origen began, however, he took a completely different tack from that of Candidus. To begin with, he expounded for a long time on the different types or shades of evil. Like love, he said, evil could take many forms. Then he went on to show that all these different types of evil could in fact be broken down into *two* basic types. One of these, the more glamorous type you could say, he said, was ruled over by the fallen Angel of light, Lucifer, and the other, the heavier, more earthly aspect, by the one known from the New Testament (especially St. John) as the Prince of this world, the dark Satan. This division, this distinction, Origen said, was absolutely crucial to any real, reasonable, and enduring understanding of the great enigma of evil. Unless one understood this, one could *never* understand the problem of evil. If, however, one did understand this distinction one could also see that even these great fallen Beings fell by will, and could, therefore, be redeemed by an act of will also.

In a further aspect of his exposition Origen went on to say that however strange it may sound, these evil Beings were a necessary part of the evolutionary growth of humans and human consciousness towards the highest good, and that the good itself was a *free choice* human beings had as their most valuable possession, and it could not be free if there was not a choice – therefore, he said, we have to contend with God's recognition of the need for evil in the world.

Loud cheering erupted for Origen when he finished this part of his exposition. Julianus' face however, as he listened to him and the growing enthusiasm for his views, went from red, to white, and finally to purple! But when the question of reincarnation came up and Origen started to speak, Julianus began to look more like a smouldering, human time-bomb than a human being.

Candidus, however, was the first to speak on the subject. Uncharacteristically he demurred somewhat. He said he believed in the pre-existence of souls all right, but when it came to the question of the soul going from one body to another, it was not his view that it could go to a lower type, or from a human to an animal body. He objected strongly to this idea, this strange doctrine of the mystical Orientals, he said. To Origen, however, he actually seemed quite uncertain of his views on the subject all round and appeared very pedantic.

Origen, immediately he began, wholeheartedly supported not only the idea of the pre-existence of the soul, but that it had many kinds of existences previous to the present one, and until it had expiated all the sins and errors of previous existences would continue to re-occupy a body. The whole Earth, he said, was a kind of perfecting school in this spiritual work, in this spiritual sense. However, like Candidus, he also denied that the soul could go, after death or in a new life, to an animal body. Notwithstanding this, he emphasised that all of the ancient wisdom and its initiates supported the idea of reincarnation in principle, and it was no less a pair than Pythagoras and later Plato himself who were the greatest exponents of it in Greece. While varying in their interpretation of the doctrine, he said, all the wisest men, ancient or modern, supported it. To deny reincarnation, Origen said in the end, was to deny the very essence of the esoteric and hidden wisdom and truth of the Gospel itself.

At this, widespread cheering and clapping erupted, and very soon afterwards Origen was declared as the undisputed winner of the entire debate.

Julianus went back to Rome in a mad rage. He hated, with an increasing intensity, all this Oriental, mystical stuff that Origen was now spewing out in volumes, wooing the faithful away from his own idea, his ideal of a neat little cut-and-dried *Kyrios* with himself and the pope of Rome as the sole, supreme authorities, the very voice of God on Earth, ruling with an iron rod of righteousness over the Empire, over all mankind, over the entire Earth, nay, over the whole damn universe itself. He set to work immediately.

He wrote to Demetrius a long letter, and after delivering a whole sheaf of minor ultimata, demanded, in the last paragraph, that Origen must immediately be banned from speaking *ever again* on behalf of the *Kyrios*, whether in Alexandria or anywhere else for that matter. The letter was signed in Pope Hippolytus' own hand.

Soon after receiving this missive, Demetrius summoned Origen to his residence and did not allow him to speak a single word while he told him of his absolute abhorrence that he, Origen, had allowed himself to be ordained without either his permission or authority. Furthermore, he said, he was absolutely appalled with his idea that Satan could be redeemed – Satan was in Hell, he said, and he would stay there for ever and ever, like everyone else who refused to listen to or accept the teaching of the holy Gospel as laid down by the legitimate *Kyrios*. And as for reincarnation – he thought it the most absurd thing he ever heard.

Demetrius then wrote to Pope Theoctistus in Caesarea-Palestina and complained to him in similarly bitter and hostile tones, saying, among many other things, that he did not even consider Origen's ordination valid. But when Theoctistus replied that he knew of no reason why it had to be Demetrius, and not any other pope or bishop who could ordain, thus calling into question the veracity and authority of Demetrius' letter, Demetrius was pushed by Julianus into calling a general council of the *Kyrios* for the whole of Egypt, in order to sort things out in his favour.

This event occurred in the following year and at it Demetrius, backed up by a large delegation from Rome, publicly denounced Origen. In Caesarea-Palestina, as well as in Greece and other provinces, however, they soon responded that they did not recognise Origen's denunciation. Thus, the first of those dreaded events which were to plague the *Kyrios* from now on, loomed large on its horizon - the schism.

Origen held his breath. For, the last thing he wanted was to be the cause of such a dreadful thing as a schism, so utterly alien to his absolutely passive nature was it. So he said and did nothing, and even published very little during this time.

Julianus and company continued to monitor things from Rome, while Demetrius busied himself by recruiting presbyters, clergy and others in the *Kyrios* in Alexandria to his side. They became ever more determined in their efforts to flush out the Gnostics and acquire for the *Kyrios* a clear and unequivocal orthodox position, especially regarding those tricky subjects to do with personal salvation. Julianus, of course, thought the threat of eternal damnation hanging over all those outside of the *Kyrios* the best possible net of fear to haul as many as possible into the fold. But, more and more he came to realize that no one was more tricky, no one more likely to thwart their efforts in this regard than Origen. Origen became a kind of scapegoat, and Julianus and company set out to silence him, once and for all! And although Origen knew of and watched these events unfolding with a growing sadness in his heart, he did nothing except write. Nothing would ever stop him doing that.

Then the final blow came. With careful and expert help from both Julianus and

Hippolytus, in the year 232AD Demetrius called a General Council of the *Kyrios*, ostensibly representative of the *whole* Empire, the first of its kind, in Alexandria. He actually promoted it as an *ecumenical* council, the idea being that it was supposed to peaceably resolve differences between various people. However, admission to this event was strictly vetted, and all was weighted in favour of a specific outcome, which they fully achieved. For, after debating in a very desultory way various controversies and issues in the presence of Origen, who was not allowed to speak at all, the Council issued a declaration at the end in which Origen was not only denounced for preaching doctrines alien to the true spirit of the *Kyrios*, but was also stripped of his status as a priest, and warned severely that if he continued to preach similar or allied doctrines he would be declared a heretic and excommunicated from the *Kyrios*.

Origen remained totally silent during and after the Council. Even in his writing he said little directly about these matters which surrounded him and weighed so heavily upon his heart. For, he loved the *Kyrios* too much to suffer a split in it, especially at such an early stage of its immensely important mission on the Earth.

Thus, it came about that in the winter of the year 235AD Origen left his beloved Alexandria for good. Though his heart was heavy as stone, he left with an ever-growing love in it for his Great Master, the image of whose suffering body, hung upon the Cross - a perfect sacrificial offering to God in expiation for the small-mindedness of men, for their divisiveness, their bitterness, their anger, their eternal lust for power and war, their utter wickedness - came ever and ever more alive for and in him, and offered to him abundant hope in his own earthly suffering and passion, as well as giving him increasing strength of will to serve his ever-loving God.

EPILOGUE

In the midst of his manifold troubles, to the astonishment and often great frustration of his many friends and admirers, the saintly and peace-loving Origen did and said as little as possible, believing that this was what was required of him by God and his Great Master in order to preserve the unity of the Kyrios. However, in a letter to his friends around this time he did say the following: *"Is it necessary to recall the discourses of the prophets threatening and reprimanding the shepherds and the elders, the priests and the princes of the people? You can find them without our help in the Holy Scriptures and convince yourselves that our own time is perhaps one of those to which these words apply: 'Believe not a friend, and trust not in a prince' (Micah, VII), and also this other oracle which is being fulfilled in our own days: 'The leaders of my people have not known me; they are foolish and senseless children; they are ready to do evil but know not how to do good' (Jeremiah, IV, 22). Such men deserve pity rather than hate, and we must pray for them rather than curse them, for we have been created not to curse, but to bless."*

Origen went alone to Caesarea-Palestina and laid as low as possible there for a long time, greatly troubled in soul, but also deeply thankful for the hospitality and kindness of Theoctistus and the congregation generally, who recognised him as a sage and a holy man of the very highest order. Ambrosius, and some of the little publishing community from Alexandria, originally wanted to follow him, but he advised against it, at least until matters settled down again. They did eventually to some degree, and only then, also, was it possible for Origen to resume his beloved work. Soon after this he invited Ambrosius to join him, and he came immediately with Gregory and a few others from the community.

Just before Origen left Alexandria he had completed the 5th volume of his great commentary on the Gospel of St. John. In the Preface to the 6th volume, which he had just started before he left Alexandria, in Caesarea-Palestina he inserted the following: *"In spite of the storm stirred up against us at Alexandria, we had completed the 5th volume, for Jesus commanded the winds and the waves. We had already begun the 6th when we were torn from the land of Egypt, saved by the hand of God the deliverer, who had formerly withdrawn his people from thence. Since that time the enemy has redoubled his violence, publishing his new letters, truly hostile to the Gospel, and letting loose upon us all the evil winds of Egypt. Hence reason counselled us to remain ready for combat, and to keep untouched the highest part of ourselves, until tranquillity, restored to our mind, should enable us to add to our former labours the rest of our studies on Scripture. If we had returned to this task at an unseasonable time, we might have feared that painful reflections would bring the tempest right into our soul.*

Moreover, the absence of our usual stenographers and copyists prevented us from dictating the commentary. But now that the multitude of heated writings published against us has been extinguished by God, and our soul, accustomed to the misfortunes which come to pass in consequence of the heavenly Word, has learnt to support more peaceably the snares prepared for us; now that we have, so to speak, found once more a calm sky, we do not wish to delay any longer in dictating the rest, and we pray God and Christ our Master to make himself heard in the sanctuary of our soul, so that the commentary we have begun on the Gospel of John may be completed. May God hear our prayer that we may be able to write the whole of this discourse, and that no further accident may interrupt and break the continuity of our Scriptures."

Theoctistus encouraged Origen to set up his school again in Caesarea-Palestina which he duly did, and which, in time, became almost as famous as the Didascaleon, Gregory becoming one of its star pupils. Gregory is actually known to this day as St. Gregory the Wonder-Worker, for he went on to develop his clairvoyant talents under Origen's guidance to such a degree that in his time he became world-famous as a psychic healer.

But in 235AD the army rebelled yet again and they had both Juliana and Alexander, the young Emperor, murdered. An unknown barbarian, who knew no Latin and who had never even been to Rome – Maximus Thrax – was then declared Emperor.

In Maximus' short reign of 3 years he brought down another persecution upon the Christians. Origen narrowly escaped becoming a victim by fleeing temporarily to Cappadocia. But, many years later, in 249AD, when yet another madman ascended the throne – Decius – the Christians suffered one of their worst-ever persecutions. This was so widespread and severe that Origen simply could not escape. He was apprehended, thrown into prison, tortured and whipped with straps. Like a beast, an iron collar was placed around his neck and his body fixed upon the rack. There his arms, legs, and feet were cruelly extended for days on end. The diabolical nature of this torture was sealed only by the failure of his torturers actually to kill him. Origen was released from these, the worst of all his tormentors, in about 250AD, but, a few years later, after a long struggle with his wounds, he died. 'He was buried in Tyre where for centuries his tomb, in the wall behind the high alter, formed the chief ornament of the magnificent cathedral of the Holy Sepulchre. Tyre was laid waste by the Saracens, but, even to this day, it is said, the poor fishermen, whose hovels occupy the cathedral site in that city of palaces, point to a shattered vault, beneath which lie the 'bones of Origen.'

After Origen's death the Empire was plunged into total anarchy and torn apart by innumerable civil wars. Over the next half a century or more there was an average of one Emperor per year. Taxation was exorbitant, inflation catastrophic, and bands of private armies or outlaws roamed the length and breadth of the Empire, plundering and killing at random. Some degree of order, however, was restored by Diocletian in 284AD, and later, when the astute Constantine acceded to the throne in 312AD he immediately issued an Edict giving the Christians their long-awaited status of *religio licita*. By this time, however, such an Edict represented little more than the triumph of common sense over pure power-mongering, for the Christians had continued to grow enormously in numbers and, moreover, had managed to organize themselves into a coherent unity, albeit a very dogmatic and narrowly orthodox one, forged, of course, under the direction of Rome whose popes and clergy hounded out the Gnostics with a fury comparable only to that which the army itself hounded the barbarians.

Thus, virtually all knowledge of the Gnostics and Gnosticism generally was wiped from the memory of western civilization, for everyone and everything, that gave off even the faintest whiff of Gnosticism, was burnt by the zealous heretic hunters. Most of what we know of this extraordinary and spiritually vibrant culture of the Gnosis comes from its orthodox and very often fanatical detractors. However, the discovery in recent times of scrolls hidden away by an enlightened and far-sighted few (The Dead Sea Scrolls, the Nag Hammadi Library, and others) has stimulated a renewed and ever-growing interest in and knowledge of The Gnosis.

Origen is reputed to have written over 5000 books! However, only a tiny fraction of these have survived the various burnings down the ages. For, for centuries after his death, long after Gnosticism was defeated, Origen continued to be controversial, and became an increasingly painful thorn in the side of the Catholic Church especially as it continued to gain ground and political power in the 5th and 6th centuries, at which time the ecclesiastical side of the movement became entirely dominant. It turned, then, from what was initially, a wonderfully far-reaching and egalitarian movement, led by the initiated, whose circles were open to all according to their ability and commitment; a movement which held out great promise of a mutual peace and friendship between ordinary, individual men and women of *all* classes, colour, and race, all sharing a common faith and knowledge - truly a world-uniting movement – from this it turned into a theocratic, dictatorial, autocratic, highly-centralized, militant, and often fiercely violent institution. Around this time also, the idea of a fortified temple or 'church' to house the faith and the faithful took hold in the minds of the clerics and ecclesiastics, and this word then became the universally accepted one to define the popular movement.

The Emperor Justinian (reigned 527-565), recognising fully the thorn that Origen represented in the side of his megalomaniacal enterprise to rejuvenate the now thoroughly spent and decrepit Empire, went so far as to issue a long Edict against him in order to hammer home the Roman orthodoxy once and for all time. This Edict was published in 553AD and soon after, under Justinian's direction, Origen was declared a universal heretic at the 5th Ecumenical Council of the Church in Constantinople, and was excommunicated from that body which he not only deeply loved but the very foundations of which he had laid.

But, despite being a heretic, Origen has not gone away! Far from it. In terms of the true and often deeply-hidden meaning of the great Christ Event in Palestine, at the beginning of our era, he simply cannot be forgotten, for in the foundation stone that he laid is contained the very essence of our understanding of it. 'As a matter of history, the seed of universal understanding we find in the esoteric circles of early Christianity did not take root as it might have done. It was not taken up by the developing Church, which needed a simplified teaching in order to carry out its own programme of spreading Christianity'. Thus, to this day, Origen continues to be a thorn in the side of the mainstream Church. Although still technically a heretic, on the one hand he is widely recognized as the foremost authority on all doctrinal and theological matters for 'by working to reconcile science with the Christian faith, philosophy with the Gospel, Origen did more than any other man to win the Old World to Christianity.'

On the other hand, the very basis of his thinking, which is the old initiation-wisdom and knowledge, the mainstream Church has, even still, no time for at all.

THE END